ABOUT THE AUTHOR

From devouring the Harlequin Superromance books on the shelves of her aunt's used bookstore to swiping her grandmother's medical romances, Liz Talley has always loved a good romance novel. So it was no surprise to anyone when she started writing a book one day while her infant napped. She soon found writing more exciting than scrubbing hardened cereal off the love seat. Underneath her baby-food-stained clothes a dream stirred. Liz followed that dream and, after a foray into historical romance and a Golden Heart final, she started her first contemporary romance on the same day she met her editor. Coincidence? She prefers to call it fate.

Currently Liz lives in north Louisiana with her high school sweetheart, two beautiful children and a menagerie of animals. Liz loves strawberries, fishing and retail therapy, and is always game for a spa day. When not writing contemporary romances for Harlequin Superromance, she can be found working in the flower bed, doing laundry or driving car pool.

Books by Liz Talley

HARLEQUIN SUPERROMANCE

1639—VEGAS TWO-STEP
1675—THE WAY TO TEXAS
1680—A LITTLE TEXAS

To the boy who once twisted my hair
around his finger, and sang me Elvis songs,
who gave me my first kiss, two beautiful children
and the life you promised me in all those notes
we passed in the halls of Webster Junior High.
I believe in soul mates.

CHAPTER ONE

BRENT HAMILTON HATED HIMSELF.

That was the only thought in his head as he sprawled on his parents' back porch steps watching a titmouse hopping from branch to branch in the scarred redbud tree.

The birdhouse he'd made last week already showed signs of inhabitancy, if the scruffy mat of pine straw peeking from the opening was any indication. At least that had worked.

Because nothing else in his life had.

In fact, it was one big royal suck.

He didn't hear the footsteps, only felt the long fingernails scraping his scalp as Tamara Beach tousled his hair.

"Morning," she said.

"Morning." He cradled his coffee mug between his calloused hands.

She squatted next to him and eased herself onto the step. She set her strappy-heeled sandals next to her.

"You want some coffee?" he asked, staring at the tufts of hair on his bare feet. He hadn't bothered with pants. Just wore the boxers he'd pulled on that morning when he'd rolled from his bed in the carriage house and padded across the backyard toward his parents' home to let the dog out.

Tamara's bright red toenails waggled as she stretched. "Nah."

Awkward silence reigned.

Apple, his parents' overweight Boston terrier, sniffed through a patch of Aztec grass.

Finally Tamara nudged him with her shoulder. "Hey."

He didn't say anything.

"It's no big deal. I mean, it happens to all guys."

Brent rubbed a hand over his face. It had never happened to him. Ever. He couldn't blame it on the liquor or the fact he hadn't really wanted to sleep with Tamara. Hell, before last night, he'd been able to get it up if the wind blew right. The cause of his failure to rise to the occasion was the damn dissatisfaction that had made a home in his gut.

It had settled in, unpacked its clothes and planted flowers out front. It wasn't going away. No matter how many chicks he picked up. No matter how many bars he stomped through, buying drinks and clacking pool balls. No matter how much he grinned and faked it.

Brent hated who he was.

Yet, to date he'd always lived with it. So what was different? The fact he hadn't been able to perform? The comments overheard at his former girlfriend Katie Newman's wedding last night? The idea that someone he'd thought so similar to him had fallen in love and tied the knot?

"Whatever," he said. "I'm sorry."

Tamara shrugged. "No biggie. I like being with you no matter what. You don't snore like most guys."

He managed a smile. "Good to know."

"I won't say anything to anyone. I'm not that girl,

you know?" He looked at her as she tilted her face to the sun. Tamara was naturally hot. Her blond locks brushed tanned shoulders and her blue eyes were a clear color that blinked innocently right before they flashed with mischief. She was lean, tight and had a rack that, though store-bought, made men lick their lips. Oak Stand's very own Playboy bunny. And she was a nice person.

"I know you won't." He patted her thigh beneath the ruffled sundress she'd squirmed into. It was wrinkled from lying on the floor, but still looked great on her.

"Well, I'd better leave while everyone else is in church. If my grandmother sees me, I'll get lectured in front of the whole family again. Roast beef just doesn't taste right with a side accusation of *whore*."

He frowned. "You're not a whore."

"Tell that to the Reverend Beach." She rose and slid the sandals onto her feet. The small birds in the tree beside her flew away. She smiled and tilted her face again to the morning sun. "Have a good one, Brent."

She waved as she slipped out the wooden gate that led to a side drive, leaving Brent to his heavy thoughts.

As the gate banged shut, the phone resting beside him on the step rang.

He didn't want to answer it. He knew who it was and what she wanted. But he picked it up anyway. Ever the dutiful son.

"Happy birthday, Brent!" The greeting launched an enthusiastic round of "Happy Birthday."

"Hey, Mom," he said into the receiver.

"Happy birthday, my handsome boy. How's everything at the house? Are you feeding Apple her sensitive stomach food?" His mother's tone sounded too cheerful for a person up at such a godforsaken hour. It was 5:30 in the morning in California.

"Let me talk to him," he heard his dad say.

His dad's voice barked in his ear. "Talked to a guy last night. Name's Russell Bates. His brother works in management for the Chargers organization. He said he saw you play your freshman year and might have a spot for you here in San Diego."

"Doing what? Selling hot chocolate?" Brent closed his eyes and pretended they weren't having this conversation again. His dad just wouldn't give up. Would never give up. Playing football was a memory for Brent. And would stay that way. "This ain't going to happen. You know that."

"Horseshit."

"Today I'm thirty-two. Thirty-two-year-olds don't start a football career in the NFL. I'm not Brett Favre. I'm done with football."

"Brett Favre is ten years older than you and still in the league. Besides, Hamiltons don't give up," his father said. His old man might as well have said, "Denny didn't give up." Because that's what Brent heard when his dad talked about Hamiltons. Always Denny. Competing with the memory of a dead brother was part of what had brought Brent to this very moment. He would never win that battle.

"Okay, fine. Give me the number."

"Ready?" his father said.

Brent closed his eyes. "Hold on. Let me grab a pencil. Okay, go ahead."

He didn't move from the step. Simply listened as his father rattled off a landline and cell number. Brent wouldn't call. The hint of interest was just a friend of a friend humoring an old man with dreams too big for his son. Brent could only imagine the conversation that had taken place when his father had learned of the tenuous connection to the Chargers organization. His father was a bulldog, pushing until people rolled over and surrendered. Brent had rolled over quite a bit in his life. Another reason for his self-loathing.

"Call him tomorrow morning. His name is Bill. Bye."

"Bye," Brent murmured into the phone. He pressed the end button. No happy birthday from his dad. Only more direction toward a future that did not exist.

He sighed and drank the rest of his lukewarm coffee. The sun already grew warm despite the cool April breeze filtering through the trees. It was a perfect day to putter in his parents' backyard, whittling out perches for the birdhouses he'd promised the kindergartners at Oak Stand Elementary. But, then again, he needed to complete the proposal for the next few books. His publisher wanted five more books in the lacrosse series, which was good because his job at Hamilton Construction was slow, mimicking the economy all over the nation.

During the day, he ran his father and uncle's construction company, a local contracting business that specialized in renovations and additions rather than new construction. But most nights, he became B.J. Hamm, author of award-winning sports fiction aimed at boys. No one in Oak Stand knew the complex B.J. Hamm. They only knew the rather simple Brent Hamilton.

His secret hobby had grown into a secret career— one that not even his absent parents knew about. Writing was a juicy secret he took pleasure in keeping. He didn't know why.

Donna and Ross Hamilton had taken a long overdue RV tour out West and suddenly retirement sounded good to his parents. For the past couple of weeks, his father had finally stopped mentioning tryouts for the Canadian Football League and started hinting that Brent should buy his half of the company. But now with the phantom San Diego Charger contact, Brent was certain his father would jump on the football bandwagon again, dreaming about Brent hoisting the Lombardi Trophy overhead.

How in the name of all that was holy could a pragmatic man like his father believe something so shaky as a dream of that magnitude? The old man couldn't let go. Of anything.

Brent had his chance years ago.

But he didn't want to think about failed dreams today. He didn't want to think about anything. Maybe he'd go back to his feather-stuffed bed. Or doze in the hammock strung between the two Bradford pear trees in the corner of the yard. He rarely had time to enjoy the peaceful oasis he'd helped his mother create between the carriage house he rented and his parents' small Victorian.

He whistled for Apple and she ignored him.

As he stood, a baseball came whizzing over the fence. It bounced on the path and crashed into a red clay planter, knocking it over, spraying potting soil into the air.

What the hell?

The ball rolled into a daylily clump and stopped.

Apple pounced on it, slobbering all over the well-used baseball.

He walked over and pulled it from Apple's mouth. She grinned up at him as if a game of fetch was about to commence.

"Hey, that's mine." The voice came from the left.

Brent turned to find two brown eyes peeking over the wooden fence. They belonged to a boy whose leg crept over the top of the fence. The boy hoisted himself up and straddled the two yards, his eyes portrayed wariness.

Brent motioned the kid to come on over and the boy tumbled down, dropping like a sack of potatoes onto the bag of mulch his mother had left in the corner.

Apple trotted close and sniffed him.

"Hey," he said to the dog, rubbing her head before standing up and brushing himself off.

Brent felt like an alien had beamed down. But it wasn't a little green person. It was a boy who looked to be about seven or eight years old.

Brent flipped the ball to the kid. He caught it with one hand. Impressive. Apple wondered off to find more frogs and lizards to chase.

"Clean up the mess," Brent said, pointing to the dirt covering the brick path.

The boy looked at the broken pottery and spilled soil. "Oh, sorry. My hand got sweaty."

Brent nodded. "It happens."

The boy didn't say anything more. He knelt and used a finger and thumb to lift a broken shard.

"You staying at the bed-and-breakfast?" Brent asked.

The boy nodded and picked up the upended planter

and started stacking the shards inside. "Yep. My mom made us come here. Right at the beginning of my baseball season. It's absurd."

Something about the boy's disgust and vocabulary made Brent smile. He knew how that felt. He'd loved baseball season. Especially in early April. The smell of the glove, the feel of the stitches of the ball against his hand, the first good sweat worked up beneath the bill of the baseball cap. Sweet childhood.

"Well, it's just for the weekend," Brent said, toeing the spilled soil with his bare foot.

The boy sighed, dropped to his knees and began scooping up the dirt. He tossed it out into the grass. "I wish. She's making us live here. I don't even know for how long."

"Oh," Brent responded, watching the boy as he labored. His reddish-brown hair was cut short, almost a buzz cut. Freckles dotted his lean cheeks and for a kid his age, his shoulders were pretty broad. He'd moved with a natural grace, like an athlete. Like Brent had always moved. "What's your name? Since we're going to be temporary neighbors."

"Henry."

"Hmm…I wouldn't have taken you for a Henry."

The boy gave him a lopsided smile. "My mom likes Henry David Thoreau. I got my name from that dude."

"You look more like a Hank," Brent said offhandedly, picking up the base of the broken planter, stuffing the flower's roots into the scant soil and setting it aside.

"Like the baseball player I saw a show on. Hank…"

"Aaron?" Brent finished for him.

"Yeah, that's the guy. Cool. I can use that name here. No one knows me yet."

"Well, you better ask your mom about that. You know moms." Henry was funny. Brent liked kids better than he liked most adults.

Henry picked up the ball and rolled it around in his hand before sending it airborne. He caught it neatly. "Yeah, my mom can be crazy about stuff like that. About sports and stuff. She doesn't think sports are important."

Brent feigned horror. "What's wrong with her?"

The boy shrugged. "I don't know. I'm good at them. I play football, baseball, basketball and soccer. I even took karate before my dad died. I liked kicking boards and stuff. It's pretty cool."

The boy tossed the ball as easily as he'd tossed out information. He'd lost his dad. Tough for a boy like Henry. He seemed headstrong and sturdy, the kind of boy who needed a firm hand. A good mentor. A man to toss the ball with.

The boy threw the ball and caught it in one hand, slapping a rhythm Brent couldn't resist.

"You know, I could get my glove, and we could toss the ball around," Brent offered. "But first you better make sure it's okay with your mother."

The boy's eyes lit up. "Awesome."

"So go ask."

Something entered Henry's eyes. A sort of *oh, crap* look. "Um, it's okay. She's making bread or something like that."

The boy's gaze met Brent's and a weird déjà vu hit him. The kid's eyes were the color of cinnamon. Like eyes Brent had stared into a million times. He glanced at the gate that had been locked for over ten years. The gate that led to the Tulip Hill Bed-and-Breakfast on the other side of the fence the boy had climbed.

"Your mom, is she by any chance—"

"Henry Albright! Where the devil are you?" The woman's voice carried on the wind into the Hamiltons' backyard.

"Oops, that's my mom. She's gonna be mad. I'm not supposed to talk to strangers," Henry said, scrambling toward the fence.

Brent closed his mouth and watched as Henry ducked beneath the redbud tree before grasping one branch and swinging himself toward the brace on the fence. His worn sneaker hit perfectly and he arched himself so the other landed beside it. But the boy hadn't been fast enough.

The gate opened with a shove because the grass had grown over the once well-worn path.

Henry froze and so did Brent.

A woman stood in the opening. Her curly red hair streamed over a blue apron that was streaked with flour and she wore a frown. Brent allowed his eyes to feast on her, for she was sheer bounty. Her cinnamon eyes flashed, her wide mouth turned down, but the body outlined in the apron was lush and ripe from the long white throat to the trim ankles visible beneath the flowing skirt. Bare feet anchored themselves in the healthy St. Augustine.

Rayne Rose.

Brent swallowed. Hard.

"Hey, Mom," Henry said, dropping to his feet. "This is—" Henry turned to him. "Hey, I don't know your name."

Brent didn't move, just watched Rayne as she registered his presence. He could see her tightening. See her shock. See her try to recover.

"Brent," she said.

Something tugged within him at his name on her lips. Her sweet lips. The first ones he'd ever kissed.

"Oh, you know him. Good. We were gonna play a little baseball," Henry said, trying to slide past Rayne into the yard of Tulip Hill. She caught his shoulder.

"I don't think so," she said, looking at the boy. "You are not supposed to wander off. And you are not supposed to talk to strangers."

"But you know him," Henry said, shrugging his shoulders in that devil-may-care manner all boys had.

"But you didn't. Pick up your glove and get in the house. You have some reading to do before we register you for school tomorrow." Her words were firm but there was a softness in her manner, in the way she patted the boy's shoulder.

"But, Mom, I—"

"No arguing, Henry."

A mulish expression crossed his face. "Fine. But I don't want to be called Henry. From now on, I'm Hank."

Aggravation set in on Rayne's face. He'd seen it every day on the face of his own mother. "Hank?"

"Yes," the boy said, disappearing behind the fence. "I want to be Hank. I hate being Henry. That's a nerdy name."

Rayne closed her eyes. Then opened them again. She looked at Brent. "I'm sure this is your doing?"

Brent shrugged and thought about crawling under the porch. "Sorry."

Her response was to laser him with her normally warm gaze.

"Nice to see you, Rayne," he said.

She stared at him for almost a full minute before speaking. "Stay away from my son."

She turned and tugged the gate closed behind her.

And that was it.

That was how he became reacquainted with the only girl he'd ever loved.

CHAPTER TWO

RAYNE SLAMMED THE GATE and stood a moment, trying to stop her insides from quivering.

Brent Hamilton had always done that to her. She'd been eleven when it had first happened. She'd spied him doing push-ups from over the fence. It was the first time she'd even noticed a boy's muscles, and she'd stared for about ten minutes before he'd caught sight of her sprawled in the tree watching him. She'd scrambled down and disappeared, much too embarrassed to confront the boy who'd been her friend from the day she'd climbed out of her parents' VW van, tripped up the front steps of her aunt's house and noticed a boy throwing acorns at wind chimes.

Brent was still a good-looking son of a bitch with a rippling body and overtly masculine aura. But the emphasis should be on the son-of-a-bitch part.

She wasn't a silly little girl, so she willed her shaking legs to obey and marched toward the peeling porch.

Henry stood there, arms crossed, brow wrinkled. He opened his mouth. "Mom, I want—"

"Don't start, Henry. You violated a big rule, buster. Haven't we talked about this before? You climbed into a stranger's backyard."

"I didn't think anyone was home. Besides, you know

him. You said so," her son said, kicking the rail, causing the rooster planter to teeter.

"Stop before you make the planter fall. It's my starter of cilantro," she said, climbing the steps. She peeked into the pot. The sprouts had given birth to the fan shapes that would become the flavorful herb. "And it doesn't matter that *I* know the neighbor. *You* don't, and to do what you did is dangerous."

"You said this town is safe. That I could run around and play and stuff. Can I go back and throw ball with him? Please?"

"Absolutely not," she said, surprised her normally cautious son would want to go. It was the baseball that pulled him. But she didn't want Brent messing around with her son. Brent was a lot of things. Charming. Egotistical. Unreliable. Things she didn't want Henry to glean from a man who'd once had the town wrapped round his golden arm, and who would no doubt do the same with her impressionable son. "Every place has dangers. From now on, you consult me before you leave this yard. Got it?"

He made a face. "Okay, but can I go throw? Please. Please. Please."

"Did you hear me?" She shook her head in wonder. Were all males born with selective hearing? "No. Now up to tackle that reading. I want you to make a good impression tomorrow."

"I hate that dumb book. It's about stupid cats and mice. You know I don't want to read that stuff." He kicked at the rail again. The planter tottered. She caught it with one hand.

She gave him the evil eye. He immediately stepped away from the rail and dumped his glove on the pew that sat to one side of the porch. "The book I bought for you is on the accelerated reader list. It's a Caldecott book. They're always good."

Henry shrugged and tugged open the door of the bed-and-breakfast. "I don't see how a book about mice can win awards. Everyone knows mice can't really talk. It's absurd."

He disappeared into the house before she could say anything else. And he'd left his glove again. He kept forgetting they were not at home. They were at an inn and he couldn't leave his things lying about.

Rayne placed her hands over her face and blew out her breath. Then she picked up the glove and sank onto the old wooden pew. Round one for the day. She could only guess what round two held.

She'd give her life for her son. She loved him with a passion that rivaled all others, but the boy was as alien to her as a Moroccan desert. Foreign. Exotic. And she didn't speak the language.

He'd been that way since he'd turned nine months old and said his first word. Had it been *mama* or *dada?* No. It had been *ball.*

And thus it had begun.

The boy's obsession with sports was epic.

And ever since he'd learned to throw, run, hit and kick, he'd reminded her of the boy who'd grown up next door to her aunt. The boy who'd climbed trees with her, studied stars with her, shared his dreams with her. He was near about the spitting image of Brent.

But Brent was not his father.

Rayne hadn't even seen her childhood crush in over fifteen years. Not since the day she'd shaken the dust of Oak Stand from her sandals and headed for a new life and a new dream in New York. She'd locked up the memory of Brent and told herself not to think of him. But her heart hadn't been good at following her head's directive. She still thought about him at the oddest times. Such as when a baby bird fell out of its nest at the house in Austin. Or when Henry had hit his first grand slam. Or when she lay lonely in her bed staring out at a harvest moon.

She'd always been drawn to Brent Hamilton.

Even on the day she'd kissed Phillip Albright in front of the preacher and all their friends, she'd been half in love with the boy who had once sung Elvis songs to her while twisting her hair around his forefinger. She supposed it had been horribly unfair to Phillip to harbor tender feelings for a boy who'd never been hers to begin with, but she suspected Phillip didn't mind. Their marriage had never been a head-over-heels, can't-keep-our-hands-off-of-each-other kind of thing. More of a mutual respect, burning desire to succeed, quiet love and amiable friendship kind of thing.

Maybe that had been wrong, but she'd been happy with Phillip. He'd been the right man at the right time for her. And she'd tried to be the same for him.

God, why is life so complicated?

The only answer was the banging of the screen door. It jarred her into the present.

"Reckon it's going to get warm today." Aunt Frances said, stepping onto the porch and shading her eyes as she perused the tangle of her yard. Rayne followed her gaze. The lawn boy had been let go in the fall and spring had taken advantage of the free rein.

Rayne shrugged. "It's Texas. It's always hot."

"When it's not cold." Her aunt laughed and sank

onto the pew beside her. Aunt Frances had faded brown hair that fell just to her shoulders and always smelled of roses. Rayne caught the scent on the April breeze and it calmed her.

"I don't want to forget about the loaves of honey oat bread. They can't bake too long," Rayne said, wondering why she constantly "remembered" out loud. Bad habit left over from her childhood.

"Mmm."

"Avery Long's oldest boy is going to help me clear the area for the vegetable garden tomorrow. But I need to get those weeds pulled. Can you keep an eye on Henry?"

"Oh, you mean *Hank?*" Aunt Frances said.

Rayne sighed. "Guess I've got something new to fight, huh?"

Aunt Frances nodded. "He's a stubborn mule, that boy. Good trait to have, though. Get him far in life."

"Maybe so," Rayne said. "We've got Brent Hamilton to thank for that little gem."

Her aunt smiled. "Brent, huh? You two were thick as thieves when you were younger. Always made me smile to see you two together. Come to think of it, that man might be what the doctor ordered, Rayne. He's got medicine that's cured a lot of gals round here."

Rayne flinched. "You're talking about the man whore of Oak Stand? No, thanks."

Aunt Frances smiled. "Always been partial to man whores myself. Know what you get."

Rayne shook her head. No way in hell was she going there. "I'd rather chew glass than mess with him. He's overrated."

Her aunt cocked her head. "You know this from experience?"

She wished. Kind of. But she and Brent had never had a chance to explore anything other than sweet kisses paired with unbridled teenage lust. "Not really. But that ship sailed long ago. Disappeared into the Bermuda Triangle. Sunk by pirates. Chopped up for firewood."

Aunt Frances gave her that look. The one that said, *baloney.* "Okay. But I wouldn't mind running my flag up his mast and I'm sixty-eight."

"And a very sick woman."

They both laughed. And it felt good to laugh. Rayne felt as though she'd nearly lost the ability. The past few months she'd been faltering, taking a step in one direction only to doubt herself and backtrack. It wasn't like her to doubt herself. To not have a clear vision. And that flip-flopping was something she didn't want to dwell upon for the moment.

"Okay, I've got to get to work. This yard won't clear itself, and we're already behind on getting things planted." Rayne stood, slipped the apron over her head and tucked it beneath her arm. "Have the painters called? We need them on the job tomorrow if we're going to have the inn ready by the middle of May."

Her aunt pursed her lips. "About the painters. Well, they went to Houston for some kind of dirt track race. I'm not sure we can rely on them."

Rayne closed her eyes and counted to ten. Her aunt moved at a different speed. The whole town moved at a different speed. She had to remember she wasn't in Austin. She was in Oak Stand. "Well, *I* can't paint the house, Aunt Fran. Tell Meg to call in professionals. She has a list, I'm sure. We can't allow Susan Lear to waltz through the door to substandard accommodations. Her article is the key to a successful launch. I pulled strings to get this feature in *Oprah* magazine."

The Tulip Hill Bed-and-Breakfast, her aunt's well-established but slightly faded business was being transformed into Serendipity Inn, a Rayne Rose exclusive getaway, part of Serendipity Enterprises. But there was much work to do before they could open the doors. Rayne had brought her assistant, Meg Lang, with her, but Meg had been bogged down with traveling back and forth from Austin overseeing the restaurant and the new project. No one else was assisting. Serendipity Inn was a family project and very much on the down-low.

Still, her aunt had insisted on using locals to spiff up the inn. The economy had been hard all over, but especially in small town America. Aunt Frances wanted to help the people of Oak Stand. Only problem was some of the people of Oak Stand didn't want to help them.

Her aunt nodded. "No problem. I'll take care of getting new painters. Someone will be here tomorrow morning. You take care of the garden, the kitchen and the menu. Meg will help me with the rest."

Her aunt disappeared, entering the house the same way she'd emerged. With a bang.

Rayne slumped onto the bench. Why had she agreed to this?

Of course, re-creating the bed-and-breakfast had seemed like a brilliant idea months ago. After twelve years of slaving like a dog to build her career, the thought of reworking the bed-and-breakfast seemed exciting and restful at the same time. A sort of sabbatical with purpose. Something about her aunt's calming touch and sitting on the front porch swing while viewing paint and fabric samples had sounded right. Rayne needed the comfort of her loving aunt, some privacy and a change for Henry.

But now she wasn't so sure.

Maybe it was being in a place bathed in memories. Or maybe it was seeing Brent. Or perhaps it was the fact she felt so not herself sitting on a pew in her aunt's backyard. So not like the woman she'd become.

Rayne Rose Albright was successful beyond all expectation with a *New York Times* bestselling cookbook, a restaurant that repeatedly made top ten lists and a possible deal on the bubble at the Food Network. She even had her own line of ruffled aprons under production with an Austin designer.

A lot of good it did her. Not when she could barely crawl out of bed some mornings. Not when her child chewed holes in his shirts for fear of being lost or left behind. Not when crazed fans penned weird letters and showed up on her front doorstep. What good was money, fame, success?

Not much if you were miserable.

Rayne opened the door and stepped into the old Victorian house. The smell of fresh bread wrapped around her, soothing her, reminding her why she was there—to recapture the simplicity of life. She took a deep breath. Then released it.

The house exuded charm from every nook and cranny. It would make a fine inn, a retreat for wealthy cosmopolitans who wished to experience a trip to trouble-free times. Most of the work they'd do over the next month was cosmetic in nature. Aunt Frances had always run a tight ship. The antiques were well-polished, the decor was country without being cliché and the house was in fairly good repair. They needed to shore up the front and back porches, repaint windows and doors, replace fabrics and purchase some new furniture. And get the backyard tamed and productive with a veggie garden, pretty herbs and edible flowers.

The highlight would not be in the surroundings, but in the smells, sensations, tastes of the bounty of the earth.

And that was Rayne's job. To create a menu of simplicity and sophistication.

She entered the kitchen and quickly set about tucking away ingredients before pulling the golden loaves of bread from the Viking ovens. They looked perfect. She set them on a cooling rack just as something brushed against her ankle.

"Ack!"

A streak of ginger raced by her. She trotted backward, banging into the baker's rack.

What the heck?

She scurried after the animal, hoping it was merely a cat and not something more menacing.

It was just a cat.

A fat ginger cat that paced at the front door.

"Rumple," Henry called from the stairway.

She looked up at her child as he ran down the stairs. "Careful, Henry."

Henry paid no heed. Simply tumbled down, tossing the book he'd been clasping onto the bench. He dropped to his knees and started stroking the fur of the now-purring cat. "This is Rumpelstiltskin 'cause he sleeps all day. Aunt Fran calls him Rumple. He lives next door. At that guy's house."

The Hamiltons' cat. They'd always had one. She remembered Sweettart, the gray tabby that followed Brent around like a dog for years. He'd stroked that ragged-eared tabby the way Henry stroked the one now curling about her ankles. The purring cat rumbled as he arched against Henry's strokes.

"Well, he doesn't need to be in the house." She swung the door open and toed the cat with her bare foot. "Out, Rumple."

"Stop," Henry cried. "I like to pet her. She loves me."

"Keep it on the porch. And take your book," she called out to the boy as he followed the cat through the oval-paned door.

Before she shut the door, she caught sight of Brent heading toward his truck. His brown hair curled over his ice-blue polo shirt collar and his jeans hugged a pretty spectacular butt. He drummed a beat against his thigh with his right hand as he'd always done. The phrase "Idle hands are the Devil's tools" popped into her mind. Yes, that man knew how to create sin with those hands. She remembered the mischief they'd stirred in her... and how much she'd liked those new feelings. But then again, lots of girls had cause to remember those hands. That thought was cold water down her back.

She stepped away from the door.

Brent had cultivated a reputation he'd been content to keep all these years. Who could blame the girls of Howard County? It would be hard for most women to resist the potent combination of Brent's charm and physical hotness. He was the kind of guy a gal would be content to watch mow a yard or unclog a toilet. He was beauty in motion. Always had been.

Hunger struck her out of nowhere.

And it wasn't for the bread she'd set out to cool. It was the same old hunger she'd first felt long ago, stirring that summer night she'd pulled on her new pink-striped nightgown, a parting gift from her parents. She'd be staying with Aunt Frances in Oak Stand for high school while her parents and sister headed north to New York State to live in a commune for artists. Rayne had tied the satin ribbons on the shoulders and moved to the window to draw the shade. Brent's shades weren't drawn and she caught sight of him across the empty darkness between the two houses. She tucked herself behind the curtain as Brent dropped his towel and ran a comb through his hair. At fifteen, his bare backside had been as intriguing a sight as she'd ever seen. A strange warmth had curled round her midsection and taken up residence in her tummy. It was the first stirring of desire, the first step she'd taken down the path of obsession with Brent.

And it was a path that had gotten her nowhere because fifteen years ago Rayne Rose had been oatmeal to Brent's French crepe with chocolate-raspberry sauce. He'd sampled her when he had nothing better to do. She'd never been important enough to acknowledge as she sat in the stands watching him play or at the dances where he hung out with the cool kids. But still, she'd loved the boy he was when he was with her. When no one else was around and he became hers alone.

She'd been such a fool.

Yet despite what she'd told Aunt Frances moments before, she still wanted a taste of Brent.

CHAPTER THREE

BRENT EYED THE BOARDS above the wide porch of the Tulip Hill Bed-and-Breakfast. "These are going to need replacing before we paint. I know they don't appear to be rotten, but they are. Won't take much time though."

Frances Wallace peered up assessingly. "How much time? Rayne's already riding me, wanting to hire people from the city to get this finished."

Something inside him started at her name. *Rayne Rose.* He'd always loved her name, loved the way everyone said her first and last name together. The vision of an orangey-pink rose like the ones his mother grew appeared in his mind. Those dew-kissed flowers were almost the color of her hair. So pure and fresh, just like Rayne. He dashed the image aside to focus on the flaking paint above his head. "Two or three days at most. Then I'll finish sanding and apply fresh paint. Two weeks on the total project."

"Okay." Frances nodded. "It'll take that long for Meg to arrange hiring someone from Dallas anyway. I'd be obliged to you, Brent. I know you're busy this time of year."

"Not too busy for a neighbor, Mrs. Frances." He shoved his hands in his pockets and looked around the half-sanded porch. Frances had given him gingersnaps when he was a kid and let him catch ladybugs in her garden. How could he not help her when she needed someone to do exactly what he did—restore and renovate? At that moment, he wondered what the cause of all this upheaval was. What was Rayne doing back in Oak Stand? And why had she pulled her son away from school and baseball to refurbish her aunt's bed-and-breakfast? He had questions, but no right to ask them. So he asked what he could. "So who's this Meg?"

Frances was about to answer when a huge rattling truck roared into the tree-lined drive. The red truck belched as the engine died. Big Bubba Malone.

The mountainous Bubba climbed from his monstrosity of a truck and doffed his cap as a tiny woman appeared at his elbow.

Everything about the woman looked severe. Straight, blunt-cut dark hair, black shirt, long gray skirt, culminating with polished combat boots. A small diamond winked in a nose that balanced Elvis Costello glasses. Her chin jutted out as Bubba graciously took her elbow.

"Hands off, Jethro," she said, pulling her arm away and stalking up the drive.

"That's Meg. She's Rayne's assistant," Frances commented from behind him.

Brent stepped back when Meg reached the steps. He didn't want to stand in her way. She looked as mad as a cat dunked in a creek.

Frances stepped forward. "Meg, what in the world happened?"

Meg cocked her head and crossed her arms. "Oh, you mean besides having a flat outside this godforsaken town and then having to walk almost two miles before someone stopped? I don't know…maybe it was that man slapping me on my ass and calling me *little filly!*"

Brent tried not to laugh. He really did, but the sound got past his lips before he could stop it.

She whirled, her dark eyes flashing behind her glasses. "What?"

He straightened. "Nothing."

Bubba stuck his cap on his balding head and sallied toward the porch. "Mornin', Mrs. Frances. Brent."

"Don't you even step one foot near me," Meg said, flinging out a small, white hand and pointing at Bubba. "I don't want any of your primordial ooze to get on me."

Bubba Malone, the slightly dim, good ol' boy of Howard County, looked down at his shirt. "I ain't got nothing on me."

Meg shivered. "Dear God, he's got the brain of a flea."

Brent could tolerate a lot. Hell, he ribbed Bubba himself upon occasion, but he wasn't about to let a snooty slip of a feminist insult a good man. "But *he* has manners. After all, he picked you up."

The termagant turned her dark eyes on him. She took him in from his work boots all the way up to his faded ball cap. He saw appreciation glint in her eyes just like almost every other woman. Then she arched an eyebrow. "So swatting a stranger on the backside is good manners around here? Really? Can't wait to find out what the ill-mannered folk do."

Bubba kicked a brick lining the walk. "Heck, it was a compliment. You got a sweet a—" he glanced at Frances "—uh, behind."

Meg snapped her mouth closed as color flooded her

cheeks. She stared at Bubba for a full minute before muttering, "I need to go make a call."

She rushed through the front door, nearly bowling over Rayne in the process.

"Ow," Rayne said, lifting a slender foot and rubbing her pinky toe. "You gotta ditch those combat boots, Megs. They're killing me."

Her assistant must not have answered, because Rayne shrugged and stepped onto the porch, barefoot and beautiful. Brent couldn't stop himself from taking her in. Her unruly red hair lay tamed in a braid that fell over one shoulder. The dress she wore looked as though it had been purchased in Mexico. It had looping bright thread in whimsical patterns on the hem. A bright pink apron depicting a mixer reading Whip it Good on the front pocket nipped her trim waist and hugged her breasts. The only thing marring the perfection of Rayne was the frown she wore.

"What are you doing here?" she said, looking directly at Brent. Her eyes looked puffy, slightly red, as if she'd cried recently. Or had an allergy attack. But her gaze was flinty and accusing.

He shrugged. "I'm going to replace some boards and paint the porch."

"No, you aren't." Rayne jerked her eyes to her aunt and gave her a look. He wasn't sure what it meant, but he thought it had something to do with the fact she hated him. She'd changed so much. Her words were direct and authoritarian. He could see her commanding a kitchen staff. *Do this. Sauté that. Move.*

"He's the only person I can find, Rayne. And he's my friend and neighbor. Besides, I take exception to your trying to micromanage every aspect of this venture. I'm perfectly capable of handling this."

Bubba clomped up the stairs. "Hey, Rayne Rose."

Rayne stopped frowning at Brent and her aunt and swiveled her head toward the large man lumbering toward her. "Oh, hey."

Bubba wiped his hand on his shirt and offered it to Rayne. Rayne ignored his hand and rose up on her toes to give Bubba a hug. "Sorry about your momma, Bubba. She was a fine lady."

Bubba nodded. He'd lost his mom a few years ago to cancer. "That she was. Everybody sure misses her."

"Especially her Seven-Up cake. She taught me how to bake my first cake, you know," Rayne said, her smile incredibly gentle. It was as if her irritation had melted away, leaving the old Rayne in its place. Brent loved her smile, the softness of it. He wanted to taste that smile against his lips.

Bubba stroked his scruffy red beard. "Yeah, she was good around the kitchen. Even taught me how to cook. Good to have you home, Rayne."

Rayne's frown returned. "Well, Oak Stand's not exactly my home."

Frances moved to Rayne's side and curled her arm about her niece's waist. "Of course, Oak Stand's your home. The place you grew up is always your hometown. And she'll be here for the next month or two. At least."

"Maybe," Rayne muttered, not quite meeting her aunt's eyes.

For a moment they all stood silent, waiting for something to break the uncomfortable moment. Luckily, Bubba knew when to make an exit.

"Shoot, guess I better get. Jack's got plenty for me to do out at the ranch. Y'all have a good mornin'."

"You work on a ranch?" Rayne asked.

"He works for Nellie Hughes's husband. You remember her. She's a Tucker. Her husband, Jack, started a ranch with his daddy raising horses for the rodeo. He raises other horses, too," Frances said, like a tour director for the Oak Stand Chamber of Commerce.

"Oh," Rayne replied, watching Bubba head toward his truck. The overgrown man opened the door before turning around and snapping his fingers. It sounded like the crack of a bat and Frances literally jumped.

"That girl left her computer bag in my truck."

Frances scurried toward Bubba. "I'll get it."

She left Brent on the porch alone with Rayne. It felt intentional.

There had once been a time when he and Rayne were like Forrest Gump and Jenny—like peas and carrots. But that time had long passed. Brent would have thought Rayne had gotten over the hurt, but one look at her yesterday as she blazed into his parents' yard to rescue her son from his total depravity told him she still nursed the anger and betrayal. He wasn't sure why it still felt so raw, but it did. For him, too. So standing beside her at that moment felt like standing barefoot in a field of stickers.

"If you don't want me to do the work, just say. I'll find someone else." He shoved his hands in his pockets and tried to pretend she was only another customer.

Rayne looked hard at him, making him squirm. He'd broken her heart nearly fifteen years ago. He hadn't realized what he'd done when he hadn't shown up at the Oak Stand High auditorium that spring night. But when he'd untangled himself from the head cheerleader, put his pants back on and uncurled the wadded paper Rayne had hurled at him, he figured out pretty quickly that he'd broken her heart and ended their friendship.

Like a dumbass, he hadn't realized her feelings for him were of the romantic variety. Not really. Sure, they'd kissed, fooled around a little when he was first trying on girls. But he and Rayne had been best buds, friends of the heart, maybe even soul mates. One look at her eyes that night, and he'd known.

He'd been a boneheaded kid, wrapped up in trying to be his dead brother, afraid to be who he really wanted to be. But he supposed the results had worked out for the best. Rayne had wiped him from her hands and spread her wings. She'd left Oak Stand and made a new life for herself, rising like a flower among the brambles to open her face to the sun. She stood as a reminder of strength and grace. He couldn't have been prouder of her…even if she hated his guts.

Rayne crossed her arms over her breasts. She was no longer a gangly sixteen-year-old. He noticed. Oh, did he notice. "I'd like to pretend your being here for the next couple of days won't bother me a bit. Thing is, it will. I'd like to say what happened years ago is so far back in the past that a mature woman wouldn't give a nickel about a boy who didn't keep a promise, but I guess I didn't grow up enough. I'd rather you find someone else to do the job. Because I don't want to be around you."

Her words hurt. As sharp as a knife, they drew blood. He nodded. "I'll see if I can find someone who can come out this afternoon. Maybe Ted Bloom's finished over at the Pattersons' place."

Rayne held herself stiffly as she stood staring at the daylilies emerging from the weary earth on the side of the house. Her eyes looked wistful. He wished he could do something to make things better, but he'd screwed the pooch long ago, and had done such a fine job that nothing was left between them but bittersweet memories of what was once so good.

"I'm sorry, Rayne." Nothing else to say, he moved to pass her and leave.

Her hand touched his arm and his step stuttered. "Why?"

The soft question hurt more than her anger.

He stopped and glanced at her elegant hand on his bare arm. Then he looked into her cinnamon eyes. Damn, but he couldn't bear to stare into the depths because he saw a mirror image of what he'd seen that night. And like that night, it made his heart feel shattered.

He knew what she asked. For the first time, she asked why he had hurt her. Even he was afraid of the reason.

"Because I was a stupid boy who grew into a stupid man. You're right. It's best if I don't do this job."

Then he left, running with his tail tucked, like the damned coward he'd always been. It was easier to run than to explain he'd been trying harder to please his parents and everybody else in Oak Stand than to please himself...or Rayne. That he was a mere shadow of the brother he'd lost. Denny had been better. Had always been better, no matter what Brent had done to fill his shoes. He'd been a seventeen-year-old boy who hadn't had the guts to claim Rayne Rose and the life he really wanted.

And the thirty-two-year old Brent Hamilton wasn't any better. He still hid behind the charming persona he'd created long ago because it was easier to pretend than to get real with himself.

Because the barbers in Oak Stand still talked about how he held the state passing record. The mechanics down at the garage still talked about the touchdown he made as a redshirt freshman against Texas A&M in the last seconds of the game. The ladies down at the Curlique Salon talked about how his body made old ladies swoon and how his huge libido made women in three counties happy they'd gone home with him. His friends talked about how they wished they had a father with a construction company to hand to them.

A local legend and only he knew what a loser he really was.

Fifteen years ago, Rayne Rose had been the only person who'd "got" him. She'd been his secret, the only person who healed him and loved him for who he was. And fifteen years ago, hurting her had killed the best part of him. And ever since, he'd hated who'd he'd become. Even though on the outside, he hid it well.

So, yes, once again he ran.

RAYNE SWALLOWED WHAT FELT like ashes. She couldn't believe she'd asked him anything about that long-ago night. Why in the hell had she done that? Years had piled upon years. It shouldn't matter. It should be water under the bridge. Sluggish, foul water not worth contemplating. She'd crossed that bridge and taken a path far away. Brent shouldn't matter anymore.

But he did.

She really wished he didn't. It would be simpler if she'd felt nothing when she'd seen him again.

But to say seeing him again hadn't unleashed the hurt, hadn't set a pining in her heart for what they'd once had, would be a lie.

Aunt Frances passed Brent on the sidewalk and exchanged a few words. The sharp look her aunt shot her said it all. Aunt Frances was perturbed. Never a good thing.

For the second time that day, tears gathered in Rayne's eyes. She was a stupid ball of emotion. Watching Henry walk into that second grade classroom had nearly done her in. He had been scared, though he'd squared his shoulders and pretended walking into a new school hadn't bothered him. He'd asked her a dozen times on the way to school about when she'd pick him up, where he should stand and if he had enough money for lunch. His lack of faith in her and in the world he lived in broke her heart.

Maybe she shouldn't have pulled him out of his old school. She simply hadn't known what else to do. Her life had felt out of control and Henry had spent every night in her bed, thrashing and crying out. She stayed awake all night and slept all day, barely creeping out of bed to stop by the restaurant before picking him up from school.

She hadn't known which end was up until Aunt Frances said, "Come home for a little bit, Rayne."

And she had.

But maybe it had been a colossal mistake.

It sure seemed like one when she'd backed out of that classroom, leaving her little boy to the care of Sally Weeks, even if she were Howard County Teacher of the

Year. Rayne had cried all the way to the inn as much for herself as for Henry. When had life gotten so intolerable? Had it been when Phillip died two years ago or when their dreams had started bearing fruit, spiraling out of her realm of control without someone to stand at her side? She didn't know, but she'd hoped this project in Oak Stand could ground her again, give her focus and help her find the grit she'd lost.

"Why the devil did you tell him to find someone else?" Aunt Frances said as she mounted the steps. "I thought getting the inn in tip-top shape was vital. Brent does good work, the kind we need."

Rayne shrugged. "I can't handle being around him."

"Oh, grow up. Whatever happened between you and Brent was years ago. You can't tell me you hold a grudge over puppy love gone wrong."

Rayne pressed her lips together. It hadn't been puppy love. It had been the real deal. At least on her end. "It's not about that, Aunt Fran. It's about Henry. I want him surrounded by good influences. Brent is…unreliable. Well, not unreliable, more like irresponsible and—"

"Available. We need him." Aunt Frances put her hands on her ample hips and gave Rayne that stare. The one her own mother never bothered to use for fear it might repress Rayne and her sister and keep them from finding enlightenment. "And don't tell me Brent's worse than the crew who worked here last week. I didn't know curse words could be used in such unique combinations. They made sailors look like thumb suckers."

Rayne almost smiled. She had to admit, the two Italian carpenters had seemed pleased with their newfound ability to pair Southernisms with the curse words they'd learned in Boston. They'd married New England girls and somehow ended up in East Texas. They possessed amazing carpentry skills and had constructed custom closets in each of the guest rooms. Rayne had nabbed them before they started contract jobs in Plano. It had been a coup since their work had been touted all over the South and featured in *Southern Architecture Today*. "True."

"Yes, true. Now pull on your big girl panties, get your tail end over to Brent's and make sure he starts tomorrow. Meg and I are meeting with Dawn Hart to look at fabric samples this afternoon, and I don't have time to bake Brent an apple cake to apologize for my rude niece."

Aunt Frances disappeared into the house as if her word was law. The woman had been alone for too many years to compromise. She'd meant what she said. Normally, Rayne would have dug in her heels, but this wasn't *normally*. It was Oak Stand.

She swiped at the mascara that had smudged beneath her eyes. Aunt Frances was right. She needed to stop acting like she was in junior high. She was a grown woman, a grown woman who'd been married, had a child and ran a successful enterprise. She hadn't gotten to where she was by being immature.

She sniffed, picked up the resolve she'd misplaced and marched down the steps, heading toward the Hamiltons' century-old house.

She could still make out the path that had been beaten into the grass between the two houses long ago. The Tulip Hill Bed-and-Breakfast had been in operation for the past twelve years, ever since her Uncle Travis had dropped dead in the grocery store with a massive coronary. Until that time, it had been Aunt Fran and Uncle Trav's house, a place full of honeysuckle and sweet gum prickle balls, a delightful place for a child to stomp and skip. Aunt Frances, heartbroken and in need of money, had turned the charming house into a place to share with others. Problem was her patrons were few and far between. Frances eked out a living, yet she seemed content doing so. Ambition had never attached itself to Frances as it had to Rayne.

A hedge of sweet olive bushes made a natural fence between the two front yards. Rayne followed the square brick pavers around to the rear of the house through the wooden gate to the charming slate-gray carriage house that sat at back of the property. The small house was unfailingly neat and simple, with only a single planter housing a sago palm squatting to the side of the French doors.

She stood on the small porch for a moment before taking a deep breath and knocking on the glass pane.

No one answered.

She knocked again.

No one.

The ginger cat leaped onto the porch nearly scaring her to death, but she saw no trace of Brent even though she'd watched him head in this direction.

She looked around. His truck was parked out front, so he had to be home.

She raised her hand and banged on the glass pane, bruising her knuckles. Still, no one came.

Where was he?

She tried the handle. It was unlocked. She pushed the door open slightly, just a crack and stuck her head inside. The room was dark but she could make out a simple couch and two armchairs. An enormous flat-screen TV hung on the adjacent wall. Very Spartan. Very male.

"Brent?" she called against the quiet of the room.

There was no answer.

She pushed the door opened wider and stepped inside.

"Yoo-hoo," she called. "Brent?"

The house was dark and silent. She felt a little like the stupid babysitter in a slasher film. Any minute a hockey-masked boogeyman would jump out with a machete.

The door clicked shut behind her and she jumped. She took a quick step backward, knocking into an occasional table and tipping over an empty beer stein sitting on the table. She caught it with both hands before it crashed to the wood floor. She placed it next to the four remote controls on the table and stepped back, relieved she'd avoided calamity.

Something hard stopped her progress.

She whirled around to find Brent standing there naked as the day he'd been born.

"Ack!" she yelped, bumping into the table and sending the stein crashing to the floor where thankfully it didn't shatter. "Good gravy, you're naked."

The room was dim, but she could make out how nicely the man fit his skin. How many times had she imagined him naked? Too many to name. For some reason, her fingers started toward the lamp switch, maybe so she could drink him in. She caught herself before she twisted the knob and plastered her hands to her eyes.

"Yeah, Captain Obvious, it's my house. And usually you take your clothes off before you shower."

She swallowed. Mostly because visions flitted through her head. Visions of her clothes joining his on the floor. Visions of sluicing water and warm, wet skin. All of which were totally…insane.

She didn't say a word.

"So you have a reason for breaking and entering?"

"Of course not. I mean, I didn't break in. You didn't answer the door." She chanced a peek through her fingers. He made no move to cover his nakedness. Of course. He wouldn't. She re-covered her eyes. "Will you put on some clothes or cover yourself so I can talk to you?"

Silence met her plea.

"Please,' she finally said, dropping her hands but squeezing her eyes closed. Or almost closed.

He moved away from her, snatching up a throw from the couch. She cracked one eye to get a brief glimpse of an ass that frankly should never be covered up. She closed her eyes again so he wouldn't know she'd peeked.

"Okay," he said.

She opened her eyes. He'd wrapped the afghan low on his hips. He switched on a lamp and grinned at her. It was a sexy, knowing grin.

"You peeked, didn't you?" he said.

"I did not," she said, crossing her arms over her chest. She hoped she didn't get struck down for lying. "And I wasn't breaking in. Just trying to…talk to you."

He tugged the throw tighter around his hips. "So talk."

Rayne looked around the room. It was clean for a

bachelor pad with tasteful bookshelves loaded with books. Was that Thoreau and Kafka next to…Debbie Macomber? She pulled her gaze away and took in a rich chocolate-and-navy-striped hooked rug that centered the room along with the pictures of various birds hanging evenly over the microsuede couch.

"Ahem." He cleared his throat.

"Oh, um, I came to apologize," she said, keeping her gaze on the print of a snowy egret. She didn't want to look at Brent again. He was more tempting than chocolate chip cookies, a virgin beach with no footprints and a kitchen utensil sale all rolled into one. Rayne was afraid she might do something insane, like kiss him. Or join him for a naked frolic around the living area.

What the hell was wrong with her? She was a deliberate woman. Responsible. Businesslike. Horny. *Strike the last thought.* She concentrated on the egret's feathers.

"Apology accepted, though I don't think you did anything wrong. You were honest. That's not a crime." His voice was emotionless. Nothing to read in the remark.

"Well, so I'm not necessarily sorry, but I did come to see if you would do the work. I shouldn't have—" She tried to recollect her thoughts. "What I'm having trouble saying is that I shouldn't have let our past interfere with the future. That's silly. We need your help." She moved her gaze to something besides the egret. This time the little blue button on the remote control.

"Rayne, look at me."

"I can't."

He sighed. "Why?"

"Because this feels like a contrived romance novel

plot. Sex-starved widow encounters hot old flame," she muttered, rolling her eyes. "So don't make me look at you."

He was silent.

She sneaked a peek. Face only. "What?"

"Are you really sex-starved?" His voice was more than curious. As if maybe he was considering dropping the woven throw. She didn't want that. Or at least wasn't supposed to want that.

She swallowed her panic and laughed. "You might as well ask me what I weigh. That's something I'd never admit to."

"Then head for the door, woman, because if you stay, we might rewrite history."

Rayne rolled her eyes. Again. "Seriously? That's the kind of line you use on women?"

Brent reached out, clicked off the lamp and moved her way. "Oh, yeah, haven't you heard? I'm the master of pickup lines."

"Oh, jeez," Rayne said, moving toward the door in case he wasn't teasing, even though part of her wanted to stay and find out. His laughter dogged her steps. The son of a gun was playing with her. She flung a last look over her shoulder. He stood framed against the darkness like a naughty ad for men's cologne or close-shaving razors.

"So will you be there tomorrow?"

He smiled. "Yeah. You can count on me."

Rayne arched an eyebrow. "Okay, I'll hold you to that."

Then she turned and made her way to the inn wondering if his promise meant as much now as it had back then. And wondering why she hadn't left as soon as she'd seen he was spectacularly naked.

She didn't know the answer to one question and was very afraid of the answer to the other.

CHAPTER FOUR

THE SOUP BUBBLED MERRILY on the stove as Rayne sliced truffles for the fennel and dandelion salad she would serve atop the thinly sliced Bosc pears. The rich smell of chicken broth made her tummy growl, but she kept slicing through the earthy pungency of the delicate fungus, while ignoring the smoky Gouda cheese sitting on the wooden cutting board. She'd found the cheese at a farmer's market in Dallas last weekend. It was divine and she'd already sampled too much of it.

"Mom, can we buy some Pop-Tarts?"

Rayne recoiled as if Henry had asked to eat a booger. "Good Lord, no. Where have you eaten Pop-Tarts?"

Henry shrugged. "Back in Austin. At Kyle Warner's house. He had all kinds of them. Strawberry, cinnamon and blue—"

"Stop." Rayne threw up her hand. "Do you know what kind of ingredients are in those things?"

Henry's brown eyes didn't blink as he stared at her. "I don't care. I saw a kid eating them at school today. They had icing on the top."

Meg dropped the books she was carrying onto the counter. "Give it up, bud. You've got the same chance as a nun getting a navel ring. Not going to happen. She'd rather you eat dirt than something with all those chemicals. Be glad you didn't eat it recently or you'd be getting purged."

"What's purged?" Henry asked, flicking little pieces of the cheese with his fingers.

"Stop," Rayne said for the umpteenth time that day.

"Making yourself throw up," Meg said, making the motion of sticking her finger down her throat.

Rayne shot her assistant a glare as Henry screwed up his face and groaned, "Gross!"

Brent stomped into the kitchen and sniffed. "What's gross?"

Meg fluttered and it made Rayne roll her eyes. Her assistant said Brent Hamilton did nothing for her. That, however, wasn't the way she acted. Her slightly Gothic, slightly punk, but wholly intelligent employee actually batted her heavily made-up eyes at Brent. "Whatever you want to be gross, stud muffin."

Rayne mimicked Meg's gagging action from a moment ago, making Henry laugh. She'd tried hard to overcome her strange feelings toward Brent over the past two days, treating him as she would any other employee. Though his gorgeousness made it plainly difficult to accomplish. After all, he'd taken his shirt off this morning inspiring Meg to use the word *yummy* way too often. The man had to stop taking his clothes off. Had to.

"Do *you* have Pop-Tarts, Mr. Hamilton?" Henry asked, sliding off the stool beside the kitchen island.

"I may have some cinnamon-brown sugar ones left over from the baseball sleepover," he said eyeing the tomato-basil soup on the stove.

"Wait. You have a baseball team?" Henry's eyes

lit up with interest. Rayne felt her mom radar start beeping.

"I don't *have* one. I coach one," Brent said. Rayne could tell he wasn't paying attention to his words. He was staring at the oat-bran muffins she'd made with the stone-ground wheat. He obviously had no idea what he'd done. How he'd unleashed a monster, one Rayne would have to deal with.

"Can I be on the team? I'm good. I promise. When I played with the Bengals, I hit it over the fence two times." Henry parked himself at Brent's boots and looked at him expectantly.

Shoot.

"Henry, Mr. Hamilton already has a team. We talked about this," Rayne said, brushing her hands on her apron and preparing for battle. Meg wisely started flipping through whatever catalogs she'd lugged in. She knew the power of Henry's will.

"Henry can still play. Hunter Todd broke his arm doing cartwheels on the bleachers, so now we're a player short. We have practice tonight at six if he wants to come along," Brent said as he slid closer to the muffins. Rayne had sprinkled them with homemade granola so they looked even more tempting than the average oat muffin.

But she didn't have time to offer him a sample of her testing ground muffins. Her son had taken to whooping, "Yes!" over and over again.

Rayne jabbed Brent in the arm. "You gotta fix this. He can't play ball this year."

Brent finally ripped his attention from the food. "Fix what? Why not?"

Henry whooped once more, performing several fist

pumps, before tearing out of the kitchen and pounding up the stairs. Rayne knew where he was heading. He'd dig his glove from the drawer she'd relegated it to yesterday. Then he'd pull all his shorts from the bottom drawer to look for his baseball pants. Then he'd bring her the cleats to untie because they were double-knotted and he couldn't pull them loose with the stubby nails he habitually bit to the quick. Hurricane Henry had set his path, but he'd forgotten that landfall wouldn't happen without her permission.

And she wasn't giving it.

Rayne glared at the daft man before her. She tried not to notice how damn good he looked in his tight jeans and the T-shirt he'd finally pulled on. How his shaggy hair looked salon-tousled. How he hadn't bothered to shave that morning which gave him a bed-rumpled, lazy movie star look. Hell, no. She wasn't noticing because he'd created a big problem and he had no clue.

"Henry can't play ball. He's behind in his reading at school. He's not up to grade level and struggling to acclimate in the classroom."

"Oh. Sorry. I knew he loved sports. I've tripped over four balls today already. I figured being on the team would help him make friends and feel a part of the community."

Rayne blinked. She'd never thought of it from that perspective. She knew Henry was lonely. She knew he'd had a hard time the past few days adapting to school. The classes were small and the kids all knew one another. He felt like the odd man out. And if anyone knew that feeling, she did. But she couldn't allow him to neglect something as important as school. It was already such a chore to get him to sit still and focus on the homework he'd been assigned that afternoon. "That's true, but he can't play."

Henry roared into the kitchen, cleats dangling in his hand. "Hey, Mr. Hamilton, where's practice?"

The boy hopped onto the stool and started trying to untie the cleats. He ignored the bits of red clay that fell from the bottoms of the shoes and confettied the floor beneath him.

"Um, sport, I can't really add you to the team without your mom's permission." Brent slapped her son on the back and cast a furtive look at Meg. Like he thought she would help him.

"Let's leave Rayne and Henry to sort this out," Meg said, jerking her head toward the dining room. Rayne wanted to kick her for helping the enemy. But was Brent really her enemy? Or was being a mom simply too tough sometimes? Either way, she wanted to blame someone for the heart she was about to break. Henry hated school and hated reading. Not a good combination for a kid in second grade. He still had a long row to hoe where academics were concerned even if he were passing at grade level.

Brent moved faster than Meg. He beat her out the door by a good yard.

Henry turned sweet brown eyes on her. "I can't play?"

Rayne sighed before slipping onto the stool next to her son. His cowlick stuck straight up and she wanted to kiss the freckles that sprinkled his little upturned nose, but she didn't. She caught his hands, stilling them. "Honey, we've already talked about sports. School comes first, and you're a little behind the kids in your class. Once you show me you're doing better then you can play baseball or football."

"But—"

"No *buts*."

"But—"

"Henry!" Rayne crossed her arms and prepared for battle. "I said no."

His eyes filled with tears. "You're so mean. You don't care about me. You took me off my team and brought me here. I thought it would be okay, but I don't like the stupid school here, either. School sucks."

"All right, where did you hear that language?"

His lips pressed together and he glared at her even as big tears spilled down his cheeks. He rubbed his eyes but said nothing.

"Henry? I asked you a question."

"Nowhere," he muttered, propping his arms on the granite counter. His elbows had dirt on them and his shirt had barbecue stains from the sloppy joe he'd had for lunch. Rayne would have to start packing his lunch. No telling what had been in that meat in the school cafeteria.

Rayne set her elbows on the counter next to her son's and settled her chin onto her hands. She blew out her breath. "I don't want you using that language again. It doesn't sound nice."

Henry rubbed at his eyes again. "Please, Mom. Please say I can play. Let me at least go to practice with them. I'll read that book. I promise. And I'll make good grades, too. You'll see. I can do it."

Her heart squeezed in her chest. She wanted to say yes. She wanted nothing more than for her baby to be happy. He'd gone through so much. He'd lost his father, had to move and suffered from separation anxiety and nightmares so severe that she cried herself to sleep for him. She wanted to watch him hit that ball and run those bases, but that was not what he needed. Sometimes it *sucked* being a mom. "I'll make you a deal. You bring home signed papers that show me you are improving, and I'll consider letting you play."

"But I won't get signed papers till next week. Can I just read the book? Come on, Mom, let's make a deal. Please. I promise I will do better."

Rayne felt the tears prick the back of her eyes. She thought about his face as he'd entered the classroom on Monday. About the way he'd fisted one hand in the fabric of her skirt. And she felt herself waver. Didn't Henry deserve something to make him happy? God, she was such a sucker. "Okay, you can practice with them. But no game until papers come home. And you have to read, starting now. One chapter before you even look at a baseball."

Henry wrapped his arms around her arm and hugged it. "Thank you, Mom, thank you. I love you."

She turned and wrapped her arms around him and pulled him to her, inhaling his little-boy scent, dropping a kiss on the back of his sweaty neck. "I love you, Hank."

He jerked back. "You called me *Hank*."

"I don't think it's such a bad nickname, but I'll still call you Henry most days."

"Like when I'm in trouble? Like when you call me Henry David?" His eyes laughed and he grinned like a deranged cartoon character. Something inside her bloomed at making him so happy, even as a little voice niggled, telling her she should have stuck to her guns.

Rayne clunked that annoying told-you-so voice over the head with an imaginary mallet. Then she drank in the sight of her son from his cowlick to his knotted cleats. He was all boy. Never in a million years would she have expected her and Phillip to create something like Henry. When she'd been pregnant with him, she'd dream of a cerebral child with blond hair and a preference for violin rather than baseball. She saw herself popping in videotapes that taught foreign languages and music. She saw herself reading books and demonstrating how to paint with watercolors.

Funny how life had played a joke on her with a rough, rowdy ball of fire. A sweet, silly Brent-like child. Well, except for the cerebral part. Rayne knew what many did not. Brent was highly intelligent. And Brent loved to read. And write. And create. And so did Henry. He simply just didn't know it yet.

"Okay, so off you go. I've got to finish my soup, and you've got a book to start on."

Henry's shoulders slumped slightly. "Okay, but can I toss the ball with Mr. Hamilton before I start on the book?"

At her look, he muttered, "Nevermind," and hopped off the stool.

She smiled and cast a glance toward the bubbling soup. She didn't want to overcook it.

"Hey, sport. I got you something."

Brent's deep voice came from behind her. She spun on the stool to see him standing before Henry holding a book aloft.

"A book?" Henry sounded a bit disappointed, but wasn't rude enough to let it show too much.

"Yeah," Brent said, squatting down and thumping the book. She could make out a boy holding a bat on the front. "This one is about a boy named Charlie who finds out he's really good at pitching, and, get this, he only has one arm."

Henry took the book and studied the cover. "How's he do that with one arm?"

"Guess you'll have to read and find out," Brent said, standing and looking at her. "All right with you, Mom? Maybe a sports book might be better than, what was the one you were reading? A talking mouse?"

Henry's eyes never left the book. "Yeah, a dumb talking mouse."

Rayne shook her head and smiled. "Well, what do you say, Henry?"

"Hank," Henry said before grinning up at Brent. "Thank you, Mr. Hamilton. I mean, Coach."

"You're welcome," Brent said, tousling her son's hair.

Seeing Brent touch her son in such a warm, almost fatherly manner did funny things to Rayne's heart. She wished Henry still had a father to play ball with, to receive books from, to grin up at. She missed that for him. "Now, get to reading. You've got practice in an hour. Can he catch a ride with you, Brent? I've got to finish a few things here."

Henry waited for Brent's nod before hauling out of the room like the devil was on his heels, clutching the book and tripping over his untied shoelace.

Rayne looked at Brent. Her heart still harbored the resentment, but she felt the block of ice around it melt a bit. Nothing like being nice to her boy to move her toward a better place. "Thanks. That was nice of you."

"No problem." Then he smiled, causing her heart to do little flippy things. Damn it. She had to stop thinking about his smile, his naked chest, the thought of being literally tangled up in him. The man had hurt her. Remember the Alamo. Or rather, the Oak Stand Literary Night circa 1994.

She moved toward the stove, picked up a wooden spoon and her control over her hormones. The soup looked perfect, nice and tomatoey. Rich and creamy. Her taste buds rioted for a little nip. She ignored them and instead added the chopped basil sitting on a cutting board beside the range. "So you happened to have a kid's book lying around?"

She saw his hand move toward one of the muffins and smiled. Men. Boys. They all were alike. Hungry. "Well, I like all kinds of books."

"Yeah, I saw the Debbie Macomber on the shelf. And, yes, you can have a muffin."

"Thanks," he said, cramming it into his mouth. "Mmm. I like these. Oh, and that was my mom's book. Don't know how it got on my shelf."

"But a kid's book?"

He licked his fingers and made her think of things other than food. "Well, I coach kids. The lessons in those books relate to kids. Or something like that."

"Oh. Well, thanks for letting Henry borrow one."

"He can keep that copy. I have a few others, so if he likes that one, he can borrow another."

She stirred the soup, scooping enough to taste, and slipped the spoon in her mouth. It needed a pinch more sea salt and then she could dish it up for Meg and Aunt Fran to sample. "That's nice of you."

"I can be a nice guy. Sometimes."

Rayne looked over her shoulder. "I remember."

"Yeah," he said, grabbing a paper towel and wiping his hands. "I gotta run. Tell your aunt I'll be back in the morning. Early this time because I got some work to do at the Harpers' in the afternoon. Send Hank over in about thirty, okay?"

Then he stepped out the back door before she could say anything else. Before she could remember how nice he'd been once. How sweet and vulnerable. So different than what others thought about him. And at one time so absolutely perfect for her.

She washed her hands and allowed the memories to follow the water right down the drain. It was easier that way.

BRENT JOGGED TO HIS PARENTS' house to let Apple out and realized he'd forgotten and left her asleep on his bed. After grabbing their mail and stacking it on the counter and riffling through the too-thin *Oak Stand Gazette*, he hurried across the backyard, thinking about the repercussions of handing Henry one of his earlier books. He hadn't thought about it seeming strange that he'd have copies of a children's book lying about his house. He'd thought only of finding something Henry would actually enjoy reading, something that would hook him and have him turning pages.

Lucky he could think fast on his feet. It was a good ability to have.

Apple trotted up to him, carrying a decorative pillow

she'd capriciously ripped apart. Fluffy white clouds covered his rug. Damn it.

"Apple, you dumbass dog. I ought to punt you to Houston, you stupid mutt."

The Boston terrier dropped the pillow his mother had painstakingly cross-stitched with his initials at his feet and smiled up at him. Then she barked.

He nudged her with his work boot and picked up the half-flattened pillow. "Damn it."

Apple barked again before clamping her mouth onto the torn pillow for a game of tug-of-war.

"Stop it," he said, pulling the pillow. Apple growled and shook her head.

"Talking to the dog again?"

Brent dropped the pillow and propped his hands on his hips. "Hey, Tamara. Yeah, stupid dog tore up that pillow Mom gave me when I moved in here."

Tam stepped inside, shut the door and propped her bottom on the armchair. He could smell her perfume as it wafted toward him, curling into his nostrils. He glanced at her. She looked fine sitting there, with her golden hair tumbling down her back and her glossy lips ready to be plundered. She wore an itty-bitty dress that tied under her breasts and high-heeled sandals that made her legs look long and tanned.

"I see," she drawled, and he could tell she had more on her mind than a cross-stitched pillow or a dog. "You wanna go over to the Dairy Barn for a burger tonight then maybe head out to Cooley's? It's two-for-Tuesday."

He picked up the stuffing and repried the pillow from Apple's mouth. "Nah, I got baseball practice."

"Oh, yeah," she said, rising and smoothing the

flimsy cotton against her upper thighs. "I forgot you coach a team."

He opened the door and whistled. Apple trotted outside, then spied a squirrel and gave chase. He closed the door as Tamara's arms curled round his stomach.

"I thought maybe we could try to fix that problem you had the other night," she whispered against his back. Her fingers smoothed themselves across his stomach. Unwillingly, he felt himself harden, but he grabbed her hands and disengaged them.

He turned. "I don't think we have time for that kind of therapy, Tam. Though I do thank you for the offer."

She smiled. Her two canines were slightly longer than her other teeth, giving her a vampy, cute smile. Two dimples appeared in her cheeks. "Well, you know, I do work for agriculture extension. It's my job to make things grow."

He chuckled, before bringing her hands to his lips. "And I appreciate the dedication you bring to your work."

"Oh, heck, Brent. I had to go somewhere. Liv's with Mark. They've been driving me crazy with all their talk of the upcoming wedding. I'm sick of tripping over bridal magazines and all the damned invitation sample books. I can't believe she's taking the plunge."

Liv Wheeler was Tamara's roommate. He'd dated her once upon a time. She was a sweet girl, not much of a conversationalist, but then again, they hadn't talked much. The relationship had lasted about a month. She came from a good family and had a sweet disposition so he'd hoped it would evolve into something serious. But it turned out they had little in common. Liv only watched reality television, and the only books she'd ever read were *The Baby-sitters Club* series when she was twelve. No conversation, only action, which had been fine for a while, but really, he was more than a piece of meat, no matter what everyone liked to say.

"Mark's a good guy. You need to find a guy like that."

She tugged at his waistband. "Maybe you. You're a good guy."

"No, I'm not." He removed her hands again and grabbed the remote control. He'd left the station on ESPN and the opening day baseball scores scrolled along the bottom of the screen. He clicked it off.

"What's wrong, Brent? You're always good for a quickie," Tamara teased, propping her hand on one hip. "Or at least you were."

Her words ruffled him. He didn't have to prove anything to anyone. He was a man. Hell, he'd gotten hard staring at Rayne lick the spoon out of the soup earlier, so he knew there wasn't anything wrong with the equipment. It was something else altogether that had him stepping away from Tamara. Something new and different wriggled inside him. A desire to be taken seriously. A wish to give up the fabled, carefree, eye candy image he'd fallen into long ago…and stayed in. He was tired of that life. And the woman before him was another piece in the puzzle of dissatisfaction.

But Tamara wasn't the sort of girl who took no for an answer. Her tenacity had served her well in the past. Usually she got her man. But the digital clock on the microwave beyond her shoulder told him it was six-thirteen. It took ten minutes to get to the ball field. He still needed to gather up the catching equipment and fill up the watercooler.

"No time," Brent said, giving Tamara a quick, hard kiss on the forehead, before unwrapping her from around his legs. "Got boys waiting on me, Tam."

Tamara narrowed her eyes. "And I have some waiting on me at Cooley's."

Brent smiled at her attempt to stir jealousy. It was an emotion he was unfamiliar with. Except for when it stirred last weekend when Kate Newman had kissed Rick Mendez beneath the flowered arbor. And it wasn't jealousy over Kate. It was jealousy for what they'd found together. Utter joy. Utter happiness. Utter love.

The only *utter* he held was utter contempt for his life. And for some reason, something inside him burned for a piece of what Kate and Rick had found last weekend.

He wasn't sure why he wanted more now, but he knew he did.

A flash of color caught his eye and broke his thoughts. He stepped from the warmth of Tamara's embrace and moved toward the French doors. Henry stood, nose pressed against the windowpane.

"Who's that?" Tamara asked from over his shoulder.

Brent didn't answer. Just pulled the door open. "Hey, Hank. Where's your mom?"

The boy shrugged. "She was right behind me. She said she'd pick me up at seven-thirty. She knows where, right?"

Brent nodded as he saw the back end of Rayne disappear behind a hedge that needed clipping. An apron tie snagged on a limb and a slender hand tugged it loose. Brent had no doubt Rayne had seen Tamara twined round him like ivy on an oak. He wished she hadn't. She already thought him the town gigolo and he'd cemented that impression in her mind, no doubt.

"Come on in, Hank. I've got to grab my equipment and then we can go." The boy stepped inside and eyed the woman studying her manicure. "Oh, this is a friend. Tamara Beach."

Henry ducked his head and rubbed the toe of his cleat in the rug. "Hi."

Tamara bent down. "Hey, Hank. You gonna be on Brent's team, huh? It's the best team to be on because Brent is the best coach."

Henry peered up at her beneath the brim of his stained baseball cap. "Um, yeah."

Brent placed a hand on Henry's shoulder. It surprised him Henry would be so shy. He hadn't displayed any unease several days ago when he'd climbed over the fence. In fact, the boy had seemed in his element.

Tamara stood and smiled at Brent, her disgruntled feelings at not getting a roll in the hay gone. "Okay, you guys have fun. Will I see you later at Cooley's, Brent?"

Brent shook his head. "Not tonight. Got a full day tomorrow. Have some fun for me."

A small furrow appeared between her eyebrows before she nodded and flicked the bill of Henry's cap. "Later, gators."

Tamara picked up the keys she'd abandoned on the end table and slipped out the door.

Henry watched. "She's pretty. Is she your girlfriend?"

Brent walked into the kitchen and started filling up the cooler with water from the faucet. Then he grabbed the equipment bag from the alcove beside the pantry. "No. Just a friend."

Henry followed him. "Do you have a girlfriend?"

"Nope. No girlfriend," he said, slinging the bag on his shoulder and grabbing two sports drinks from the fridge. It wasn't too hot yet, but Henry might need some extra electrolytes.

"So are you funny?"

Brent shut the fridge door. "Huh?"

"You know. Funny. Like this one guy who works for my mom. He likes other guys and stuff." Henry's brown eyes were so matter-of-fact. Brent had no clue kids his age knew about homosexuality. He was knocked for a loop.

"Um, no. I'm not funny…in that way. But I know some good knock-knock jokes."

"Me, too." Henry smiled and Brent noticed he was missing his two lower teeth. It made him look even cuter. "Hey, I read one whole chapter of that book all by myself."

Brent motioned him toward the door. "That's great. Chapter books can be hard. Only big kids read those."

Henry nodded. "I feel bad for that kid in the book. He didn't get born with a whole arm. That's gotta stink."

Brent felt a flash of satisfaction. Just what he had thought when he'd met a college teammate's son who'd been born with a congenital heart defect which resulted in an underdeveloped limb. He'd intentionally written that book to celebrate the fact his friend's son Reese hadn't allowed his handicap to keep him from playing sports. It was one of his favorite books.

"Yeah, but the kid doesn't let his disability hold him back. You'll see that he's pretty brave, especially when some kids make fun of him. Even his own teammates."

Brent unlocked his truck, tossed the equipment bag and cooler in the bed and helped Henry climb into the cab.

"Well, I'm only on chapter two, but I guess it'll make me mad if they're mean to Charlie. It doesn't seem fair to not be like other kids. It probably makes him cry at night when no one is around."

Brent opened his mouth, then shut it as he cranked the engine. He wondered if Henry knew firsthand about crying in the privacy of his room. It seemed unfathomable that a strong, funny kid like Henry could suffer humiliation at the hands of others. He seemed so cool. So talented. So innocent and wonderful.

"Maybe," Brent commented, reversing out of the driveway. "You'll have to read and find out."

Henry propped his chin on his elbow and watched the passing scenery of Oak Stand. They rounded the town square, braked for a squirrel and headed south toward the Oak Stand Athletic fields. "Do you think my mom will be early to pick me up?"

Brent shifted his gaze from the road to the boy looking way too contemplative for a seven-year-old.

"Sure. If not, we'll call her. Or you can ride back with me."

"Oh," Henry said, fiddling with the glove he held in his lap. "Okay. I think she'll probably be early."

Brent waved at his friend Margo, who swept the steps of Tucker House, then saluted the new police chief, Adam Bent, before swinging toward the highway that would take them to the sports complex outside the city limits.

"So you like books, huh?"

Brent grabbed a dusty ball cap from the dash and crammed it on his head. "Sure. I love books."

Henry studied him. "Really?"

Brent nodded. "Really. Books take me to new places. Places I can't go—pirate ships or secret rain forests. Besides, I learn about people who are like me and people who aren't. It's like taking a trip, but you don't have to pack."

Henry frowned. "I don't really like books. I'd rather be doing something. Playing ball or watching TV. My mom reads stuff all the time. Sometimes she cries when she reads books. I hate when my mom cries."

The boy turned and looked out the window as if he knew he'd said too much.

Brent wasn't sure if he should respond. So he let a few moments go by. Nothing but Miranda Lambert on the radio crooning about love gone wrong.

They drove into the parking lot adjacent to the ball field. A few of the kids on his team already tossed the ball, warming up.

"You know, there's nothing wrong with crying, Hank."

Henry's head whipped around. He met the Brent's gaze. "Do you cry?"

Brent shrugged. "If I need to."

Henry's brow knotted. "Oh."

Brent didn't want to tell Henry the last time he'd cried had been when he read in the *Oak Stand Gazette* that Rayne Rose had married Phillip Albright. That when he'd read those words and saw her smiling face staring out from the page something had crumbled inside him and the world faded several shades dimmer. Because up until seeing Rayne's and Phillip's names linked together in holy matrimony, Brent hadn't realized how much he'd believed in a second chance with Rayne…until that chance had disappeared. The dream of somehow finding himself in her good graces again had been blown out like a candle, leaving the recesses of his heart dark. And that knowledge had caused tears to prick the back of his eyes and sadness to burn deep inside his gut.

But over the past day or two, he'd been looking for matches, contemplating a way to light the candle of hope again. If he could move past her anger and disappointment in him, then maybe, just maybe, he had a shot with Rayne. As crazy as the idea seemed.

And it seemed crazy.

Rayne was going to leave Oak Stand. Her life was too grand for the simplicity of the town. Besides, their past was a hopeless tangle of fierce emotions, emotions born of angsty teenage lust and love.

But he couldn't stop the thought that had anchored itself inside him. Fate wasn't a fickle lady. She knew her mind. The cards had been dealt the moment he'd sat on that porch step days ago, hating himself and his life. Then a ball had landed in the backyard and things had changed. Maybe Fate was on his side this time, even if she wasn't ready to show her cards yet.

He turned to Henry. "Game on. Let's play some baseball."

CHAPTER FIVE

RAYNE PULLED INTO THE parking lot of the baseball field and girded herself against stepping into "real" Oak Stand. Nothing like a pack of former schoolmates to make her feel like a gauche little nobody. She knew it was asinine to feel vulnerable again, but that didn't help. Thinking and feeling were two different things. She cracked the windows in her Volvo SUV before sliding on sunglasses and climbing out.

Remember. You're not the pathetic, awkward Rayne Rose. You're the successful, intelligent owner of Serendipity. You have products with your name on them. You have the power now. No one can take it from you.

Why was she giving herself a rah-rah pep talk just to pick up her son? The word *nutty* came to mind as she scanned the area.

The ballpark had seen improvements since the last time she'd been here. The stands had coverings and the concession had been painted a bright blue highlighting a mural of a baseball sprouting arms and legs. The park looked neat and well-tended, not a scraggly weed in sight.

"Rayne Rose!" said a voice to her left.

Rayne turned and saw a plump woman wearing a visor and tugging a toddler heading her way. She paused on the curb and tried to figure out who the woman was.

"My gosh, it's been years. I use your recipe for guacamole all the time. I saw you on *Good Morning America*."

Rayne nodded, but had no clue who the woman was. She had apple cheeks and brown eyes the color of rich chocolate ganache.

"You remember me, don't you? Stacy Darling. Well, Harp now. I was a year ahead of you."

Rayne took a step back.

Stacy Darling had been one of the meanest girls in all of Oak Stand High. She'd been lithe, trim and amazing with a basketball. She'd also reduced many a girl to tears, and Rayne had been a favored target. *Come on, retard, can't you catch a ball? What did your hippy mamma eat when she was pregnant with you, Knobby? Grass? 'Cause you're about as ugly as a goat's ass.*

Being the awkward daughter of a pair of artisan hippies had been challenging. Her parents had traipsed across the country, unmarried and unrepentant, dragging Rayne and her sister, Summer, with them. Sometimes Rayne and Summer had been homeschooled. Sometimes dumped in an elementary school near whatever commune her parents were visiting. Her father blew glass and her mother worked pottery or made clothing. Not the ideal lifestyle for children. Rayne had come to live with Aunt Frances and Uncle Travis when she was ten. The six years she'd spent in Oak Stand had been the most stable in her life, even if she had to deal with bullies and mean-spirited people who forgot they were good Christian folk when it came to bastard children.

"Oh, Stacy, of course." Rayne turned her head toward the field and away from the memories. Henry had rounded second base and headed toward third. The boy flew like wings were on his feet. If only she'd had a smidgen of Henry's ability when she'd been young. She wouldn't have had to "forget" her P.E. uniform so often. And she wouldn't have been in Stacy's line of fire every day of her sophomore year.

"I'm picking up my son." Rayne started moving toward the fence surrounding the field. Several mothers sat along the chain-link length in camp chairs, surrounded by younger children.

"Oh, me, too. I'll walk with you," Stacy said, tugging the toddler by the hand and falling into step with Rayne. Stacy's little girl had a runny nose and droopy pigtails. She also didn't seem to want to go with her mother. She kept planting her feet and sliding as Stacy tugged her. "My son plays on Brent's team, too. He's a good coach."

"Oh, okay. This is Henry's first practice," Rayne murmured as she watched Brent bend and curve one arm around Henry's shoulders as he stood on third base. Her son nodded and looked intently at the slim boy batting.

"I was so glad Camden got on Brent's team. The scenery's nice, if you know what I mean."

Rayne knew exactly what Stacy meant, but she wasn't going to comment on Brent's obvious attributes.

Stacy cracked a smile. "Hey, I may be married, but I'm not dead."

Rayne really wanted Stacy to go away. She knew the woman had likely grown out of mean girl mode, but the last thing she wanted to do was make small talk about Brent Hamilton and how amazingly he filled out a pair of shorts. It seemed almost cliché. And she knew the only reason Stacy deemed her conversation-worthy was because of her minor celebrity status.

"So are you visiting? Or moving back? Or what?" Stacy asked, waving at a platinum blonde woman wearing next to nothing. "There's Brandi McCormick. You remember her?"

Of course she did. She'd been Brandi Patterson in high school. Rayne remembered how the captain of the dance line had tripped her in the hallway and proceeded to make fun of Rayne's granny panties when her skirt had flown over her head. Nothing like the whole school whispering about your underwear. Talk about scars. "I remember her."

Brandi ended her conversation and headed toward them. The only relief Rayne felt was that she'd avoided answering Stacy's question about being in Oak Stand. Mostly, because she didn't know the answer. She had no clue how long she would stay. She'd allow Henry to finish out the school year, of course, but she didn't know if she'd stay much longer. Tulip Hill should be transformed to Serendipity Inn by the first of June and technically Rayne would be back in Austin…or apartment shopping in New York. Depended on an offer coming through from the network. Her agent still hadn't gotten definite word. The last time her agent had gone to the mattresses with the network, she'd been turned down. Rayne had dreamed big about having a show of her own like Rachael Ray or Giada. This might be her last shot at negotiating with the Food Network.

So she had no answer for when she'd leave Texas. Or if she'd even have the opportunity to do so.

"Well, Rayne Rose, you grew up good," Brandi drawled, sliding her hair behind her ear. A big diamond glittered on her tanned hand. Oversize designer glasses hid her eyes, but Rayne could smell bourbon on her. She wore a small tennis skirt and sleeveless athletic shirt. She looked like every suburban mom Rayne knew rolled into one parody. The phrase "trying too hard" came to mind.

"Thank you," Rayne murmured, seeking out her son once again. She could make nice with the other moms if only for Henry. She didn't need their boys being as mean as their mothers had once been. "You look good yourself."

Brandi preened, tucking another lock behind her ear. "Thanks. I work out most days."

Then she delivered a pointed look to Stacy.

"Don't start, Brandi. I don't have time to work out. With four kids and a part-time job doin' nails at the Curlique, my hands are full." Stacy narrowed her eyes at Brandi. "Brandi owns the Anytime Fitness and thinks everyone in town should belong."

Brandi surveyed her manicured nails. "Not everyone."

To say Rayne felt uncomfortable was an understatement, so she stepped around the two women and waved at Henry who delivered a thumbs-up.

Brent saw Rayne and jogged her way. She could feel the two women behind her tighten with expectation.

"Hey, Rayne. Henry's doing great. He's a natural." Brent stopped in front of her and propped his arms on the top of the fence. He wore a pair of athletic shorts, a sleeveless workout shirt and an old ball cap. He looked about as fine as a man could. She could almost hear

Brandi and Stacy sigh. He peered over her shoulder. "Oh, hey, ladies."

The women stepped forward and Brandi literally elbowed her way in front of Rayne. Something inside Rayne snapped. She pictured Brandi trying to put her in her place. Maybe it was infantile, but she knew what they'd once thought of her. Skinny little no-nothing Rayne. Well, no longer. She'd handled bigger egos and bitchier women in the back of every restaurant she'd worked in. She shoved her glasses atop her head, walked to the other side of the overly done woman and beckoned Brent with her eyes. She also licked her lips. Like a very good boy, he stepped her way. Rayne smiled. "I'm glad Henry's doing so well. And I appreciate your giving him a lift."

Brent, a connoisseur of the game of seduction, gave her a toe-curling smile. Damn him. His dimples were weapons of destruction, hammering the defenses of any woman within twenty feet.

"He's a funny kid. Told me some good knock-knock jokes. And he's a great ballplayer. I'm going to work him at—"

"What about Camden?" Stacy interrupted. "Do you think he needs more batting practice?"

Brent ripped his gaze from Rayne's. "Nah, he's doing fine, Stace."

Brandi's perfume drifted into Rayne's nose. "Well, Colby's been having trouble with learning shortstop. Do you think I could get you to give him some extra practice? I'll be glad to bring him to you."

Not so subtle. Rayne couldn't stop her lips from turning up. She clamped them together and tried to look concerned that Colby was having trouble at shortstop.

But Brent saw through Brandi's plea. His knowing gaze met Rayne's and she fell back through the years. It had always been this way. Girls chasing Brent. Her laughing at their blatant attempts.

Until the girls had succeeded. She sobered at the thought. Hadn't Tamara Beach portrayed a boa constrictor at his house hours ago? And Brent hadn't seemed too bothered by it. Same old Brent.

She wasn't going to stand around and watch women fall all over themselves trying to secure a spot in his bed. She had way better things to do. And it wasn't jealousy rearing its ugly head. Merely Rayne refusing to play the role she'd played years ago. She and Brent would share no secret looks, make no private jokes. They weren't friends. They weren't anything.

Rayne stepped away from their chatter and crooked a finger at Henry who stood staring at the other boys trying to douse each other with water. He looked lonely.

"Hey, tiger. Ready to head home? Maybe get a bubble bath in Auntie Fran's big—" She stopped when a horrified expression crossed Henry's face. Oops. Maybe she shouldn't have offered that bubble bath in front of all those boys.

The boys stopped trying to soak each other and stared at her. Henry looked as if he wanted to sink through the third base and disappear beneath the red dirt.

A dark-headed boy who only came to Henry's chin, grabbed another one of the boys, secured him in a headlock, and sang, "Yeah, Hanky wanky, wanna bubble bath, boo-boo?"

Rayne nearly slapped herself at the tragic look in

Henry's eyes. He shot her a glance that said, "Thanks for nothing," then lifted his chin and headed toward where the boys still tussled on the pitching mound. The boy who'd teased Henry struggled against a bigger boy who'd tripped him and planted him in the dirt. Uh-oh.

Henry halted in front of the boy. "Yeah? Well, I'd rather take a bubble bath then suck the way you do playing third base."

Then her son jumped over the boy's feet and headed her way. Rayne opened her mouth to say how sorry she was for stepping into her Mother of the Year shoes at the absolutely wrong time, but didn't get the first word out. Henry crossed the first base line and then he hit the dirt. The dark-headed boy rolled him over and punched him in the face.

"Henry!" Rayne yelled.

Brent pulled himself from the two mothers and ran to the tussle. He had the two boys pulled apart before any other adults could react. The other boys gathered round the two squirming kids, who shouted a couple of obscenities at each other.

Rayne didn't know Henry even knew some of those words, though she knew her head chef used them often enough. Henry had learned from a master.

"Cut it out," Brent commanded as the two boys struggled to reach one another. Henry's eyes flashed ire. He was as pissed off as Rayne had ever seen him. Blood trickled from his nose and something painful seared across her chest. This was her fault.

"Oh, my gosh! Camden!" Stacy said, tugging the toddler once again toward the gate. "Camden, are you hurt?"

Rayne didn't move. To hurry over and wipe Henry's nose would only make it worse. She clutched the top of the fence and watched as Brent dragged both boys toward the dugout.

The other kids, along with Stacy, tried to follow, but Brent turned around and stopped them with a look. "I'll handle this. Everyone else wait for me on the mound. No roughhousing. Stand and wait."

Then Brent disappeared into the dugout, dropping both boys onto a bench and standing over them. Rayne couldn't hear his words. But she knew they were getting an earful. And she knew it was what Henry needed. A man doing a man's job. Teaching boys about being boys.

It made Rayne feel so inadequate.

Henry needed a father.

A longing crept into her heart as a dangerous thought flashed in her mind. Brent would be a good father.

Strike that.

Not an option.

The last thing Rayne needed was the itty-bitty idea of a Brent as a "keeper" creeping into her brain and taking up permanent residence. She already had plenty of fantasies about Brent, ones she'd had for so long she was comfortable with them even if they wouldn't amount to a hill of beans. The picture of Brent as a father, as a man to depend upon, couldn't exist with her kinky ones. Because she suspected he could deliver on the tangled sheets one, but couldn't on any daydream that involved her, Henry and a cute little picket fence.

She and Henry were leaving in a matter of months whether it was back to Austin or to New York. And she and Brent were no longer friends. They weren't anything.

She'd repeat that mantra fourteen thousand times over in order for her heart to accept it as true.

Stacy tapped her on the shoulder, drawing her from her affirmation regarding Brent.

"What's with your son? He started this, you know."

Rayne turned and pretended Stacy was a sous-chef. She set her gaze on subzero and leveled it at Stacy. "I don't think so. Your son struck my child. I do believe that is the definition for *starting it*."

Stacy sputtered. "Listen here, Rayne. You may be a famous chef, but I know you. Your momma and daddy wasn't even married and you think you can come back to this town and bring your kid. What is he? A bastard, too?"

Rayne's hand curled, but she did nothing more than look down her nose at Stacy, as she stepped so close to her that the chubby woman had to step backward. Rayne made her eyes crackle, then narrowed them. "What you may not realize is I'm not the same girl you tortured in school, and I won't stand for you or your son picking on my child. If I have to get an attorney, then I will. You're nothing but a bully, and I've learned how to deal with bullies. You smack 'em right in the mouth."

Stacy opened her mouth again, but Rayne stepped even closer. She could smell the garlic on the woman's breath. "Go ahead. I dare you."

The cheerful, chubby Stacy didn't look so friendly anymore, but she snapped her mouth closed. "Whatever. Just make sure your boy stays away from mine."

Silence sat between them.

Which was not good. If she didn't play nice with Stacy, Brandi and every other Oak Stand mommy, Henry would suffer. She needed to pull out her negotiating skills and tip the balance back in her favor.

Rayne stepped back, crossed her arms and smiled. "You know, we're old friends and we shouldn't have to treat each other this way. It's going to be hard to stay away from one another since our children are on the same team, isn't it?"

Stacy didn't look convinced but nodded anyway.

"I think we need to put this behind us. After all, we want our children to get along, don't we? We've got to model good behavior," Rayne continued, consciously uncrossing her arms and assuming a nonthreatening demeanor.

Stacy's eyebrows knitted together. She was confused by Rayne's tactics. Rayne knew she was manipulating the woman, but she needed Stacy to play nice, the way she expected her staff to play nice. Everything under control. Everyone doing his or her part. Stacy had to feel she was doing Rayne a favor by extending the olive branch.

"Well, sure," Stacy said, pressing her lips together and visibly relaxing.

"Good. I knew you were the kind of mother who understood how boys can be," Rayne said, smiling a sweeter smile. "Now, I've been wanting to try a new recipe for guacamole. What do you think about adding poblano pepper instead of jalapeño, and trying out a few Texas heirloom tomatoes to balance the avocado? If I whip up a batch, would you give me your opinion? I'm thinking of featuring it in my new cookbook that's dedicated to Tex-Mex cuisine."

Stacy's eyes sparked. "I'd love to help you test it."

"Terrific," Rayne said, knowing it was a bit evil to use her fame as a vehicle to make Stacy behave. She watched as Henry and Camden followed Brent from the dugout toward the pitching mound. Their heads drooped like flowers after a storm.

Brandi sidled up to them. "You know, if you're whipping up some food for taste-testing, I'll bring the tequila."

I bet you will.

Stacy clapped her hands together. "Yes. We'll have a girls' night to welcome Rayne Rose back home. Perfect. When can we do it?"

Rayne sighed inwardly. The only side effect of manipulating people was overdoing it. Looked as if she'd be making dips and taking sips with Oak Stand's soccer moms...the same women who'd likely stood by years ago while girls like Brandi and Stacy hacked Rayne to shreds. "Sure. I'd love to."

The women excitedly talked about who to invite and where they should have the girls' night. Rayne listened with half an ear as she watched Brent talk to his team. Occasionally, they'd all nod their little heads and shuffle their cleats in the dusty mound. Then they all put their hands together and Brent counted, "1-2-3..."

"Warriors!" the boys shouted in unison.

They scattered like beetles, scrabbling left and right, snatching up batting bags and tossing their gloves into the air. All but Henry. He followed Brent into the dugout, like a miniature version of the man picking up paper cups and tucking a clipboard into a gym bag. Henry had the same physique. Broad shoulders, trim waist, muscular legs, but it was more the swagger in his walk and the lift of his chin that spoke of the same self-assurance.

And yet he was not Brent's child. He was Phillip's child. Even if the only things Henry shared with his dead father were his flat feet and dimples.

Now Henry was hers alone and had been for the past few years.

Weight descended upon her, and she wished for the umpteenth time Phillip was here to share the burden of raising a strong-willed, scared little boy with her.

Phillip had always been a good partner, a good friend and a good advisor. And he'd been a fantastic father, taking Henry to karate, on fishing trips and to the zoo while Rayne worked. She missed him. Especially now when she felt so incompetent, so confused about what direction she should take. Their five-year plan was at its conclusion, and she didn't know which way to go.

Henry appeared at her elbow. "Come on, let's go home, Mom."

For now she went with her son.

CHAPTER SIX

BRENT STARED AT THE BLANK page and wondered why the words wouldn't come. He'd outlined the chapters, knew his main character down to his SpongeBob undies and had a deadline looming. But, obviously, those things weren't going to help him meet his daily word count. The page mocked him with its perfect blankness.

"Hell," he muttered rubbing a hand over his face and pushing his rolling chair across the wood floor toward the massive bookshelf behind him.

Apple's nails clicked on the floor as she responded to his curse. Thankfully, no pillow or similarly fluffy item dangled from her mouth. Not that he had many fluffy items left. Apple had wreaked havoc on socks, slippers and his memory foam neck pillow the first week his parents left. All he had left were a few feather pillows he'd tucked in the top of a linen closet. She ignored the rubbery dental bones he'd bought.

Just like a woman. Didn't know what was good for her.

Immediately Rayne came to mind. He suspected she was the reason his usually energetic muse had abandoned him. Raine was like his flighty muse—fickle, teasing and infuriating without meaning to be so.

He still couldn't figure out why she was in Oak Stand. Sure, the inn needed some spiffing up, but it

seemed odd Rayne would take the time out of her busy
schedule and pull Henry out of school to splash some
paint on the old house. Something more was going
on at that bed-and-breakfast. Too much activity and
he sensed it had something to do with Rayne's newly
acquired fame.

And here he was, yet again, mixing himself up in
thoughts of Rayne. The sensible part of Brent knew he
should have found someone else to do the work on the
house. Should have kept his nose out of the baseball
business with Henry, not to mention he shouldn't have
fetched one of his books for the kid. But something
niggling in the back of his mind told him he'd done the
right thing by Henry. The boy, as capable as he looked,
had a vulnerability about him that made Brent want to
take care around him.

Just like Rayne.

She seemed capable as hell. So unlike the girl he'd
once known. A girl with a silly grin and romance in
her soul. This woman was so different he almost didn't
know her. The Rayne he'd known stopped to smell the
flowers and got lost in them. This new Rayne would
have cut the flowers, arranged them into an acceptable
bouquet and displayed them on a weathered farmhouse
table next to a perfect round of brie. Efficient, tamed,
controlled. It was almost too much of a change. Almost
enough to make him want to stay away from her. But
he suspected the old Rayne, the dreamy, romantic waif,
was somewhere inside this new woman.

So his heart wasn't buying the notion of keeping
Rayne Rose at arm's length. In fact, his heart wanted
her close. Very close.

He pushed his chair toward his desk, tugging with

him the book he always grabbed when words defied him. It was a beaten, ragtag textbook full of American poetry. He'd bought it his junior year of college when he'd signed up for a poetry class. It was the semester after he'd ridden the pine through most of the football season, the season he'd disappointed everyone. Something about the words he'd read in the tome had allowed the fetters of his life to fall away. He'd felt emboldened and full of conviction in a way he'd not felt since those hours he'd spent with Rayne reading Longfellow and Poe, playfully trying his hand at crafting internal rhyme or drawing caricatures of their teachers. Doing things his father said were "girly things." But they were things Brent had found value in.

He thumbed through the dog-eared pages past the words of masters, opening to the page that held the crumpled paper. He lifted and unfolded the much-handled poem. The handwriting was spidery with periodical fanciful loops. A small red heart sticker had been affixed to the upper left corner of the page. His finger traced the title "The Courage to Be He."

He smiled and tucked it back between the pages, hiding it as much as he hid himself. Closing the book of poetry, he stared at the blank page on the monitor before fingering the mouse. Maybe some research would motivate him. Or not.

A knock interrupted his lack of progress.

Brent glanced at the clock. It was well after nine.

He padded barefoot into the living area, drawing together the strings of his pajama pants.

Rayne stood outside, worrying her bottom lip with her teeth. She'd been showing up on his porch way too often for comfort. This, too, was a new habit of hers.

The old Rayne hemmed and hawed, ducking behind trees and hiding behind curtains. This new Rayne invaded.

He unlatched the French door. "Hey."

Her gaze hit his then dipped to his bare chest. She swallowed and redirected her gaze, but not before he caught the interest that flared in the warm depths of her eyes. "Hey."

A frisson of awareness skipped up his spine. She'd looked at him as though he was the last scoop of ice cream in the tub of rocky road. It made his body tighten with anticipation even though he knew it wasn't a good idea. Screwing Rayne wouldn't get him what he wanted. Well, it would get him something he wanted, but he wanted more than sweaty sheets and sexual satisfaction. He wanted a piece of what he'd once had with her...and that had nothing to do with lust. He stood a minute waiting for her to say something. She didn't. "Rayne?"

"Huh?"

"You knocked."

She blinked. "Oh, yes. Sorry. My mind has been wandering lately." She paused, as if to give herself a mental shake. "I wanted to say thank you."

He wanted to invite her inside so he could turn the glimpse of desire he'd seen into something full-fledged and worthy of bleary eyes in the morning. But that sort of behavior was his standard way of operating. Rayne wasn't just any girl. He couldn't go there with her. At least not yet. Or maybe never. He pulled logic in front of his libido and propped a hand on the doorjamb, blocking the entrance.

The scent of Rayne's perfume skated on the night

breeze. Vanilla. Her scent was almost enough to make him fling logic to the corners of the earth and throw open the door. "Thank me for what?"

"For taking Henry to task for the…incident at the ballpark. And for giving him a ride. I didn't get a chance to thank you again before you left the parking lot." She caught her lower lip with her bottom teeth and fidgeted with the hem of her shirt. She blazed into his yard, interrupted his writing, for what? This woman clung to her dislike of him, yet here she was. Talk about a big ol' bag of mixed signals. Maybe she was tempted to treat him like the man she thought him to be. A sure thing. Yeah. Maybe Rayne wanted to cash in on her old lustful feelings.

Any other time he'd let her. But not now. Not when he was actually committed to looking for something more than a glass of whiskey and a quickie in the backseat. He wanted that something more with her, even if the whole idea of pursuing Rayne for a permanent sort of relationship seemed ludicrous.

"You came here at—" he checked his wristwatch "nine twenty-six to thank me for something anyone would have done? It couldn't wait?"

She straightened. "What?"

"What do you really want?"

After the comment she'd made the last time she stood in his house, he was wary of asking what she wanted. She'd said barging in on him while he was naked was cliché, but there was a spark of desire that had ignited when she'd looked at him two days ago. And there was one now. She kept turning up at odd moments. Such as when he was naked or half-dressed. With contrived reasons.

Rayne propped her fists on her hips. "Okay. Fine. I used it as an excuse. Are you going to invite me inside?"

He shook his head. "We almost made trouble the last time you came inside. I nearly dropped the blanket and threw you over my shoulder."

She gave him a wry smile.

"Me ape man want pretty girl." Nothing like humor to put her back at arm's length.

"Didn't stop Tamara Beach from stepping inside earlier," she said, with a lift of her shoulder.

Ah. He almost smiled at her obvious female reaction. "I'm used to making trouble with Tamara."

A frown gathered and something flashed in her eyes. "Don't worry. I'm not Tamara."

He smiled. "No, you're not, are you? Tam's reliably uncomplicated."

"If that's what you want to call it," she quipped, crossing her arms and lifting her eyebrows. Something about her pose softened him. Rayne was a woman. And all women wanted to be desired. If only she knew how badly he longed to show her, to spread her on his bed and memorize every new hill and valley he'd noticed beneath those tight aprons she wore.

He stepped back and motioned for her to enter. "Okay, but when you're raking your nails down my back, don't say I didn't warn you."

Her head jerked and the foot she'd been about to put inside his house hovered midair.

"Kidding," he said, shepherding her inside the small living area and closing the French door behind her. "No matter what people say I'm not a sex-crazed nymphomaniac."

"How disappointing," Rayne said snappishly. She turned and tossed him a smile. It was a smile he'd never seen before—an I-got-this-under-control smile. "Doesn't matter. I know karate."

"Do you?" he asked, shuffling aside a sports magazine he'd left on the couch. "You seemed to have learned a lot since you left Oak Stand."

She tugged the hem of her shorts down and perched on the cushion. "Yeah, lots to learn out in that big, bad world."

Silence descended. Rayne's irritation over Tamara seemed to vanish as quickly as it appeared. A mask of control was in place. Once again he marveled over the coolness she brought to the table. Or living room if he wanted to be literal. The second hand of the clock in the short hallway leading to his bedroom and office ticked off fifteen seconds.

"So?" he said.

"I wanted to ask— Well, this may sound strange." She seemed to weigh her words. "You spend a good amount of time around boys Henry's age through your coaching, and I wondered if you thought Henry was normal."

It was his turn to feel caught off guard. Henry, normal? Why the devil would she ask something like that? "Yeah. He's like any other kid, I guess."

Her shoulders sank a bit. "I know, but he's been having trouble sleeping and he's terrified of being left behind or forgotten. I haven't been around boys much. I don't know how obvious it is that he suffers from anxiety issues. Did you notice if the other boys sensed his unease?"

All other emotions between him and Rayne faded

to the background. He'd sensed something in Henry, but nothing of this magnitude. "I haven't been around him enough to render a verdict on how he handles his fears, and I'm not qualified to give you an opinion. To me he seems as normal as any kid. Are you sure you aren't overanalyzing it a bit?"

Rayne shook her head. "He has horrible nightmares. He panics if I leave him alone. We saw a therapist after Phillip died, and I've been doing everything she suggested, but he's not any better. He still has nightmares and crippling anxiety. He masks it well, I guess. And he seems ultracomfortable with you. But I wondered if the boys on your team had picked up on it. Wondered if maybe they teased him because he acted scared or nervous."

"Darling, he popped off to Camden Harp, and that kid is the unofficial leader on the team. Henry seems to hold his ground well enough. He practices with good effort, has a firm knowledge of the game and seems cool with the other kids. He's not chatty, but neither is he antisocial. Totally normal."

Rayne sighed. "Good. I know I'm probably being overprotective. I haven't had a chance to talk with his teacher about it yet. I thought you could give me some perspective before I meet with her next week."

Brent couldn't stop himself from sinking on to the couch beside her and taking her hand. Once again, warm vanilla tickled his nose. "Rayne, why are you in Oak Stand?"

Rayne pulled her hand from his. He knew he'd likely overstepped the bounds of their tentative relationship. His thoughts were confirmed when she stiffened like a soldier at attention. "That's none of your business."

"You made it my business when you came to me about this. Why would you take a kid who's having trouble from the normalcy of his everyday life?"

"What if his life isn't normal anymore? What if mine isn't, either?"

"So you've quit your other life? Your career?"

"No," she said, relaxing slightly and looking out the large windows into his parents' yard. Her mind was turning cartwheels. He was certain of it. "I'm still running the restaurant, albeit from here, and I have a new project, a new cookbook. Lots of fantastic things going on in my professional life. More on the horizon."

"So this is personal?"

She sat there for a moment, looking absolutely lost. "I don't know."

"You don't know why you came to Oak Stand?"

"No," she said, shaking her head. "Well, yes, I do. The inn is my newest venture, but it was mostly to take a break. I needed to take a break."

She looked at him and her eyes were naked. It was almost as if she sought to convince herself. He rose and put distance between them, mostly because his hands itched to touch her, to soothe her. "A break?"

"Yes, a break. Since Phillip's death, I've been struggling to keep my head above water. Not financially. Just mentally. He was my partner, kept everything under control so I could be creative. With him gone, I—"

She lifted her hands. "Why am I telling you this? I haven't even talked about this with my therapist. It's not your problem. Really, I wanted to ask you about Henry. That's all. Not dump all my doubts and troubles into your lap."

"Isn't that what friends are for?" he asked.

The moment broke. Rayne leaned forward, setting her elbows on her knees as her chin jutted forward. She slid her gaze to him. "But we're not friends. We're not anything. We're two memories of a friendship."

He stilled at her words. "Memories. Yeah, I guess that's what we are."

Silence once again reigned over them.

He watched her as she struggled to find something to say. Something not as harsh as implying he meant nothing to her. The words hurt, and the flicker of hope he'd held earlier that day waned. Why had he thought there could be something more between them? His yearning was of the heart not of the reality of the world. She'd always done that to him. Made him believe in things he had no sense in believing. Things like beauty, honor and purity. Things no one would associate with the man he was. Brent was sex, sin and cowardice. He lived a lie because he was a lazy chickenshit. Was there any good reason to change now? Surely he could live the rest of his life screwing, drinking and hiding behind a secret identity.

Rayne had moved on in life, even if she were taking a temporary detour, so he needed to stop trying to make something out of nothing. It was too late to chase that dream. "You shouldn't have come here. I'm the contractor. I'm Henry's coach. Nothing else."

She rose and tossed loose curls the color of pennies behind her shoulders. "You're right. I don't know why I came. I do and I don't, you know?"

He shrugged but didn't say anything.

"Thank you for helping with Henry. I'm glad you're aware he's having problems. I would have told you anyway. Since you're his coach."

He nodded and held his ground, a statue before the glinting panes of the windows.

Rayne walked toward him, her eyes soft in the light from the single lamp. "I shouldn't have… I didn't mean to hurt your feelings." She stopped in front of him, reached out and squeezed his shoulder.

"You didn't hurt me. You're right. I'm just a memory."

A small smile slipped to her lips. "You forget. I know you."

"You think you do, but you don't. Not anymore." Then he lowered his head swiftly and covered her lips with his. Hard, punishingly so, he kissed her, using her surprise to his advantage, grabbing her ass and hauling her against him. Her lips were soft and her body hit him at all the right places.

It was agony and ecstasy for ten whole seconds.

He forced himself to rip his lips from her yielding ones. He pulled back and studied her glistening mouth as if it were the finest art before moving his gaze to her cinnamon eyes. They were soft with desire, and he could feel the heat slough off her. "No games, Rayne. The next time you walk through my door, I'll know what you want. Stop toying with me."

She straightened. "I'm not toying with you. I'm not that same pathetic girl anymore—"

"I noticed." He allowed his voice to drop to a silky purr, all the while hating himself for stooping to such tactics. She wanted him. If anyone knew a woman's desires, it was Brent. So he asserted control the only way he knew how, using the gift God had given him to its fullest. Like a cat with a mouse, he'd toyed with her desire for him, the desire she'd always held for him, weakening her because she'd hurt him.

Her eyes hardened. "You forget that of all the women in this town, I know you. And because I do, I know exactly what you're doing. It won't work on me."

"Oh, yeah?" He purred again, wrapping a curl around his finger and tugging her forward so he could reach out and flick one of the nipples outlined against her T-shirt.

She inhaled, but caught herself. Then something happened, something that had happened only once before. Rayne smiled, and it was a devious smile. Her brown eyes filled with power and naughtiness. The mouse had turned the tables on him. "Know what?"

He frowned.

"I can resist you."

She rose on her toes and pressed a kiss to his lips. It was hard, fast and sexy. She allowed one hand to brush the front of his pants, brushing against the raging erection beneath the thin cotton. Then she patted his cheek. "But can you resist me?"

Brent watched Rayne flounce out the door. He was aroused and confused. Not a good combination.

Apple padded into the room as the door shut. She held his newest leather driving moccasin in her mouth.

She dropped it at his feet, sat and looked up at him.

He groaned and picked up the wet, twisted mess. "Bad girl!"

But he wasn't talking to the dog.

CHAPTER SEVEN

THE MORE BRENT THOUGHT about the way Rayne played him, the more pissed he got. So he shut down his computer right in the middle of chapter eight and went to Cooley's.

He needed a beer and some company that didn't make him think about his feelings. He needed a game of pool and a nice rack to contemplate. And he knew he'd find all he needed at the honky-tonk that sat on Highway 1 between Gilmer and Oak Stand.

The parking lot was full and he had to park in the pasture next to the bar. With a tin roof, tinted doors and flashing beer signs, Cooley's was the equivalent of pulling up a chair to Grandma's apple pie. Pure comfort.

"Yo, Brent," Bones called as Brent stepped inside the dark, crowded bar. A cacophony of clacking pool balls, country music and scruffing boots met his ears. Ah. Sweet music.

"What's up, Bones?" Brent called back at the owner bartender who held two ice-cold beers in each hand. He slid them to a couple of boys who worked on oil rigs a county over. One of them was good at shooting pool. Brent knew because the son of a bitch had beaten him the last time he'd been in.

"Hey, darlin'," Brent said to Tamara when she appeared at his side. Everything felt damn familiar.

"You're here. Thought you had stuff to do."

"Yeah." Brent nodded, signaling the usual to Bones as he hunkered onto a scarred bar stool beneath a flat screen televising the Lakers' game. "Didn't pan out."

The dance floor was packed with a gaggle of women doing a line dance. One wore a weird-looking hat on her head. Or was it a veil? Yes, a veil of condoms. That meant a bachelorette party. No wonder some of the good ol' boys stood around nursing beers when they likely had to get up before light the next morning.

Nothing like a bunch of loaded gals looking to be naughty to keep a guy yanking out his wallet and buying fruity little drinks. Brent always called the fancy martinis that Bones served panty-droppers. Because they worked.

Tamara sat next to him, leaning forward so her breasts brushed his bare arm. He felt nothing. Not a smidgen of interest.

Damn.

Rayne had really screwed with his head.

"How about we dance?" he said, finally focusing on the blonde next to him. She'd changed out of the little dress and now wore tight jeans and a vest thing that bared her arms. She wore slouchy cowboy boots and dangling earrings that brushed her shoulders. Her hair looked blonder and her skin too tanned for early April, but her body was kicking. He should have felt interest stir at her sex kitten vibe.

But he didn't.

"Okay." She grinned and placed a manicured hand on his arm. "I love this song."

It was an old Dixie Chicks song that took him back about ten years. He wished the deejay would play something current. Nothing from the past. Nothing that made him recall who he'd been ten years ago. Or who Rayne had been—the blushing new Mrs. Phillip Albright.

"Fine," he said, setting his nearly empty beer on the bar and following her toward the dance floor. Large-bulb Christmas lights dangled from the ceiling over the worn wooden floor, giving the area a festive feel. Brent wished he could enjoy the music and his very own Dixie chick gyrating in front of him. He wished he wanted to take Tamara out back and pound out his frustrations in a round of hot, fast sex. But at this point, he figured he might have the same problem he had the night Katie Newman got hitched.

He wasn't sure he could handle the shame again, so he pasted on a smile and stomped around trying to appear like he was dancing. A slower song came on and he spun Tamara into a two-step that took them around the perimeter of the floor. He caught sight of a few buddies as he slid his boots and whirled the pretty lady in his arms. He needed a game of pool.

Anything to keep his mind off the fact his life was in the crapper.

The song ended and he tromped back to his stool. "I'm gonna get a game of pool up if I can rip one of these boys away from trying to get lucky with the tipsy bridesmaids."

"Okay," Tamara said, before ordering a beer. She turned to one of the roustabouts and ordered him to meet her at the pool table. The man's eyes glinted with interest as he set his empty beer bottle and followed her toward the three pool tables that squatted in back of Cooley's.

Brent followed with a second beer in hand, the last

he could have for the evening and still make it home un-affected. Lord knew he wanted more, wanted to drink until he didn't feel anything. But those kind of desires led people to twelve-step programs.

The oil-field worker was named Rusty, a wholly ap-propriate name considering his hair was auburn and he wore a Rusty Wallace NASCAR cap. He racked up the balls and chalked his cue tip as though he'd done it every day of his life. Brent was probably toast, but he really didn't give a damn. He needed distraction. And not of the female variety.

"You break," Rusty said, eyeing Tamara as she leaned against the unoccupied table beside them. She stretched and the vest she wore expanded, threatening to spill out her very nice rack. Rusty swallowed hard and ripped his gaze from the blonde. "What are we playing for?"

Brent shrugged. He didn't like to play for money and he'd probably lose anyway. "How about a drink?"

Rusty looked like he wanted Brent to put up Tamara as part of the wager. Which was stupid for many rea-sons. First, she didn't belong to Brent and, second, they were living in the twenty-first century. But the man nodded. "'Kay."

Brent broke and the balls spun in all directions. He pulled stripes and set about working them into the vari-ous pockets. For some reason he was on tonight, sinking tough shot after tough shot. Rusty barely had a chance to lift his cue stick before Brent sank the eight ball. The oil worker didn't seem to mind. He'd spent much of his time watching Tamara stretch and brush back her hair from her shoulders. Brent wasn't sure but thought the man actually wiped drool from his chin.

Brent accepted the beer as part of his win, even though he knew he shouldn't have another. He took a swig and the liquid slid down his throat, icy and seductive. After beating Rusty in another game, he found himself four beers into a good time. Before he could drop the cue stick, the bridesmaids had him out on the dance floor shuffling around doing asinine dance moves even though he knew he looked incredibly stupid. But he didn't care. It was better than staring at his ceiling thinking about Rayne and how she wouldn't piss on him if he were on fire.

But even through the haze of the booze, he hated that he was doing what he'd vowed not to do. He'd tossed out his intention to make a new start and pulled on the same old cloak he'd donned for the past fifteen years. He laughed, he flirted, he drank. And he pretended he hadn't a care in the world. He let people think he was nothing more than what he'd always presented himself to be.

And it caused shame to course through his body.

What he was doing wasn't fun. Not really.

And it damn sure wasn't satisfying. Had no shot at bringing him joy.

As a new song started, he knew he wanted to go home. Too bad he'd had four beers and couldn't drive. Stupid. That's what he was. He'd allowed the pain of Rayne's rebuke to get to him. Instead of doing the adult thing, he'd stomped out the door like a child with an "I'll show her" attitude. And what had he proven?

Nothing other than the fact this neon life wasn't cutting it anymore. He should have left Cooley's and the tipsy chicks to the oil-field workers and stayed his ass home. It was time for change. He knew it in his gut.

And if Rayne couldn't be a part of his life, he'd find someone who could. He wanted more than lukewarm beers and drunken sex. He wanted more than honky-tonks and bar fights. He wanted more than empty rooms and a silent house.

He smiled at the pretty bride-to-be doing some sort of crazy jerky dance, saluted and then exited the dance floor, swerving around other rowdy patrons before making it to the exit. He had to find a way home. Maybe Tamara. Or maybe he'd have to call someone.

Rayne's image appeared in his mind.

Her soft, wide mouth and cascade of curls brushing her alabaster shoulders. Lord, he was poetic when he was half-drunk. He wanted her. It burned inside him, consuming him. And he didn't know what to do about it. How to proceed with her. He knew she was aware of him, both sexually and spiritually. But she'd dug in her heels. She clung to the fact that they could be nothing to each other.

"Where'd you go?" Tamara said, sticking her head out the glass door.

"Needed some air," he said, wishing she hadn't interrupted his thoughts. He felt close to figuring something out about Rayne. Besides he knew what Tamara wanted.

She slid out the door and moved so she stood beside him. "Pretty moon tonight."

He looked up at the moon. It was pretty. "Yeah."

"Wanna come home with me, B?" she said, sliding a hand up his back, smoothing his T-shirt against his skin.

He ripped his gaze from the night sky and looked at

the girl who'd been his sometimes lover but all-the-time friend. "I don't think so, sugar."

She frowned. "What's wrong with you? You're not acting like yourself."

He shrugged. "I don't know, Tam. I think I want something different than what I've been doing. I can't go on spending all my time at bars, indulging in meaningless relationships, going home to an empty house."

She pressed her lips together. "So I'm a meaningless relationship?"

Shit. He figuratively spat out his boot. "No, that's not what I meant. You've always been a good friend to me."

"That's the definition of a friend to you? So I guess you screw all your friends?" Her mouth had formed a straight line. Frost edged her words.

He reached out and rubbed her shoulder. She jerked away. "Hey, that's not what I meant. You're a sweetheart."

"But you could never love me. I've been wasting time trying to get you to see me as something other than a booty call. Guess you think I'm not good enough. Why buy the cow and all that."

He felt a little panicky. He'd always thought their friends-with-benefits relationship mutual. Never in a billion years had he felt Tamara's interest was anything more than passing. "I'm not sure I understand. You—"

"God, I'm an idiot." Tears glistened on her lashes and she crossed her arms defensively. "I get it. You're looking for someone wholesome and pure. Someone like Rayne Rose."

He felt himself stiffen at her conclusion. "No. I'm

not sure how staring at the moon led to this, but you are a terrific woman. I've just never...I mean..."

"You're not in love with me," she finished. "Yeah, I get it."

He turned to her and gently grasped her upper arms. "Don't make this something it's not. This is not a judgment against you. I care about you, Tamara. You're a good person, but I can't make myself fall in love with you any more than you can make yourself fall in love with me."

Her eyes were bright blue in the light of the moon. Tears streaked down her cheeks and he felt like total dog shit for hurting her. He'd had no clue she was seeking more from him.

"Whatever," she muttered.

"You're not in love with me, Tamara. You're looking for something you can't force, sugar."

She shrugged loose. "Maybe so."

He let her walk away. He knew the hurt she felt. He'd been there hours before when Rayne declared they were nothing, not even friends.

Damn, life was complicated.

"See you around, okay?" he called at Tamara's back.

She flipped him off.

"Crap on a cracker," he said to the flashing beer sign to his left. He'd had too much to drink and hurt a friend. How had the night gone so wrong?

He stared up at the moon. It held no answers.

The glass door behind him flew open and several members of the bachelorette party tumbled outside.

"Hey, you disappeared in the middle of our dance," the cute brunette who'd dragged him to the dance floor said, wagging a finger at him. Her eyes were glassy from the booze, but she had a warm smile. "Bad boy. You're not supposed to leave a gal hanging like that."

He managed a smile. "Sorry. Needed air."

Another girl, this one a blonde, yawned. "Yeah, we did, too. Not used to these kind of nights. I got car pool in the morning, you know?"

The brunette nodded. "Don't know why we chose a weeknight. I'm beat."

The door opened and the bride staggered out. "Come on, girls. Let's blow this joint and go to Shreveport. I feel the need to roll bones."

The blonde wrinkled her nose. "What?"

"Craps, baby. At the casino," the bride said, snapping one of the latex condoms drooping in her eyes.

The blonde groaned but the brunette jabbed her in the ribs.

The condom-crowned bride looked at him. "Wanna go with us, hottie? We got room in the Suburban."

He shook his head. "Not feeling lucky tonight, but if you got a designated driver, I'll take you up on a ride into town."

Two more women staggered out, each of them enthusiastic about playing the slots and getting free drinks. The blonde dangled the keys. "Okay, I'm designated driver. We'll give you a ride home. That is if you don't mind being crowded. Janie wouldn't take the car seat out."

The brunette narrowed her eyes. "Have you ever tried to put one of those things in? Well, let me tell you, the car seat stays put no matter what."

Ten minutes later, after having stopped so one of the girls could buy a six-pack for the trip, they pulled up to

the front of Brent's parents' house. The brakes squealed
on the large SUV and, frankly, it was a wonder he could
hear them with all the squealing, sisterly squabbling
and giggling going on inside the vehicle.

"Is this it?" the blonde said. He'd since learned her
name was Doreen, she had three kids, and was the
sister-in-law to the bride-to-be. She seemed the most
reasonable of the bunch. Or maybe she seemed smarter
because she'd stuck with Diet Coke all night.

"Yeah, thanks," he said, shifting one of the women
so he could climb out. Janie yanked the latch for the
door before he was ready and he fell out.

"Damn it." He tried to plant his boots on the curb,
but slipped and fell onto the grass. Right on his ass.

The car window slid down and laughter interrupted
the serenity of the night. "Oops. Sorry."

He waved off the apology and lurched to his feet as
one of the condoms hit him on the shoulder. The bride-
to-be rose through the sunroof, wearing a naughty grin
on her face as she sling-shot another condom his way.

"Just in case," she called out with a laugh.

Doreen tooted the horn and the Suburban pulled
away with a chorus of "Byes" in its wake.

He brushed an errant leaf from his pants and turned
around. He half expected Rayne to be standing there
with a disapproving frown and a smart-assed comment.
But she wasn't. It was twelve forty-eight in the morning
and she was likely fast asleep in the house to his left.

He trudged toward the gate that led to his house,
noticing that his parents' yard needed cutting already
and that the cat had killed another field mouse and left
it in the driveway.

As he pulled the gate open, a fluttering above him

caught his eye. He looked up and caught sight of Rayne in the window. She stared at him for a moment before disappearing.

He shook his head and stared down at the two rubbers he held in his hand.

Fat chance of needing a condom any time soon.

CHAPTER EIGHT

"SO YOU WANNA TELL ME AGAIN what we're doing here?" Meg asked Rayne as she picked up a spotted cherry tomato and tossed it into a plastic sack filled with other similarly blighted fruits.

"We're culling the bad fruit from the good," Rayne said, studying the plump fruit she'd purchased from a farmer outside of Tyler earlier that day. The farmer's market had been a lovely find. When she managed to circumnavigate all the obligatory rosebushes for sale, she found a sprinkling of homegrown vegetables paving the way for more variety as the spring progressed. She'd even scored some lavender-infused honey.

"Oh, yeah?" her assistant said, wiping her hands on the damp flour sack towel beside the sink. "Because it feels like some kind of weird back-to-the-future thing."

Rayne made a face. "What do you mean?"

"This." Meg waved a hand around the kitchen. Her fingernails were painted turquoise and she wore a pair of striped purple tights with a black puffy skirt and tight ballet-style top. Rayne wondered how Meg picked out her outfits each morning. It was either with little thought or too much.

"This is a kitchen," Rayne said.

"Yes, I have a brain. I meant Serendipity Inn. Henry. Brent."

"Brent?"

Meg blew out a breath. "I got eyes, sister. I see what's going on."

Rayne could feel irritation rise within herself. She was not doing anything with Brent. Not really. Her parting action several nights before had been rash, a way to gain control over the way he made her feel. She shouldn't have turned the tables…her words had been an invitation to a man like Brent. And the fact she'd seen him climb out of a SUV full of women was reason enough to remind herself Brent Hamilton had always been a simplistic ball of self-serving machismo with a side of sex appeal. His sexy bad-boy grin may have made her knees weak when she'd been sixteen, but as a grown woman she could fight against the feelings he stirred in her. "Nothing going on, Megan."

"When you use my real name, I know I've hit a nerve."

For a moment the kitchen fell silent. The only noise reaching Rayne's ears was the sound of Brent's hammer on the front porch followed by the whine of a table saw. He was nearly done repairing the rotted boards. He'd finish sanding soon.

"Seriously, what are we doing here? Why aren't we in Austin talking to a real estate agent about scoring us a pad in Manhattan? The network would be stupid to pass up the idea for the show. It's brilliant. Rayne, this has been your dream, our dream, for the past few years and it feels like you're losing focus. All this feels wrong," Meg said, sliding onto a stool and contemplating her BlackBerry.

Meg could rearrange a schedule, scold a hostess and plan a menu all at the same time. No one could line up people and events the way Meg could. She'd stepped right into Phillip's shoes without blinking. Rayne didn't know what she'd do without the girl she'd hired right out of the University of Texas, the girl no one else would give a job to because she looked different and had a colorful past that included a stint in rehab.

But as much as Rayne respected Meg, it didn't mean that her assistant knew what was right for her.

"I made this decision based on many things. I'm worried about Henry. And Aunt Frances is not getting any younger. I don't want her scrambling to make ends meet." Rayne finished culling the tomatoes and tied the handles of the plastic bag together. She'd deliver the unworthy fruit to the compost bin Brent had hastily constructed for her the day before. By the fall, she should have a nice rich layer of soil ready for the winter garden. Of course, she wouldn't be here in the fall. "It doesn't matter if it feels wrong to you. It feels right to me."

Meg narrowed her gaze, causing her smooth white forehead to crinkle. She tapped her chin. "So I guess I shouldn't point out that Aunt Fran could sell this house and live nicely on the profits? And her dear niece has plenty of money to resettle her adored aunt into a nice retirement community with no yard to mow and planned activities like golf and bingo. And Henry is seven. Every seven-year-old is scared. Methinks this a diversionary tactic. Like you're afraid to move forward."

More than irritation bubbled within her. She didn't need Meg pointing out the fact she currently was floundering around undecided about her direction. But she would gain control and move forward. Soon. The past weekend she'd gone to Austin to check on the restaurant and do a Saturday-morning cooking show. She'd talked to her agent and expected word on the network deal by the first of next week. Two weeks at the latest. Maybe three. The thought of not getting the offer made her stomach hurt, but there was little she could do about it now. So she was taking steps in a direction. Even if she didn't know what direction.

"First, I'm not scared. Just cautious. I have many people to think about. Henry. You. All my employees. It's not me taking off on a new venture. It's all of Rayne Rose Enterprises. I have to be sure," Rayne said, unwinding the band from her braid. She got a headache if she wore it too long. Or maybe Meg was giving her one.

"Fine. I'll shut up and do my job."

Meg's expression was unreadable. Rayne wasn't sure if her friend gave up the battle or the war. Who knew with Meg? "Good. Agreeing with me *is* part of the job description."

Meg shook her head, slid off the stool and headed toward the door. "No, my job is to keep you straight. Totally not the same thing."

"Are you going to pick up the extra fabric for the place mats?" Rayne asked, transferring the tomatoes to the sideboard beside the huge Viking stove. The cushions for the front porch rockers should be complete and Meg would use the excess fabric to make matching place mats for the table they'd use in the magazine spread. Dawn Hart, who currently served as a senior care center director, had once owned a furniture redesign center in Houston and still did extra work on the side. Work that was incredible. In fact, she was so good, Rayne had sent several antique armchairs to her workshop for refurbishment.

Meg turned around. "No. I'm going fishing."

Rayne blinked. "Huh?"

"Fishing. I believe you put a worm on a hook and drop it in the water. Then you wait for a fish to bite it."

"Yeah, I get the concept. But why are *you* doing it? Dressed like that?"

Pink swept across Meg's cheeks. "I've always wanted to try it, and Bubba Malone said he'd take me. Besides, I'm wearing boots."

"Bubba? Malone? The guy who slapped your butt?"

Meg shrugged. "What? I feel sorry for him. I was mean to him and he was nice enough to compliment my ass. And being that it's rather large, I don't get many compliments on it."

Rayne smiled. "Oh, now I see."

Meg flipped her off.

"Have fun," Rayne called as Meg tromped off in her black combat boots. At least she wouldn't come back with chiggers. Heck, even snakes would be deterred by Meg's steel-toed boots.

Rayne glanced to the Persian walnuts she'd imported from the Balkans. She'd spent the past few days working on a basic menu for the launch of the inn. She wanted the menu to be modeled after her flagship restaurant, yet simpler, with a smidgen of home cooking. This inn would be her first attempt at branching out since the Austin restaurant had taken off nearly five years ago.

Only one shot to prove she wasn't a flash in the pan. One shot to prove she could make magic again.

Her thoughts swung back to Meg's words. Was she using this project as a diversion? As a way to slow down the careening roller coaster of her career? Her success had happened fast. One day she labored under Claude Feret, one of the best chefs in the South. The next she and Phillip were leaving Atlanta to fill out loan forms and pick out cutlery. Serendipity was the culmination of blood, sweat, tears and dreams. And Phillip hadn't lived long enough to see his part of the hard work bloom into a success.

He'd shared her vision. From the very beginning. It was what had drawn them to each other. That, and the fact they were both from Texas. She a lowly line cook fresh out of culinary school, alone and unfamiliar in a new city. He, the assistant to the front of the house, fresh out of University of Texas business school with an MBA and an accounting degree. They'd commiserated over leftover wine late at night when the sous-chef slipped out for his date with the dishwasher. It became a nightly habit that grew into a healthy respect and shared goal. Then two years later, she was the sous-chef and he ran the front of the house.

One thing led to another and before they knew it, Rayne wore a diamond wedding band and Phillip held the deed to a deceased aunt's farmhouse in a burgeoning section of Austin. They left Atlanta and embarked on a journey that earned them rave reviews from critics all over Texas. Then all over the country.

Phillip and Rayne had done what many couples sought to do—they bought a house, grew a business and made a beautiful baby boy.

Neither of them had been head over heels for the other. But they loved each other. They liked the same movies, laughed at the same comedians and had pretty decent sex once they scheduled it into their weekly list of demands. She hadn't needed a grand, all-consuming love. She and Phillip had suited each other just fine.

And she still missed him fiercely. Missed his warm hazel eyes and good foot rubs. Missed the way he drummed his fingers on the steering wheel in traffic intent on recreating the drum solo from his favorite Rush song. Missed the way he took care of the bills, the dry cleaning and her.

But her wishes couldn't stop the freak aneurism that had claimed her husband at the age of thirty-four. One minute they'd been talking to each other on the cell phone while he was en route to pick up Henry. The next she was calling a funeral home.

Rayne shrugged off the memories and focused on the salads lying before her. Arugula? Perhaps the Bibb lettuce divided into even wedges? A fresh creamy buttermilk drizzle would complement the buttery flavor of the lettuce. She quickly cut the Bibb lettuce with the knife, artfully arranging it on the uncomplicated purity of the salad plate. She halved the tomatoes and lined them in a semicircle on the plate.

Too simplistic?

But wasn't that the theme?

She leaned against the counter and closed her eyes, drawing in a deep breath. She counted to five and released the breath.

"You okay?"

Rayne jumped, opening her eyes. "Oh, hey, Aunt Fran. You scared me."

"Sorry," the older woman said, slipping her arms around Rayne's waist and giving her a squeeze. She peered over Rayne's shoulder. "That doesn't look as if it took all the starch out of you. That's just lettuce and tomatoes."

Rayne stared at the plate. Perhaps Aunt Fran was right—the salad was too plain. Still the buttermilk dill dressing needed an uncomplicated background. "Don't worry. I've still got my starch."

"Good." Aunt Fran tugged one of Rayne's curls. "I'm tied up in a meeting with the landscaper, and Dawn Hart called for the second time today requesting we pick up the cushions and chairs. She has another project and needs the space. Brent said he'd swing by and get them. Why don't you ride with him and settle with Dawn?"

Because Rayne didn't want to ride with him. Didn't want to smell the scent that was his alone. Didn't want to see the way the denim stretched across his toned thighs. Didn't want to make awkward small talk after their encounter last Thursday evening. Didn't want to remember staring at him from her bedroom window like the morality police. But most of all she didn't want to ride with him because she was tempted. He made her want to jump into a place she'd never been before—his bed. And that might be temporarily satisfying, but not lasting.

She'd learned long ago that Brent spelled absolute heartbreak to any girl who did a half gainer into his bed. And several nights before as she'd stared out the window at the full moon, she'd been seriously contemplating stepping onto the springboard to perform that dive. Thinking about going over to his house and stepping through the door.

But then she'd seen him fall out of the Suburban full of women. He'd been drinking and holding a condom. It was the equivalent of an apple falling on her head, knocking sense into her.

Brent was forbidden fruit and she wasn't going to take a bite of him. No matter how nice he was to Henry or Aunt Fran or to her.

"Rayne?" Aunt Fran's voice checked her back into reality.

"Get Brent to pick up the cushions and chairs for us, if he's willing, and I'll run the payment over to Dawn later today."

Aunt Fran frowned. "I would think since this venture is so important to you, you'd want to check the job Dawn did before we haul them all the way here. Not to mention, she'd probably appreciate payment on delivery."

Point for Aunt Fran. It did make sense. Rayne looked at the salad experiment station like a lazy chef de garde manger. The second salad on her menu would have to wait. She untied her apron. "Fine. Just make sure the landscaper puts marigolds around the veggie garden in back. They are natural deterrents and since we're all organic—"

"Right-o," her aunt said with a rather satisfied smile. Rayne knew that if it were up to Aunt Fran she'd have Rayne wrapped in a satin bow and delivered to Brent's bed. For some messed-up reason, her aunt thought Brent would be good for Rayne. But Rayne knew she couldn't play with him like all the other women in town did and not fall under his spell. Her heart was too vulnerable.

Rayne sidestepped the new bedside tables that had arrived via UPS earlier that morning and glanced at the antique grandfather clock in the foyer. Only five minutes until Henry jumped from the top step of the bus into the cushion of the St. Augustine at the curbside. Lucky her. Henry could ride with them and provide a buffer.

She stepped onto the porch. Brent wasn't there, but she heard clanging sounds coming from the truck he'd parked at the side of the house. She slipped on the flip-flops she'd left sitting on the front porch steps and headed toward him.

"Damn it!" were the words that emerged from behind the construction-scarred truck.

Brent stood staring at a length of board. He threw the tape measure down. It clanged against the scratched metal of the truck bed.

"Measure twice cut once," Rayne said, moseying up and propping her arms on the truck bed as if she stalked sexy contractors every day.

"I taught you that," he said, rubbing a hand over his dark hair. Small flecks of sawdust stood out on the velvety richness like dandruff on a black dress. He had taught her the rule when they'd made birdhouses and feeders one summer. He used the kit his uncle had given him for constructing the houses and she'd painted them bright colors. They'd taken most of them to the Shady Oak Retirement Village to place outside the atrium. The feeders had been a hit.

"I knew I'd learned it somewhere. I put that into practice when I'm cooking, too," Rayne said, noting that the man looked extraordinarily good for someone who'd been working all morning. His shirtsleeves had been rolled up and she could see the veins on his forearms. She didn't know why it was sexy. It just was.

Brent opened his mouth to respond, but at that moment the squealing of brakes interrupted the tranquility of the afternoon. The bus ground to a stop in front of the driveway, opening the doors before actually stopping. Henry flew out, taking five steps before spinning and throwing a wave toward a window at the back of the bus. Rayne saw the flash of a small hand along with a blond ponytail. A girl's voice shouted. "Bye, Hank."

Rayne rolled her eyes. The boy already had the eye for cute blondes.

A smiling Henry ran their way.

"Hey, Coach!" he shouted, heaving his backpack onto his shoulder as he pounded toward them. He swerved around a root, and the backpack shifted and fell from his sturdy shoulders, hitting the ground and spewing its contents on the grass. He stopped and tried shoving everything inside, but pencils, erasers and papers littered the ground.

Rayne sighed and moved toward him. He never zipped up his backpack. She'd told him a dozen times.

Henry rifled through the workbooks and binders, pulling his copy of *Throwing the Stinky Cheese* from the depth. "I finished the book!" he crowed.

Brent tossed the board he held into the back of his truck and strolled toward Henry. "Good job."

"I can't believe Ben was so mean to Charlie. I mean, he was on his team and everything. I felt real bad for

Charlie." Henry handed the book to Brent. "Thanks for letting me borrow it. It was way better than that mouse book."

Rayne knew the look on Henry's face. He wanted to ask Brent something more, but didn't know how to do it the right way.

"So you wanna borrow another one? I have one about a kid who thinks he's bad at sports but finds out lacrosse is his game," Brent said.

Henry cocked his head. "What's lacrosse?"

Brent smiled. "I guess you'll find out."

Henry nodded. "Cool."

"Henry, get this stuff back in your binder and next time zip up before you bail off the bus," Rayne said.

Her son shot Brent a look that said, "See? This is what I get all the time," before squatting and shoving papers in willy-nilly. Rayne almost smiled but instead she redirected her gaze to Brent. "Aunt Fran said you were going to the hardware store and would be willing to pick up some items from Dawn Hart. Do you mind if I ride with you? I want to settle up with Dawn and check the work before we haul everything back here."

"Can I come, too?" Henry asked, biting his lip in effort to seal the bulging backpack.

"Sure. Let's grab an ice cream at the Dairy Barn," Brent said, digging in his pocket for his truck keys.

"Yes!" Henry abandoned the bag to give a fist pump. "I want a chocolate shake."

Rayne watched as her son scurried toward the front porch, dumped his backpack and leaped into Brent's truck. She blinked. Then looked at Brent. "Where does he get all that energy?"

Brent shrugged. "I think the government puts something in the school milk."

Rayne shook her head. "So let's go give him more sugar."

BRENT VEERED OFF THE SQUARE and looked for a place to park in front of the Dairy Barn. No spaces out front, but there was one close to the bank. He pulled in and cut the engine.

"I think I want chocolate. But maybe strawberry. What about you, Mom?" Henry hadn't stopped talking since they got into the car. Rayne had told him the child had nearly crippling anxiety, but Brent couldn't tell there was anything wrong with the boy.

"I'm probably going to pass, bud," Rayne said, climbing out. He liked what she wore—a pretty skirt that swirled around pink flip-flops. Her shirt was one of those that poofed out. He thought they called it peasant-style. Rayne wore them a lot and they suited her. Delicate, thin material that draped gently across her breasts, but gathered at her slim waist. Her curly copper hair looped around her shoulders to frame her face. He'd never seen a prettier woman. Truly.

"Aw, come on, Mom. You never eat good stuff," Henry said, leaning down to tie his shoe into a knot that Brent knew would not hold for ten paces. He needed to teach the boy how to tie so the laces stayed tied and didn't drag on the ground.

"I beg to differ. Everything I eat is good. And good for you."

Brent laughed at Henry's face. The boy had looked up and crossed his eyes. Funny guy.

They strolled down the street and Brent held the

diner door open as Rayne and Henry entered. The place wasn't too busy. Charlie Mac, the ancient owner, stood behind the counter wearing a white apron and white paper cook hat. He pulled a pencil from behind his ear. "What can I get you, Brent?"

Brent looked up at the board. "Hank here wants a—" he looked at the boy "—a chocolate shake?"

Henry nodded. "A large one."

"Rayne?"

"Um, a bottled water," she said.

Charlie Mac made a face. "We ain't got no bottled water, but I can get you some outta the soda foundation."

Rayne shook her head. "Nothing for me, thanks."

Brent shrugged. He thought she took healthy eating a bit too far. Didn't she know water was water? "I'll take a banana split with chocolate sauce, butterscotch and caramel. Oh, and a cheeseburger, all the way, hold the onions. And a root beer."

"Can I have fries?" Henry peered over the counter at Charlie Mac.

"I got curly fries," the old man said, scratching on his order pad. Henry nodded with the same enthusiasm Apple showed when it came time to eat her kibble. Concentrated hunger.

Rayne opened her mouth, looked at Henry's face, then pressed her lips together. She crossed her arms and tried to seem vaguely disgusted, but the twinkle in her eye when she glanced at her son gave her away.

Brent took out a credit card, pressing Rayne's hand back as she tried to hand him a ten-dollar bill. "I got this, Rayne."

Charlie Mac swiped the card and stared hard at the

pretty lady standing slightly behind him. "I do declare. Rayne Rose, ain't it? Ain't seen you since you was a girl."

"Hi, Mr. Charlie," Rayne said. Brent turned to look at her. She wiggled her toes and twirled one curl around her index finger. "It's nice to see you again."

Charlie Mac grunted. That was the end of the conversation.

Brent took the plastic number set on the counter and scanned the place for a good table. He grabbed the soda and Henry's shoulder and steered toward a nice booth by the window where the sun tumbled in to warm the zealously air-conditioned diner.

Henry hopped onto the faded red faux leather and Rayne slid in next to him, pinning him against the squeaky-clean glass of the front window. Brent sat and took a swig of his soda.

"Been a while since you've sat here and looked out at the park, huh?"

Rayne glanced out the window at the square that held a huge fountain flowing at the feet of Rufus Tucker, the founder of Oak Stand, and the broad swath of newly green grass. Pansies still flourished in the raised beds at the square's entrance and squirrels scampered left and right, digging frantically for stored acorns. "It's still a pretty place."

Henry stabbed the windowpane. "Where are the swings and junk?"

"It's not that kind of park. Just a town square with paths and flowers, and though you can't see it, a small gazebo to the left of the footbridge spanning a dry creek bed." Brent pointed in the direction of the structure where he'd given Rayne her first kiss. He still remembered how sweet she'd tasted. How surprised she'd been.

"Oh." Henry glanced at the counter. Obviously, school had made the boy ravenous and he couldn't wait for his food. He looked at his mother. "Did you play in that park?"

Rayne nodded. Brent thought back to the park where they had gathered acorns for a war with Bubba Malone and Talton Drake nearly every day one summer. And many afternoons he and Rayne had ridden their bikes to the library which sat across the square, stopping in the park to kick off their shoes and climb the ancient oaks bending toward the stone paths radiating from the fountain. They'd detached locust shells and covered themselves with them, splashed in the fountain until an adult ran them off and raced across the footbridge to climb on the roof of the gazebo.

"I've got an idea," Brent said, scooting out from the bench and heading toward Charlie Mac.

He looked back at Henry and Rayne. "Charlie, make that order to go."

CHAPTER NINE

RAYNE WATCHED AS HENRY sloshed his milk shake onto the brick-paved street that encircled the square, wincing when it dripped on his uniform shirt. Chocolate milk shake on white knit. Great.

"Henry, watch your shake," she called as they darted in front of a small SUV looping the square. Traffic had picked up as the five o'clock hour neared.

"I've never been on a picnic," Henry shouted, catching up with Brent. Her son's words shook Rayne. Had she never taken the boy on a picnic? That couldn't be right, but she knew it to be true. She'd always been busy. What a horrible excuse.

Henry glanced at her. "Come on, Mom."

The child's face looked lit from within, like a hundred fireflies had taken up residence. It struck Rayne, the reason for his joy. He was thrilled to be with Brent. Just as she'd always been, dogging Brent's footsteps, worshipping at the altar of the all-state quarterback.

A bleep of alarm sounded inside her, but the sight of her son's smiling face overshadowed the fear. She wanted Henry to be happy, to smile rather than chew his shirt or check obsessively for the note card of emergency numbers he carried with him in his pocket like a security blanket.

What would some hero worship hurt?

She didn't answer that question. Just hurried her pace to catch up.

"Follow me," Brent said, carrying the two white bags with the red logo of a barn. Already grease marks formed on the outside of the bags. She suppressed the inclination to snatch them and toss them in a trash can.

They filed into the park like ducks heading to a pond. The brick pavers of the path matched the ones in the street, and the oaks greeted them with a friendly wave of leaves. Rayne's hair whipped in the wind, and she impatiently pushed it from her eyes. Here and there, people moved around them, but no one sat on the park bench or wandered over the well-trod paths. It felt much as it had when she was younger, a magical little oasis in the middle of reality.

"How about here?" Brent motioned with a bag. He indicated one of the benches. A copper plate read In Memory of Edward Monk. May He Forever be a Part of our Lives. A balding man in a checked sport coat materialized in Rayne's mind. He'd carried wrapped bubble gum in his pocket and gave it to kids who gave him a high-five. His wife, Betty, had trimmed Rayne's hair at the Curlique.

"Y'all sit on the bench," Henry directed, snagging a fry from the sack that gaped open in Brent's hand. "I wanna sit by the fountain."

The fountain that gurgled at Founding Father Rufus Tucker's feet was about twenty yards away. Rayne nodded. "Okay, but no playing in the fountain."

Henry shot Brent another suffering look. The child was getting good at demonstrating disgust at his mother's pampering, but Rayne was okay with it because he was taking a step in the right direction. Usually he'd insist on sitting right beside her as if she might gallop away and leave him behind. The separation anxiety he'd been struck with reared its ugly head at the oddest times. But today wasn't one of them.

Brent rooted through the sack and pulled out Henry's fries, handing them to him along with a packet of ketchup. "Here you are, sport. And mind your mother."

Henry scarfed down three fries while nodding. He ran toward the fountain, clutching his treat.

Brent plunked down on the bench. "You want some of my banana split?"

"No, thanks," she said, still standing. She raised her face to the blue sky peeking through the trees. "We better not spend too much time here. Dawn wants us to pick up the chairs and cushions."

The leaves shimmered in the breeze, a soft rebuke to her need to rush. She inhaled the scent of spring in the air, allowed the splash of the fountain to soothe her, remind her that time marched at a clip, and she'd sought to slow it by coming to Oak Stand.

She tore her gaze from the bark of the oak and the spark of new, sticky green on the silver-leafed maple to find Brent watching her. His mouth was full of cheeseburger, but his eyes showed a deep hunger.

It made her mouth dry.

He seemed to sense her reaction and shoved his soda her way.

She took it and sipped. Root beer. How long had it been since she'd indulged in a soda? According to her taste buds, too long. Then she recognized the moment as a mirror of the past—she was sneaking sips of Brent's root beer while watching him wolf down a Dairy Barn cheeseburger. Déjà vu waylaid her like a linebacker.

She shoved the soda at him. "Thanks."

He nodded as he scooped up a huge bite of vanilla ice cream drizzled with caramel and shoved it in his mouth. Rayne felt her knees get mushy. The man's mouth was seriously wicked. Sensuous bottom lip, framed by a scruffy five o'clock shadow that would make a Hollywood hunk envious. Then to further demonstrate the power of his sexuality, he licked his lips.

Damn it.

Rayne felt heat gather in her stomach. Her hand curled into a fist as if it remembered the feel of that hardness beneath those cotton pajama pants only nights ago. The air hummed with tension.

He took a scoop of chocolate-glazed ice cream and held the spoon toward her. "Want some?"

Rayne couldn't stop herself, she took three steps and lowered her head and opened her mouth.

Brent's eyes glinted. He knew what he was doing. The bastard. He said he wouldn't play games with her. Then what the hell was this? He slid the spoon in her mouth, his lips twitching with amusement. Still, she knew by the gleam in his eye he felt the heat, felt the deliciousness of their play.

So Rayne swallowed the icy sweetness then took great pains in licking the chocolate sauce off her bottom lip. "Mmm. Good."

She could hold her own in any game.

Brent closed his mouth then looked at the spoon, before dropping it into the plastic container that held the pooling ice cream and decadent sauces. He set it beside the half-eaten cheeseburger. He raised his hands to do what? Reach for her? Pull her into his lap?

Her mind raced with the possibilities before the water hit her in the face.

"Bull's-eye!" yelled Henry. Rayne stumbled backward, wiping the cold water from her eyes.

She looked at her son. He grinned mischievously, holding a faded water gun.

"What? Where'd you get that?" Rayne said.

Brent dropped his arms, just as a stream launched toward his head. He ducked.

Henry squealed. "I found it under a bush. Awesome! I totally got you guys!"

Another stream hit Rayne in the shoulder before Henry lunged behind the azalea bushes growing behind the bench. Another blast of water arced over the tiny buds atop the bushes and hit Brent in the back of the head.

"That's it!" he cried, leaping up, encircling the bush. Henry's cry of laughter floated out, as another stream of water whizzed over Rayne's shoulder. She ducked behind an oak tree. Brent jogged out with a laughing Henry slung over his shoulders. Henry still pulled the trigger of the water gun but the waning streams of water flew wildly with no target in mind.

Brent jogged toward the fountain. "Hmm. Where shall I set him down? Here?"

Rayne reached the fountain as Brent pretended to toss Henry in the tiled pool surrounding the fountain. Henry shrieked and clutched Brent's shoulders.

"Get him, Mom!" Henry shouted, wiggling and kicking his feet.

The water gun clattered to the pavers below and

Rayne snatched it up and pressed the barrel to Brent's back. "Put the boy down, Hamilton, before I make you look like you wet your pants."

Her statement caused Henry to dissolve even further into giggles. Brent lowered her son. "You sure you want me to put him down?"

He dropped Henry down within a foot of the gurgling waters, still cradling the laughing boy. Henry yelled. "Not here!"

Laughing, Rayne prodded Brent in the back. "If you get those new school shoes wet, someone's gonna get hurt."

Brent swung around and waggled his eyebrows. "You talk a big game, Mrs. Rayne Rose Albright, but I don't think you have it in you."

Rayne lowered the gun toward his stomach.

"Do it, Mom!" Henry cried, giggling in Brent's arms. Rayne smiled at the glee her son took in her being silly. How had she failed to show him that she had a sense of humor?

Rayne smiled and cocked an eyebrow. "A mother must protect her son."

She pulled the trigger but missed the mark. Brent grabbed the gun, set Henry on the bricks and gave her a wicked smile. "Now, your mother's going to pay."

"Run, Mom!" Henry shouted, reaching for the water gun in Brent's hand. Brent let the child have the toy. His eyes were on her.

He lunged toward her. Rayne shrieked, hiked up her skirt and ran to the other side of the fountain while Henry dunked the gun beneath the water in the pool.

The sound of Brent's deep laughter joined hers as they raced around the monument. The founding father glared his disapproval as Henry joined in the fray with a reloaded water gun. Rayne ran left and Brent met her. She spun and ran round the other side, but he was there before her.

Brent grabbed her upper arms and spun her backward. "You're going to pay for trying to make me look like I peed my pants."

Rayne could barely talk past the laughter. "Don't do it, Hambone."

He laughed at the nickname he'd earned in high school that made him sound like the hound dog he'd become. His laugh was low and luscious. Shivers crept up her spine. Then he scooped her into his arms. "Or what?"

"I'll tell everybody that you cried during *Rudy*," she said, digging her fingers into the softness of his shirt. Her fingers slipped so she wrapped her arms around his neck to keep from falling into the water he now held her over.

"Everybody cries during that movie," he said, allowing her to slide down to his forearms.

"Eek!" she cried twisting away from the depths of the fountain. She could feel the spray on her arms. She looked down. Six inches from submersion.

Brent played dirty.

But then a stream of water hit him full in the face. He sputtered and stepped back. "What the—"

Henry delivered a Sioux warrior battle cry. He'd perfected the call to arms over and over in his room one Saturday. He did it rather well. "That's what you get for trying to dunk my mom!'

Eyes shut against the water running down his face,

he laughed then whispered, "That's not all I want to do to her."

Heat unfurled inside her and she grew keenly aware of being held in his arms. Of the flirtiness of his words. Of how good his lips had felt on hers several nights before.

Rayne tried to ignore the feelings stirring inside her and turned her head to see her son darting toward the azalea bushes. Smart boy. He was taking cover.

Brent seemed content to hold her. Her hands were still locked behind his neck in a death clasp. She could feel his heart beating right next to her breast. Something more than heat fluttered inside her. She looked up at the man that a mere week ago she'd sworn to despise.

Something shifted. It was that feeling she got when doing a jigsaw puzzle. Like when she slid one big blob of linked pieces over to another big blob of pieces, and then suddenly she could see where they linked and matched up. A revelation.

Brent's gaze met hers, and she caught her breath at the expression in his eyes. Water droplets dripped from his dark brows and rivulets of water streamed down his face, but his ice-blue eyes seemed almost…serene.

"I swear Hank is about as aggravating as I was at that age. How'd you put up with me?"

And just like that, with one flip-flop hanging off her right foot and her hair caught painfully between Brent's arm and chest. With a giggling seven-year-old still zapping Brent with a water gun. With all of Oak Stand toodling around the square going to the post office or the grocery store, Rayne felt herself go under.

For the second time.

What it was or how to describe it wasn't important. All she knew was that she didn't hate Brent anymore.

Maybe it was acceptance. Or lust. Or a connection that never went away. She didn't know. And putting a name to it wouldn't help. All she knew was her feelings had changed toward him and she saw him differently. Saw him the way she used to—as someone good, as someone more than what everyone else expected.

Even if he'd come home in the early hours of the morning, drunk and carrying deflated condoms.

BRENT LOOKED AT THE beautiful creature he cradled in his arms and felt satisfaction creep over him. Or was that contentment?

Whatever it was, it was something he'd not felt in a long time and it felt like putting on a favorite coat and finding a twenty in the pocket.

Rayne hadn't commented on his observation of her. Instead she stared at him with a contemplative look in her brown eyes. He loved her eyes. They were exactly the color of cinnamon, warm and spicy with a hint of imp. This was the Rayne he remembered. This was the Rayne he wanted back.

And nothing beat standing in the middle of the town, holding her in his arms while being drenched by a seven-year-old sharpshooter.

Another blast of water hit him between the eyes, showering Rayne with a fine spray. She blinked against the assault, and the small droplets caught in her eyelashes.

Damn, she was pretty.

He allowed her legs to fall to the brick path beneath them. "Okay, let's go get this rogue assassin."

Henry's giggles had moved farther away.

"I lost a flip-flop," Rayne said, dropping her arms from his shoulders and hopping around on one slender foot.

"Huh?"

She bobbed her head in all directions. "Flip-flop. I'm missing one."

Brent caught sight of the hot pink shoe floating in the fountain. "There it is."

The sandal bobbed beneath the curve of the statue. Brent could tell that it was too far away to reach.

Rayne frowned and called for Henry to come to them. The boy trotted up, water gun at his side. "Darn it, I'm out of water."

After a moment's contemplation Brent tugged off his well-worn construction boots. The water was cold, but he'd have few opportunities to play valiant knight with Rayne. "I'll get it."

"No," Rayne said. "I'm already barefoot."

"Can I go in?" Henry said, dropping onto his behind and pulling at his shoes.

"No!" Brent and Rayne shouted at the same time.

Rayne had already hitched her skirt up to her thighs. The sight caused lust to flare in regions he couldn't acknowledge standing in the middle of town with a seven-year-old in plain sight. But he couldn't help taking notice of how toned her thighs were. How pale and tempting. He ripped his gaze from her legs and looked at the flip-flop bobbing in the fountain.

He tossed his socks atop the boots and rolled his jeans up to his knees. He tugged Rayne's hand as she lifted a leg to climb over the fountain rim. "No, you don't."

She stayed put.

He hissed as he sank his feet into cold water. April in Texas was fickle and they'd gotten a cold front a day ago. He was sure people in Alaska swam happily in the temperature of the fountain water, but Texans were thin-skinned when it came to bailing into cold water. Or maybe it was him.

As he grabbed the flip-flop, he caught sight of Henry perched on the opposite side. The kid tottered on the edge of the fountain, preparing to jump in. Rayne reached for him but her fingers missed.

"Henry!" she cried.

Brent reached out and scooped the boy out of midair.

"I told you not to—" Rayne started fussing, but a whistle rent the air.

They all froze. Rayne, skirt still gathered around shapely knees, dropped her mouth open. If he hadn't been standing in subzero water, the sight of her pink lips and the tip of her tongue might have launched a raunchy fantasy in his mind. But he was holding a bright pink flip-flop, balancing a seven year-old on his shoulder and freezing his toes off in subzero water. And longtime Oak Stand police officer Roy Killough regarded them, hands on hip, whistle between his lips from the entrance of the park.

Officer Killough allowed the whistle to drop and perused the situation with amusement plainly evident on his worn face. "I got a call about vandalism."

"Vandalism?" Brent said, stepping over the edge of the fountain and setting Henry onto the pavers at his mother's feet. Rayne dropped her skirt. "You haven't taken Old Lady Taylor's binoculars away yet?"

Roy smiled. "No. In fact, Fred bought her a new pair last Christmas. She can see a flea bite a dog across town. Without Greta Taylor, half the news wouldn't make it to the front page of the *Gazette*. She's Fred's sure thing."

Brent wiggled his toes to restore circulation. "No vandalism. Simply fetching a shoe and a kid."

Roy shrugged. "I'd let you off with a warning, Brent, but this ain't the first time I've had to chase you and Rayne Rose out of the fountain. And it plainly states right over there that you are not allowed inside the fountain."

"Officer Killough, that was almost twenty years ago. We—"

"I don't suppose you'd want to teach the boy here that it's okay to break the law?" Roy gave Rayne a stern look.

She snapped her mouth shut, but Brent could see the anger in her eyes. It crackled and burned, but she managed to mind her smart mouth. Of course, Roy *was* being ridiculous. Any other officer and they'd all laugh and talk about old times. Not Roy. For all his outward harmlessness, he nursed a grudge against Brent held over from a dispute they'd had about the cost of the sunporch Brent had constructed for Roy's mother. The older policeman was a notorious cheapskate, not to mention paranoid about being swindled.

Roy pulled a pad from his back pocket and started scratching out a ticket.

"Are we going to jail?" Henry said, curling an arm around his mother's legs. He looked wary. A little scared.

Brent forgot about cold feet and the fact Henry had

disobeyed. He didn't think twice,. He scooped up Henry and held him at eye level. "Of course not, Hank. Just a citation. We were being silly and forgot to read the sign over there." Brent pointed to the sign warning visitors to stay out of the fountain. "No problem. I promise."

Henry looked at Roy then his mother. "Mom?"

Rayne stopped shooting daggers at the obtuse policeman long enough to look at her son. Her face softened. "We're not going to jail, pumpkin."

Brent felt Henry relax in his arms. Then the child did something uncharacteristic, at least for as long as Brent had known him. Henry curled his arms around Brent's neck and laid his head on his shoulder. The absolute trust and small token of affection settled a delicious warmth around Brent's heart. Henry was big for seven, but merely a kid. And he was scared. And something about the child's breath on his neck and sweaty grubby hands locked around him caused something wild and wonderful to move within Brent.

Then Henry whispered something in his ear that seared Brent to his gut. "I wish you were my dad."

CHAPTER TEN

RAYNE SIPPED THE OVERLY sweet chardonnay and watched Oak Stand's Junior League women in action. The scent of gardenia wafted among the women—a gift from the flickering candles strategically placed around Brandi Patterson McCormick's newly constructed Acadian house. It was standard Texas upscale—wood floors, khaki walls dotted with black-and-white photographs of smiling kids, fleur de lis doodads, expensive drapes and overstuffed furniture. It could have been cloned from every other house on the block. Even the Yukon sitting in the garage and the pepper jelly cream cheese on the pewter Arthur Court plate at Ryan's elbow felt standard.

"What do you think of the wine, Rayne Rose?" Stacy inquired, filling her glass. "My husband brought this back from a vineyard in California. He went to a conference out there last year. Said it was gorgeous."

"Mmm," Rayne said taking a sip. "Very good. And, yes, California wine country is beautiful."

Women swirled and talked, propped on wide chair arms and sitting on plaid ottomans. A huge plasma television took up the space above the fireplace and was set to the Disney Channel. Three little girls, mouths slack, giant bows affixed, stared as a preteen wearing too much makeup danced and sang. The women stepped around the little girls as they moved around the room talking about test scores, smocked clothing and fundraisers.

Meg appeared at her elbow, wearing thigh-high black boots and a bemused expression. "So we're among the real housewives of Oak Stand, eh?"

Stacy grinned, oblivious to Meg's sarcasm. "Well, we don't usually sleep with each other's husbands."

"At least not often," Brandi quipped, sliding along- side her friend. The woman gave a secret smile that made Rayne feel a bit nauseous. "Like the wine? I went to a conference out in California and picked up a case. Stacy's husband went, too. Good, isn't it?"

Brandi was like a cat with a crippled mouse. It was plainly obvious to everyone but Stacy that the woman had an inappropriate relationship with Alex Harp. Rayne would feel sorry for Stacy but the girl had been an absolute bitch in high school. Hard to feel any sympathy for a girl who'd thrown playground balls at her head then laughed when Rayne had nearly been decapitated.

Meg made a face, drawing Brandi's attention.

"Oh, so you're Rayne's assistant?"

Meg nodded, meeting Brandi's assessing stare head-on.

"Nice boots. What are they? Vintage?" Brandi said in a voice that didn't sound exactly complimentary. Her tone implied Meg had dug them from some dusty bin in a Goodwill store.

"You have a good eye," Meg said, with a twitch of her lips and a gleam in her blue eyes. "Original Masiero Lorenzo. A bitch to take off, but so worth it. You should see my patent leather Doc Martens lace-up combat boots. They're totally hot and useful for kicking ass."

Brandi's response was interrupted by the arrival of Nellie Darby and Kate Mendez, two others Rayne had attended Oak Stand High with, though they'd been a year ahead. Kate looked as intensely beautiful as she always had, and Nellie looked better than Rayne ever remembered her looking. Marriage and motherhood obviously agreed with her.

"Rayne," Nellie murmured, a warm smile curving her lips. She grasped Rayne's hands. "Sorry I'm late. Had to wait on Jack to pick up Mae. It's so good to see you."

Rayne had always liked Nellie. As a girl, she had been pragmatic and plain to the point of dowdy, but no longer. Her light brown hair was streaked with caramel highlights, and her clothes spoke of style and elegance—she'd definitely gotten herself together.

"Good to see you, too." Rayne squeezed her hands before acknowledging Kate, the girl who'd been tangled up with Brent the night she'd hurled the poem she'd worked so hard on, the poem that exposed her love. There had been many a night the year after she'd left Oak Stand that she'd lain awake and imagined a variety of ways to humiliate and torture Kate Newman. It still felt odd playing nice with a girl she'd hated for a long time. "Hello, Kate."

Kate gave her a genuine smile which surprised Rayne. Years ago, Kate hadn't bothered with her at all, hadn't seemed to even realize Rayne existed. "How's it going, Rayne Rose? Though I guess I know. I just bought your cookbook. It'll probably collect dust."

Nellie playfully punched her best friend. "I'm trying to teach Kate how to cook for her new husband."

Kate rolled her bright blue eyes. "*He* can cook. That's why I married him."

But then Kate smiled a sweet smile, one that spoke of a woman smitten with a man. Wow. Kate Newman, the rabble-rousing backseat legend, was in love. Amazing.

"Hey, I'm Meg, the feminist assistant." Meg offered her hand to both Kate and Nellie, making Rayne feel rude for not making introductions.

Kate narrowed her eyes, dropping her gaze to Meg's black boots with the drawstring and flaps. "Are those Ferragamo?"

"No, vintage Masiero Lorenzos," Meg said.

Kate raised an eyebrow then linked her arm though that of Rayne's assistant. The two paired off speaking a language not understood by anyone who didn't have a life-long subscription to *Vanity Fair* or *Vogue*.

Nellie shook her head. "Fashion escapes me. I wear what Kate tells me to."

Rayne shifted in her not-so-designer sandals and wondered as the guest of honor how long she'd have to stay. How strange it felt to be feted by these women who once seemed almost disdainful or at the very least disinterested in her. Fame cured lots of evils, and the hypocrisy of it ruffled her feathers a bit. If she'd been an accountant, would half of them be there?

She watched as Brandi drifted off to speak with a few women who were discussing the Spring Fling gala. Stacy melted away leaving Nellie and Rayne alone. No way she and Meg could leave until at least half of the women present gathered up their Dooney & Bourke purses and declared they needed to get home to laundry and packing lunches for the next day.

So she spent a few minutes catching up on Nellie's life—the man who'd followed Nellie home from Vegas, their wedding on the porch of Tucker House and the birth of their daughter and the expected arrival of a new baby in a few months. Amazing how life changed so quickly. The last time Rayne had been in Oak Stand, Nellie had been taking care of her sick grandmother and, honestly, looking resigned to a life of loneliness.

"So enough about me. I hear you and Brent had a little fun in the town fountain. Way to make a splash." Nellie's eyes sparkled. Any other person and Rayne would have been peeved, but the woman in front of her had a heart of gold, along with an impish need to tease.

"Well, we weren't having fun," Rayne said, before pausing. But they *had* been having fun. More fun than she'd had in forever. The sound of Henry's laughter had stayed with her as she pulled the sheet to her chin and snuggled into the soft mattress in her old room. Then her mind had turned to Brent. The way he'd looked at her.

Had he looked at half the women in this room that way?

Probably.

No doubt he'd perfected that mixture of passion and sincerity in his mirror and then applied it on whatever poor creature tottered his way in her too-high heels enveloped in a martini haze.

So why was she being taken in by his practiced seduction routine? Once she'd known it was all an act, a way to be what his father and the town expected. The boy who threw touchdowns and winked at fawning cheerleaders. The boy with the golden arm and tarnished reputation. But then that night had come. The night where she realized he wasn't pretending. He'd become that person.

And he hadn't changed. Pieces of the sincere boy he'd once been, the boy he'd been with her, might still float inside him, but he embraced the life he'd made for himself. A life of honky-tonks, easy women and few ties. A life that would never include her. She didn't fall out of cars, half-drunk in the middle of the night. She didn't sleep around. And she damned sure never hid her light under a barrel.

"Brent went in after my flip-flop." Rayne stared at the half-empty wineglass in her hand. The chardonnay tasted better for some reason. Maybe she'd have another.

Kate popped up at her shoulder holding a plate of Goldfish crackers. Obviously, her former arch nemesis had been snacking from the kids' table. "But the question is—what was it doing in the fountain?"

Rayne looked at the tiny woman with the fashionable leggings and oversize patterned shirt. She looked happy. Something about her glow made her more approachable, less snarky and brash. Kate's mischievous blue eyes slid to Nellie's and she grinned like a naughty elf.

"Well, I—" Rayne snapped her mouth closed. "You two are trying to create smoke where there's no fire."

Kate shrugged and took a sip of the bottled water she held. "Oh, I don't know. Brent usually does more than take a gal's sandals off."

Rayne stiffened and looked across the room at

Heather Breaux demonstrating something her little girl had done at ballet. Or at least that's what it looked like. "Yeah, that's the problem with Brent, isn't it?"

Nellie made a face. "Well, some would say it isn't a problem. More of an ability."

"But Brent has always had a thing for you. Since, like, grade school or something," Kate said, her gaze sweeping the room. Her sharp eyes landed on a few women and something stirred in the depths. "Yeah, he was all gaga over you, sister."

Rayne choked. Surely Kate was exaggerating. Years ago Brent had showed no compulsion to acknowledge his friendship with Rayne.

Nellie thumped her on the back. "You okay?"

Rayne cleared her throat and wiped the moisture from the corner of her eyes. "Sorry. Wrong pipe."

Kate narrowed her eyes as though she knew it wasn't the wine. It had been the words. "I'm serious. He had it bad for you. I could have my hands around that guy's—"

Nellie punched her friend.

"—um, shoulders and he'd be talking about this butterfly Rayne had found under a crepe myrtle. Or a new recipe Rayne had come up with on her own. He talked about you all the time except when he talked about how his dad wanted him to gain more yards on each carry. Or how his brother Denny had been better at avoiding sacks. Football and Rayne. Two opposite things, huh?"

Rayne didn't know what to say to that little tidbit of info. She assumed that when Brent had been with Katie Newman he'd done very little talking. But chatting about her when he was making out with another girl? Strange. She always thought the relationship she'd shared with Brent had been a secret. As though he was one way with her but ashamed to acknowledge her when he was out with others. She'd been merely his gawky, skinny, socially awkward neighbor. She'd had no idea he'd even mentioned her to anyone, maybe other than his parents. "I—uh—don't really know what to say.…"

She trailed off. Damn, she wanted to go back to the inn. Snuggle with Henry and watch a Harry Potter movie. Whip up a batch of popcorn.

Nellie gave Kate a slight shake of her head before turning back to Rayne. "So I hear Brent's doing work on your aunt's bed-and-breakfast. He did the kitchen in Tucker House. Did a good job."

It was an open invitation to discuss a myriad of things—the renovation of the inn, her reason for being in Oak Stand and Brent's role in all of the above. But Rayne didn't want to talk about Brent any longer. This whole night was too much and she was tired of pretending to enjoy it. "Lots of conversations start with *I hear* around here, don't they? Like people don't have anything better to do."

"I'm sorry, Rayne. I wasn't prying. Just trying to shift the conversation away from something that obviously made you uncomfortable. Another thing we are polite enough to do around here." Nellie lifted her chin.

Touché.

It was Rayne's turn to feel like crap. "I'm sorry. I feel like an ass. Not used to standing around chatting. I'm used to running a kitchen. No one questions me."

Nellie flashed a gracious smile. "That must be nice.

All I get are questions all day long from Mae." Nellie's voice assumed the plaintive whine of a toddler. "'Momma, why can't I have jelly beans for lunch?' Or, 'Momma, what's that fat man eating?' All day long, questions, questions, questions."

Kate wrinkled her nose. "I think all kids should be shipped off to boarding school at age three and then brought back when they can carry on a semi-intelligent conversation. Say, about eighteen years old?"

"Oh, you do not," Nellie said.

"Well, don't tell me there aren't days you don't wish you could pack that chattering three-year-old off to camp or something? She's got more to say than a preacher. Or a lawyer. Or a late-night talk show host."

Nellie laughed. "She *is* precocious."

"You think?" Kate smiled, making it obvious she respected the chatty Mae Darby.

Meg reappeared and lowered her voice. "So how much longer we gotta stay here? I nearly got hives when they started talking about cracked nipples."

Kate's mouth twitched. "I think I'm in love with your assistant, Rayne. Can she come over and play sometime?"

Meg gave Kate a droll look. "You know, of course, that I'm not a lesbian?"

Kate snickered. "You're too funny. Bubba had lots to say about your being very heterosexual."

Nellie looked like she'd swallowed a fish and snapped, "Big mouth!"

Meg lifted a well-shaped eyebrow over one kohl-rimmed eye. "Oh, so Bubba likes to kiss and tell, huh?

Better make sure I give him something really good for next time. Just so you gals can live vicariously."

Kate looked at Nellie. "See? I love this girl."

Brandi floated back their way, her lapdog Stacy right on her heels. Kate gritted her teeth.

Brandi laid a perfectly manicured hand on Nellie's arm. A diamond bracelet glittered in the track lighting over the mantel. "So glad you could stop by, Nellie. Oh, and you brought Katie. Never a party without her."

Kate's smile could have shattered glass. "Says the Kappa Sigma keg stand champion of 1998."

Brandi forced a laugh. "Still bitter I beat your time?"

Kate showed her teeth again. "Nah, it was a perfect record to set on the *Girls Gone Wild* video. You look good upside down."

"Meow," Meg murmured, drawing a nervous laugh from Nellie.

Kate merely shrugged one shoulder. "You know we like to have fun with each other. Wouldn't be a party without a little scratching and biting."

Brandi nodded and flashed a smile as brittle as her colored hair. "So I heard Brent mentioned over here. What's new with our favorite boy toy? You playing with him, Rayne?"

"Playing with him?" Rayne asked. When had Brent become merely a toy? She knew what people thought of him, and maybe he'd not done a good job of dissuading them from their beliefs, but it seemed a little unfair that he be whittled down to something so insignificant as the whip-thin viper's plaything.

Brandi raised her eyebrows. "Can't say I'd blame

you. I hired him to build an arbor by the pool just so I could ogle him while he worked."

Kate whistled. "Desperate much?"

Rayne felt irritation gather inside her. Though she knew Brent was perfectly drool-worthy, she also knew he was so much more. That very afternoon, he'd patiently explained base-stealing to Henry when she knew he needed to get over to Justus Mitchell's house for some repair work. He'd also continued building birdhouses for the retirement home. The trees outside the kindergarteners' windows at Oak Stand Elementary held four or five squirrel feeders he'd constructed. He gave his time to coach Little League and took a seven-year-old on his first picnic, earning himself a citation in the process.

Why did everyone in Oak Stand have him only filling the slot of town skirt chaser? When they looked at him, was that all they saw?

Then she felt guilt flood her. Hadn't she called him a man whore recently? Hadn't she put him in that slot, too? She wasn't any better than Brandi, Stacy or the rest of the women, clinging to the assertion that Brent Hamilton was good for a couple of things—construction and seduction. Rayne felt ashamed she wasn't prepared to let him be anything other than what his reputation said he was.

"I don't have to be desperate, Katie. I like distractions. That's all." Brandi patted Kate's shoulder then sauntered off to torture someone else. Her favorite target bobbed off behind her, throwing a cheery wave.

"Bye, Stacy," Nellie said, shaking her head. "Poor woman doesn't realize Brandi isn't a true friend."

"Quite the opposite. She's a menace," Kate said,

popping a cracker in her mouth. "But she's right about ol' Brent. He does look good building things."

"Stop," Rayne said, shaking her head. "Everyone treats him like he's nothing more than some hunk of meat."

"He went through my underwear drawer," Nellie said absentmindedly.

"What?" Meg stifled a choking noise similar to the one Rayne had made earlier.

"When he was working on Tucker House several years ago he went through my underwear drawer."

Rayne actually took a step backward. "No. That's... that's—"

"Perverted?" Meg filled in. "Hey, I like a little perversion but that borders on sick."

Rayne shook her head. "No way. Why would he do that?"

Nellie shrugged. "I don't know. It's just, well, I know my lingerie wasn't the way I'd left it. I'm particular about my panty order."

Kate laughed. "You're particular about everything. I'm sure undies are no exception."

Rayne didn't know what to say. This was why so many persisted in believing the worst of Brent. Pawing through a woman's underwear? Why? It didn't sit right with her. There was no way he'd done something so bizarre. If he'd wanted to see underwear, there were plenty of women around town willing to model theirs.

"There's some logical reason. Did you ask him?" Rayne set the empty glass on a coaster and crossed her arms. She felt defensive. She didn't doubt Nellie, but she couldn't believe such a thing.

"Well, I didn't ask. I accused," Nellie said, now

looking a bit sheepish, as though she wished she hadn't brought it up. Too late. "But he played it down. Said he liked the red ones. He didn't deny it."

Something that felt close to pain ripped through Rayne. Here she was ready to chastise all of Oak Stand for treating Brent as less than what he was, and he'd done something so…weird. "I don't know. It doesn't seem like him. I can't believe he'd be so twisted."

Nellie gave her a gentle smile. "Maybe, but then again you're a bit biased. You've always seen him differently than the rest of us have. It could be a good thing, but then again, it could be dangerous."

Rayne felt tears clog her throat. Nellie's words hurt, and once again, she found herself doubting the man who'd held her so tenderly in his arms a mere two days ago in the town square. Had she picked up the blinders she'd always worn where Brent was concerned? Had she set them on a shelf fifteen years ago and now they were dusted and ready to view him in the light she preferred? Was she once again building him in her mind so big that she'd be unable to see his obvious flaws from her place at his feet?

Maybe she was the biggest idiot in Texas.

Maybe, once again, Brent had her under his spell.

But maybe everyone was wrong about him.

"Seeing people differently is not a bad thing. People in this town tend to put labels on others without giving them the benefit of the doubt. I never wanted to be that way."

"Gotta respect a lady who thinks outside the box. No one likes to be stereotyped," Kate said.

Something flashed in Nellie's eyes. "You know, I never liked being the poor little rich girl, the girl who always did the right thing. Maybe you're right, Rayne. Maybe Brent doesn't like being who he is."

Rayne looked Nellie right in the eye. "I'll agree with you on that."

CHAPTER ELEVEN

THE COOL SPRING BREEZE whipped through the stands surrounding the baseball field, hurling empty soda cups to the concrete below and stirring up the yellow pollen coating the bright blue bleachers. Several fans sneezed as the Oak Stand Warriors took the field.

Rayne cheered as Henry ran out and took his place at shortstop. Aunt Frances blew an air horn.

Everyone jumped. One woman screamed.

"Sorry," Aunt Frances said, sporting a Warriors T-shirt that said Hank's Aunt on the back.

Rayne gave her son a thumbs-up sign. It was his first game and he'd earned the privilege of playing when he brought home signed papers showing significant improvement along with a computer printout that relayed he'd scored a nine out of ten points on his accelerated reading test. Rayne had been stunned. Henry had given her a told-you-so shrug and said, "I didn't like dumb ol' talking animal books, but I can do good on the ones about sports."

She'd hugged him, after correcting his incorrect adverb usage of course, and let him eat one of the Pop-Tarts Brent had sent over for him via Meg.

"Oh, he looks so little," Aunt Frances said, waving at Henry. Her son gave a quick wave and then focused on the batter lining up at the plate. A bright blue pitching machine whirred on the pitcher's mound. A coach from the other team stood behind it and began threading balls into the slot. Brent emerged from the dugout, tugged the batter out of the way and crouched to catch the balls. He was making certain the strike zone was right.

Brent wore a red-and-black coach's shirt that declared he was Coach Brent on the back. All the parents wore the red shirts with the black battle-axes crossed on the front beneath the word *Warriors*. His shirt looked much better on him than Rayne's did on her. Wearing battle-axes was so not her thing.

As the thunk of the ball hit Brent's glove, Rayne wondered for the tenth or eleventh time about him going through Nellie's panties.

She was afraid to ask him, but more afraid not to ask.

What right did she have anyway? And what would it even mean to him if she asked about his reasons for digging through a woman's panty drawer? She thought about the night she'd kissed him and brushed against his pajama pants just to play with him. Just to gain the upper hand with him. Then she thought about the day at the fountain when everything had shifted and she'd fallen into the infatuation she'd always had with him. Why was she moving in his direction? Why was she tempting him? Flirting with him? Letting him back inside her heart?

Was it fate? Or perhaps she simply wanted to get naked with him and call it a day? Or was there something more.

She suspected the latter, but was afraid to explore it too much. Afraid to label her feelings. And Rayne liked to label everything. She liked a plan, a path and a goal. But outside of her career, which hung in the balance, she had no idea about what to do with the burgeoning feelings she had for the man standing in the huddle of little boys giving a pep talk.

Confused was the word of the day. Who was she kidding? It was the word of the year. She felt bewildered about everything. Her career. Her relationship with Brent. Her new fondness for Pop-Tarts. Yes, she'd polished off the last two in the box and then hid the evidence from Meg. She knew she'd never live it down that she'd eaten chemically injected pastries if Meg found out. Not after she'd forced her assistant to throw out the Halloween candy last year.

Meg stood with Bubba Malone alongside the chain-link fence skirting the ball field. Rayne had never seen a couple look so misfit as those two. Bubba wore unlaced construction boots, stained jeans and a well-washed T-shirt. A ball cap faded from the sun sat backward on his head. He'd shaved his scruffy beard into a neat goatee that suited him much better. Meg wore a long skirt, a tight Ramones T-shirt and, of course, her patent leather combat boots. Her nose ring caught the sunlight just right.

Yet the two looked content to merely stand next to one another. No words. No forced conversation. No confusion. Simply being.

A referee clad in protective armor took up residence behind the plate and the game began. Good defensive play had the Warriors running to their dugout after a three up, three down inning. The parents cheered as if it were the World Series.

"Do you think Henry will get a hit?" Aunt Frances

asked as Henry sauntered to the batter's box. "I think they should let them bat until they hit the ball. I hate this whole 'out' thing."

Rayne laughed. "That's how you play baseball, Aunt Fran."

"I'm not sure it's good for their self-esteem."

"You sound like Glenna," Rayne said, deliberately drawing the comparison between Frances and her sister. Rayne's mother was so very different than her aunt, but somehow they shared a gentleness in their nature. A demand for things to be just.

"I'm not like her at all," Frances said before letting loose with the air horn again.

The front row ducked and a baby started crying. Several fans glared at her aunt. "Y'all were raised by the same parents. Merely pointing that out."

"That doesn't mean a thing. You're nothing like Summer."

Rayne smiled. Her sister was a fireball with a flair for drama. Yes, Summer was a bit over-the-top. "I'm a little like her."

"Maybe," her aunt conceded, "but don't lump me in with that crazy hippy."

Rayne laughed. "Okay, but you *are* a crazy fan."

They both let the conversation rest as Henry pulled the bat over his shoulder and crouched in his hitting stance. Brent stood behind the pitching machine and directed Henry, moving him first forward than backward, closer to the plate then back again. Finally, when Henry was in the exact same spot he'd started in, Brent dropped the ball.

And Henry swung.

The ball connected and went sailing…right over the fence.

The crowd erupted as her son dropped the bat to the ground and took his jog around the bases. Rayne stood and clapped as Aunt Fran unleashed the air horn yet again. No one seemed to mind this time.

Brent's eyes met hers from across the field. He mouthed, "Wow."

And just like that, Rayne knew Nellie had been very wrong. Most of Oak Stand had been very wrong. Brent wasn't a gigolo looking to get into every girl's pants. He wasn't some dumb jock with multiple passing records. He wasn't perverted, irresponsible or callous. He wasn't what he was painted to be at all.

She didn't know exactly how she knew it. She simply did. And she wasn't ready to put to words what she knew him to be exactly. But right then, she was content to believe Brent was better than everyone had given him credit for.

But she still wanted to know about the panties. For good measure.

Her son crossed home plate and his team met him for a good old-fashioned dog pile. Brent jogged toward the dugout entrance for some knucks. Henry's smile could run the town on its wattage. He ducked his head under all the praise, but the smile stayed.

A crazy bubble of joy rose in Rayne.

"I think I want some nachos," she murmured to Aunt Frances. "With extra jalepeños."

Aunt Fran stopped clapping and stared at her. "What did you say?"

Rayne laughed. "I'm going to get nachos. You want something?"

"You're going to let people see you eat processed cheese? This isn't Pop-Tarts in the closet. We're in public." Aunt Fran didn't meet her eyes. Instead she gave Henry a fist pump.

Rayne blinked before waving to her glowing son and mimicking Aunt Fran with the fist pump gesture. "How'd you know?"

"I found the foil wrappers. You can't fool me, Rayne Rose."

"Guess I never could," she said, grabbing her wallet from the depths of her purse and fishing out a twenty-dollar bill.

Aunt Frances pushed a curl from Rayne's face. "You know, sometimes what you think is bad for you turns out to be good."

Rayne frowned. "You're not talking about Pop-Tarts or nachos, are you?"

Aunt Frances gave her a wink. "You always were a smart girl."

Rayne rolled her eyes and slid out from the bleachers. She waved to Stacy and Brandi, who'd had the foresight to bring camp chairs. She'd written them each a thank-you note for her welcome-home party, but would stop by after the game to make another personal gesture of appreciation, even if she didn't care for them much. Being nice meant keeping their boys from pestering Henry. She looked out at the field of play and caught Brent's glance as the new batter stepped to the plate. He winked.

The gesture made her tummy flutter, and she wondered if they sold candy bars in the concession stand.

BRENT LOADED THE EMPTY cooler and bucket of balls into the back of his truck, glad they'd pulled off the first win of the season. The boys had whooped, hollered and then ran for the bathrooms. They'd drunk all the Gatorade he'd mixed and put out.

Henry popped up at his elbow. "Thanks for coaching me. It was awesome."

"You're welcome. I had fun, too. Good play you made to get that out. Your throw to first was on target."

Henry nodded. "Mom wanted to know if you want to join us for a burger at the Dairy Barn. She wants some onion rings."

"Seriously?" Brent looked up and saw Rayne talking with a few other mothers. Something caught in his chest at the way her hands moved as she talked. At the tilt of her chin. The animation in her eyes.

"Yeah, I know. She never eats fried stuff." Henry joined him in staring at his mom. "You don't think aliens abducted her, do you?"

"Abducted. And, no, I don't think they exist."

"I saw some in a magazine. They had big heads and weird eyes. It said they suck people's brains out of their ears," Henry said, looking as if he totally believed everything he'd read in the pages of the magazine.

"You're a funny kid," Brent said, tossing the catcher's equipment bag over the side of the truck bed and pushing up the tailgate.

He nodded. "I know. I checked out a joke book in the school library. I got better knock-knock jokes for you."

Brent ruffled Henry's hair, tugging the bill down over his eyebrows. "Good. I need more material."

Rayne broke away from the group of mothers and

walked toward them. Her hips swayed gently. She wore a skirt and sandals with the T-shirt. On most women the outfit would have looked strange, but on Rayne it looked right.

"I hear you're in the mood for some of Charlie Mac's onion rings," Brent said, pulling off his visor and pushing his hair from his eyes. "Hank thinks aliens abducted you and replaced you with a replica."

Rayne looked down at Henry. "Oh, yeah? You're a funny guy."

"That's what Coach said," Henry said, flipping his glove into the air.

Rayne's eyes met his and something passed between them. Her gaze was warm, cinnamon with a hint of tenderness. Maybe Rayne had finally gotten past "We're not really friends. We're not anything" and had moved on to something. He wasn't sure what that might be, but the invitation for onion rings seemed a step in the right direction. "Well then, your mom and I agree on something."

Rayne tore her gaze from him and looked at her fidgety son. "Stop before you hit someone."

Henry stopped. "Let's go already."

"So," Rayne said, "do you want to go for a burger?"

"Have I ever turned down food?"

She smiled. "Not in this lifetime. I'll treat. To celebrate the victory."

He shrugged. "Even better. I'm a cheap date. I'll only eat two burgers."

"Can I ride with Brent?" Henry said, running to the passenger side of the truck before she could even answer him. He jerked on the locked door. Then frowned when it didn't budge. "It's locked."

Rayne ignored her son and looked at Brent. "You want to leave your truck here and ride with us? Aunt Frances is going to Myrtle Wilson's for bridge and finger sandwiches, so we've got room."

"Sure, as long as you're good with swinging me back here afterward."

She nodded. "Sure."

"You can ride shotgun!" Henry whooped, nearly tripping over his shoelaces as he lunged to grab Brent.

Henry packed a punch, slamming against Brent's legs and wrapping his arms about Brent's hips. Brent stumbled, took a step away and patted the boy's back. The impromptu show of affection should have felt awkward, but it didn't.

"This is the best day ever," Henry said against his legs. Immediately Brent's mind tripped back to several days before, the whispered words against his neck at the fountain. *I wish you were my dad.*

Alarms clanged in his brain, so Brent retreated another step and tugged Henry's ball cap over his eyes the way he'd done earlier. "Any day you hit a home run is a good day, sport."

He lifted his gaze to Rayne. She looked so sad and resigned. A prickling of awareness surged between them. It wasn't passion or any sort of sexual energy, though he knew that to be lurking beneath the surface. It was more of a human, Hallmark-card sort of moment. A poignant moment of understanding. Of a boy. Without a father. Wishing it was different.

Brent swallowed the sudden emotion that clogged his throat as Rayne turned and clicked the button that unlocked the doors on the Volvo crossover sitting four spots away from his truck. It was a somber navy blue car, the kind mothers who were way too protective drove. He bet Henry still had a booster seat in the back.

"Let's grab those burgers," she said, walking away. It was nearly a trudge, as if the heaviness of the moment weighed her down. Henry, ever light on his feet, bounced behind her. Brent pocketed his keys and tried to decide whether his going was a good idea.

He could feel Henry getting attached, and on any other month of Sundays he'd not mind a bit. Henry was a terrific kid, only second to his mother. But things felt too fast too soon with the boy. Especially since the future perched precariously on the ledge of uncertainty. He wanted Rayne but not at the risk of Henry's heart. Didn't seem fair for a kid to be the casualty of their messed-up relationship. So maybe he should forget trying to push something with Rayne. Maybe the risk to Henry was too great. He and Rayne could deal, but a seven-year-old? Not so much.

He wavered.

Then Rayne turned back to him. "You coming?"

And despite his reservations, there wasn't much more he could do but start walking toward her.

THIS TIME THE DAIRY BARN was packed. Half the people there were clad in parent shirts declaring whose "Maw Maw" they were while the decidedly smaller other half wore various uniforms with dirty knees and dusty cleats. The atmosphere could only be described as mixed with some kids jubilantly hopping around the

Formica tables and the others modeling how it looked to lose a best friend.

Henry pointed to a small boy with a sad-sack expression. "That's Tyler Ratcliff. He's on the team we beat."

"Why don't you go say hi to him? Make him feel better," Rayne said, giving Henry a small shove.

"No, I don't even know him. He's not in my class."

"So? Doesn't mean you can't be friends." Rayne gave Henry another push, wondering why her son was so shy around kids his age. Adults she could understand, but other kids? Surely they weren't intimidating? Henry eased away from her reach and made no attempt to move toward any other kids in the diner. Not even when one of the boys from the Warriors waved at him.

She started to march Henry over to the boy's table, but then she thought to when she was seven and how awkward she'd felt. Her parents had dragged her from commune to commune, only venturing to Oak Stand when money got too low or there was a nearby art show. Otherwise, she played the role of new girl in elementary schools around the country. And with red curly hair, pale skin and knobby knees, it hadn't been a glamorous role. She'd only felt herself when she'd come to live with Aunt Fran in her rambling house.

And met her first true friend. Brent.

So on second thought, she backed off. Like her, Henry would have to make his own way. Even if it pained her to see him without friends his age. "Why don't you and Brent find a table? I'll order."

"You sure?" Brent said, taking her son by the shoulder to guide him toward the seating area. He gave her a detailed order, leaving off onions and tomato then steered Henry toward the back of the diner.

She hadn't spoken much to Brent on the way into town. Henry had filled the silence with the review of all the awesome plays from the game. It proved a good thing because her emotions felt too raw from the sight of Henry twined about Brent's legs, the tender way Brent patted her son's back. A bittersweet longing had swamped her, and it hadn't gone away. She kept thinking about Brent and why she'd come to Oak Stand. About fate and those damned panties of Nellie's. About who she was and who everybody thought Brent to be.

Rayne got in line behind a girl texting on her phone and perused the order board, choosing a chef salad for herself and a small plain burger for Henry. He'd have to do without the fries.

"Hello, Charlie Mac," Rayne said, stepping toward the register, changing her mind on the salad as she opened her mouth. "If my regular customers find out I've been wolfing down onion rings, I'll tell them you forced them on me."

Charlie Mac cackled like a rusty rooster. "I'm gathering you want an order of 'em?"

Rayne nodded. "And a side salad. Dressing on the side."

"That'll help," he said, sarcasm very much intended.

Rayne took the number, then headed toward her son and— What? Friend? Former friend? What was Brent? Oh, yes. Contractor. Coach. Could she put a name to him? Maybe he was just Brent. That could be enough. Maybe.

Eyes followed her winding path through the maze

of tables. A few people waved, some rudely stared and a few didn't bother looking up from their steak fingers and country gravy platters. They were probably people who'd never met Rayne. Or the chicken fried steak fingers were that sinfully good. Could be both.

Rayne sank onto the metal chair, glad they'd forgone the coziness of the booth. "Here's the number."

She sat the tented plastic number where it was visible as a boy appeared next to Henry. He had disheveled brown hair and a cast.

"Hey, Hank. I'm Hunter Todd, remember me? We played kick ball at recess. Wanna come sit at my table?"

Henry looked at her. He looked a bit shell-shocked and uncertain. "Mom?"

She smiled and gave his arm a squeeze. "That's a nice offer. You can sit with Hunter Todd if you want."

Henry looked at the boy and then back to his mom. "You won't be lonely?"

"Nah," Brent interrupted. "She's got the old Coach here to keep her company. You go on with Hunter."

Hunter Todd grinned at Brent. "I got some new magic tricks to show you. Only it's hard 'cause of my cast." He looked back at Henry. "You coming or not, Hank? Tyler's gonna sit with us, too. He's got a magazine that shows all the new PS3 games."

Henry looked wary but slid out and followed Hunter to a booth with two other kids whose gazes were locked on a magazine. He cast only one glance over his shoulder at where she sat with Brent.

"That's good for him, huh?" Brent looked at her.

Rayne nodded. "He hasn't had as many nightmares recently. His grades are good. He seems to be flourishing in Oak Stand. Just what I hoped."

"So what's going to happen when you pull him away again?" Brent's words sounded accusing.

She didn't want to talk about the future. She gave a shrug. "He'll deal like any other kid."

Brent frowned and fingered the red plastic number. "But you said he wasn't like other kids. He suffers from a disorder that obviously needs routine. Have you talked to the counselor yet?"

Irritation gathered inside her. "It's none of your business what I do with my son."

Brent leaned back. "You're right. None of my concern."

A hard silence fell. Uncomfortable, hard silence.

Rayne pressed her lips together and watched Henry as he quietly took in the rambunctiousness of the other boys wiggling in the booth. He nodded periodically at something Hunter said. He looked not exactly happy, but maybe a bit more accepting at being away from her.

He turned his head and caught her gaze. Then gave her the most endearing smile she'd seen in a while. She smiled back. Then looked at the man across from her. He watched her with a guarded expression.

"I'm sorry," she said. "I'm not good with people questioning me."

"You think?" Brent leaned back and crossed his arms, making him look broader, more masculine, more alpha male. She swallowed at the way her body reacted. She'd automatically leaned toward him. Nervously licked her lips.

"So what are we doing here?" Her words were the same as her assistant's words days before.

"You mean between us?" he asked, pointing to her then to himself.

"I don't know how to label you. Are you my friend? My contractor? My kid's coach?"

"Or something more?"

She swallowed again. "How? We can't be something more. It's not like I can date you or something."

"You can't? Why?" His words were flung like a challenge.

She studied him, knowing the answer. Afraid to tell him. He'd break her heart. That's what he did, didn't he? What he'd done those fifteen years before. Taken her childish first love and ripped it to shreds. She wasn't different than any other woman Brent had taken to his bed. The only difference is that they'd once shared an almost magical friendship. He'd hurt her once. He'd do it again.

And she might not survive this one.

So she didn't answer. She turned from him and watched a teenage boy bob their way with a laden tray.

"You won't give me an answer?" Brent was pissed. Why? Why did it matter to him what label she gave him? Why did she have to declare him anything?

"Rayne?"

She smiled at the waiter. "Leave us these two baskets and take this meal to the little boy in the red baseball jersey at that table over there." She pointed in Henry's direction before turning to the irate man sitting across from her.

What to do? What to say to Brent wanting something

more? Maybe she should lay it out. Let him see why she couldn't go there.

"Truth?" she asked, shuffling the double cheeseburger his way and setting the onion rings and salad in front of her.

Brent uncrossed his arms and leaned forward. "Yeah, that'd be good."

"Because *something more* scares the hell out of me."

He flinched. "Why?"

"Because if I walk through those French doors of your house, I'll end up in your bed. And I have little doubt what will happen between those sheets would be very good. In fact, in my wildest daydreams, it's more than good. But the thing is, I can't climb in your bed without risking my heart. It's too dangerous. And I have to protect myself. Henry, too."

Brent didn't react for a moment. Then he smiled. "What if I don't want your body? What if I want your heart?"

Rayne felt herself reel backward. "What?"

"What if I want all of you, Rayne? What if I want more than sex? What if this thing between us is meant to be?"

"I—I— Are you serious?" She couldn't stop her voice from shaking. She looked down at the crispy onion rings. He couldn't be serious. Brent wasn't that kind of guy. He was a good time. Nothing more.

She looked at him.

He nodded.

"Well…" She tried to smile. It probably came out as strained, as if she had a stomach cramp or something. But it was way stronger than that. Her heart thumped

against her rib cage and her palms felt sweaty. It was
the strangest of moments. And she felt all Alice down
the rabbit hole. What to do? "I guess the first thing
I've got to ask is, did you go through Nellie Darby's
underwear drawer?"

CHAPTER TWELVE

BRENT CHOKED ON HIS cheeseburger. After several hacking coughs and a few sips of root beer, he was finally able to stammer, "What?"

"The choking was my reaction, too."

He blinked. "Where'd you hear this?"

"Nellie Hughes, I mean, Darby, said you went through her underwear drawer when you were remodeling her kitchen," Rayne said, picking at her rings and not meeting his eyes.

"What the hell do you gals talk about at those get-togethers?"

Something about the way he said it made her feel small. She hadn't been gossiping. Someone else had given her the info. She had to ask because his answer mattered. She couldn't fathom him actually doing something so perverted. Didn't even want to think about what it meant if he'd done something so absolutely creepy. "It just came up."

"What does this have to do with our relationship, or rather lack thereof?"

"I need to know you wouldn't do something like that. Before we go any further."

She felt him move forward. His elbows appeared on the table. His voice sounded strained when he said, "Look at me."

She raised her gaze to his ice-blue eyes. In the depths of his eyes she saw it. The hurt. It made her heart pinch.

"Are you asking me this because you think I poked through Nellie's panties? That I rifle through women's underwear like some kind of pervert? Or are you asking because you want an explanation? Because it does make a difference."

She swallowed. "I don't think you're a pervert. But, she said you never denied it. What kind of man allows people to believe that sort of thing about him?"

"A man who is accustomed to people thinking what they want about him. People will believe what they want regardless of the truth. Take a look around the world. Hell, take a look around this room." His eyes masked his emotions, rendering his whole expression indistinguishable. She could get no read on him.

Neither of them spoke for a few moments. People laughed, kids cried, Charlie Mac yelled out numbers, but she and Brent were frozen in place. Rayne tried to cipher his meaning, wondering how cynical he'd become over the years. Realizing his words were true. People saw what they wanted.

Rayne turned her head when she heard Henry laugh. He was fine, giggling with Hunter over a face one of the boys at the table made. Boys being boys.

"Why didn't you tell the truth? Why do you let people think you are less than what you are?" Her words fell between them. It was the heart of the matter. The elephant in the room between them for fifteen long years. Could they strip themselves bare and be what the other person knew each to be?

"That's always been my problem, right? Never showing who I am to anyone except you. I wish I knew. Maybe I'm not strong enough to break the ties that bind me to my image. It's been easier to be the charming Brent Hamilton. The guy you grab a beer with and hide your sister from. Everybody likes that guy. Well, most people."

"But you don't deserve to be thought of as some pervert." Rayne embraced the anger that rose in her. She couldn't fathom not standing up for herself. Not clearing the air. She didn't understand him and maybe that was the biggest obstacle.

"Nellie left her laundry on the dryer. Her laundry room was next to the kitchen where I was working. We were removing old drywall that day. Dusty job. So I picked up the stack of clean clothes and took them upstairs. I couldn't leave her underwear out for all the guys to see."

Rayne took a sip of her soft drink, very glad she'd skipped water and gone for the Dr Pepper. This kind of conversation demanded twenty-six secret ingredients.

"I started to leave them on her dresser, but I know that women keep their panties in that smaller top drawer, so I shoved them in, closed the drawer and went back to work."

He shrugged, but didn't meet her eyes. "She didn't ask me. She accused. So I said something about liking the red ones with the bows. Don't know why. Just kind of pissed me off she thought the worst of me."

"But you don't give people reason to expect the best," Rayne said, finally pulling an onion ring from the basket before her. "For instance, no one knows you make those birdhouses for the retirement village. Or the squirrel feeders I saw over at Oak Stand Elementary. You are a nice guy, but you don't let people know it."

He shrugged. "People know. It's just that *nice guy* is not the first thing people think of when they hear my name. They think about the records I set or the way I didn't put the cornice board over their kitchen sink the way they wanted it. Or how I broke their cousin's heart when I didn't call her for a second date. People see what they want to see, Rayne. I learned that long ago. Why exhaust myself fighting against opinion?"

"For self-respect."

Brent's mouth twisted and he shut down. She'd hit a nerve and didn't know whether to pull back or run with it. Brent didn't say anything else. He picked up his cheeseburger and took a bite.

"Am I making you uncomfortable?" she asked.

He said nothing. Just glanced over to where Henry sat with his new friends. Then he looked around the Dairy Barn. Rayne wondered what he thought as she unwrapped the plastic from her fork and ripped open her dressing.

Finally he looked back at her. "Yeah, it makes me uncomfortable. I know what I do. I don't know why. Maybe I'm still trying to be someone I'm not. I guess I am. If I pull back and look at myself, I can see what went wrong. Denny. My dad. My hopeless quest to be who my brother was. Deal is Denny died because of who he was. Everyone knows he'd been drinking the night he wrapped his new truck around a tree. But I couldn't stop myself from trying to be him. I was screwed up. Guess I still am."

He looked at her as if he wanted her to challenge those words, but she couldn't disprove them. Maybe he was still screwed up. So she said nothing.

"I was fourteen when Denny died. A stupid snot-nosed kid. I couldn't tell my father no when he pushed me. I'd seen him sink to his knees sobbing when the sheriff knocked on the door. I'd seen my mother so devastated she couldn't get out of bed."

He shook his head and she watched as he crawled into his memory. "I'd always been different, and it never bothered them. They had Denny. So I got no flack for climbing trees and writing stories. My mother was happy to put the pictures I'd taken with that camera you loaned me on the fridge. She even bought me art kits and a word processor. But at that moment, the moment they told us Denny was dead, I knew. They valued Denny more because he'd been such a good athlete. He was their idea of a perfect son. They'd spent years laughing at his exploits, shaking their heads over his subpar grades, but declaring it didn't matter because his arm would get him into college."

Brent had never talked much about his older brother or his parents' lack of expectations for their younger son. She'd known, of course. She'd been there. She'd seen Brent change, pick up the challenge of being better than his father's wildest dreams for his oldest son. She'd seen him glow in his father's praise. Revel in the town's praise of his prowess on the field. But she'd never really understood the seduction of pleasing a parent. Her parents set very few expectations. They wanted their daughters to grow where they were planted and experience life as it came at them.

"I stood there that night as they cried, talking about Denny. How great he was, how there'd never be another like him, and I knew I had to fix it. I knew I could be as good as Denny, maybe better."

Rayne slid her hand to where his rested on the table. During Denny's funeral, she'd sat in the back with Aunt Frances and Uncle Travis feeling as if her place was beside Brent, thinking she could make things better by holding his hand. She remembered the distinct feeling of knowing he needed her and the knowledge she had no right to be with the family. He'd looked lost in a suit two sizes too big for him. She remembered everyone had cried. Everyone except Brent.

"So I became who you see before you. It's been easy to keep him around. He's an uncomplicated sort of guy."

He looked away from her. It was a heavy conversation for what should have been a celebratory feast. But such was life. Rayne knew there were times a person had to roll with what came her way. And her one small question about what they were doing had broken loose baggage of epic proportions.

"Except you're not uncomplicated," she said with a small smile. She squeezed the hand beneath hers. It was so different from hers. Long, squared-off fingers with calluses, wholly masculine with veins and scars from construction gone wrong. These hands had thrown record-breaking passes and stirred the first fledgling love inside her breast.

Brent met her gaze. "Guess not."

Rayne's smile grew bigger. "Needed to get that off your chest?"

He delivered a sort of embarrassed smile. "Guess so."

She released his hand and picked up the fork she'd left in her salad. She took a few bites, chewing as she contemplated the quite complex man before her.

He, in turn, tucked into his meal, looking not comfortable but perhaps a bit lighter. She wondered why it had taken him so long to come clean behind his rationalization for becoming the man he was. And how many layers would she have to peel back to find the man deep inside?

And did she want to start that job?

Common sense told her she didn't need anything more on her plate. Henry was doing better but still obsessive about knowing where she was at all times. He'd called her ten times in a three-hour period when she'd left him with Meg to do the television spot in Austin last weekend. She had a restaurant to oversee, an inn to debut and the possible deal at the Food Network. Adding the complexity of Brent, their past and a potential future seemed a very bad idea.

"What do you mean when you say you want something more?"

Brent looked up at her question. A fleck of mustard hung out on his top lip. She grabbed a napkin and handed it to him. He immediately wiped his mouth. Damn, they were telepathic.

"Do you always place labels on everything?"

She frowned. "Labels make me comfortable. I know what I'm getting."

"Why can't we move in a direction without defining it?" He looked so sincere, so utterly unprepared for what his words would cause.

"Spoken like a man who doesn't want to be pinned down." Irritation flashed inside her. Not labeling was what had caused problems to begin with. "Fifteen years ago I didn't have a label, did I? Wasn't your girlfriend, though you kissed me like I was. Wasn't a friend, otherwise you would have talked to me in the halls at school. Maybe I would have liked a label. Maybe then I wouldn't have expected you to care."

He shook his head. "That's not what I meant. I meant that you've changed."

"Yeah, you're damn right I have. I don't like floundering around and seeing what happens. I don't need a commitment from you, Brent. Not sure I want one. But I would like a definition for what we have going on. It's the way I work."

It was his turn to frown. "Well, maybe that's not a good way. Life happens, Rayne. Trying to define it makes it harder."

Rayne gave a brittle laugh. "Says the man who commits to little, who sashays through life with a beer in one hand, a woman in the other and a secret revulsion for what he is."

His body tensed. "I don't repulse myself, Rayne. I have worth."

"Did I imply you didn't?" Irritation turned to ire. Poured into her. He dared to judge her because she demanded a plan? A label? Some guidelines for living her life? What she wanted made sense. It's what every rational person wanted. What she and Phillip had done. Mapped it out. Made it happen. Prepare for the worst but expect the best.

"You—"

"Hey, you gonna eat those, Mom?" Henry leaned over and pulled a cold onion ring from the basket and popped it in his mouth. "What's wrong with you guys? Why are y'all yelling at each other?"

Brent closed his mouth. A furrow cropped up between his normally amiable blue eyes.

Rayne clued in to where they were. Clued in to the fact that every person at the surrounding tables, with the exception of the two-year-old Taylor kid, was eavesdropping on their conversation. And why wouldn't they? She and Brent had raised their voices to a near yell.

"Nothing," Rayne muttered, shoving the basket toward her son. He grinned and happily dived into the artery-clogging rings. "Just a difference of opinion."

"Oh," Henry said, with his mouth full.

"Don't talk with your mouth full," she said.

"Okay," Henry said with his mouth still full.

It made her smile. Or maybe it was the panicky loss of control over the situation. She felt slightly hysterical. And totally out of control. She hadn't felt this way in so long. Not since she'd left Oak Stand, not since she'd left Brent waiting for her in his backyard. She hadn't said goodbye. She'd simply climbed into Aunt Frances's old Crown Victoria and shut the door on her old life.

And she'd taken control. Took her GED. Applied to college. Then culinary school. Then went to work. She'd not wandered anymore. Wouldn't allow herself to be left hanging out in the wind undecided about what direction she might blow next. Rayne had set her path and stayed on it.

Until Phillip died.

Because that hadn't been in her plans. And months afterward, things had unraveled. Her career had sky-rocketed yet she had no barometer. Then Henry had started clinging to her and she'd stopped sleeping.

No, she'd come here to gather her wits, reassess and form a new plan for her and Henry. Brent would muddy it with his "Let's not make a plan. Let's not put labels on things." It would be beyond stupid to even consider such a prospect.

She took a deep breath and met Brent's gaze.

Undecipherable.

Okay. What good had this conversation been? She didn't know where she stood with Brent. What he wanted. What she wanted. None of it made sense.

She was once again where she'd started. Confused. No, strike that. Even more confused.

Henry's brown eyes swung from her to Brent. "What's wrong? Are y'all mad at me?"

Brent shook his head. "No, sport, why would we be mad at you?"

"Cause I didn't eat with y'all?"

Rayne curled a hand around her son's waist and tugged him to her. "You know we're not mad at you for not eating with us. I'm glad you're making new friends. That's good."

"'Cept I'm not going to stay here, so it doesn't matter. They're not real friends."

Rayne couldn't prevent the emotion that rose in her throat. "That's not true. We make friends along the way wherever we go. Having friends is a good thing. No matter what."

"No matter what," Brent echoed.

Brent's eyes met hers and she nodded over Henry's head. At the very least, she knew she and Brent were friends. It was as good a starting-out place as one could get.

"Friends?" she asked.

"Until you decide you want more."

CHAPTER THIRTEEN

RAYNE WATCHED THE BERRIES burst under the intense heat. It was a bit early for blueberries at the farmers' market, but she'd found the ones she stirred in the saucepan in her aunt's freezer. In her aunt's neat handwriting, the label had said Hartner Hills which Rayne knew was in Avinger. She'd picked blueberries there when she was a girl. Her aunt must have gone with friends last summer. They'd been frozen for a while, but would serve the purpose well.

She grated a hint of nutmeg into the compote and added a pinch of orange zest.

The kitchen was quiet except for the tapping of the occasional bug against the window screen. Rayne reveled in the silence, allowing it to wring out the tension in her shoulders.

The digital clock on the microwave read 10:23 p.m. Nighttime was her favorite time to test new recipes. Something about the gathered darkness around her, the freedom to sauté and purée dressed in nothing but a cotton nightgown. No bustle, no shouting of the line cooks, nothing but her mind and her art.

A muffled thump sounded on the back porch.

Rayne laid her wooden spoon on the spoon rest and glanced in that direction. The door was closed and locked, but something about the windows open with only a thin screen between her and the night made her feel vulnerable.

She eased toward the door, glad she was barefoot and wouldn't make noise.

She heard another thump then a muffled curse.

Her shoulders sank in relief.

Brent.

She unlocked the door and unlatched the screen. Like a magician—sans cape—he appeared in the doorway.

"What are you doing?" he whispered. "It's almost ten-thirty."

"I'm not the one creeping around someone's porch at this hour. You are. What are *you* doing?" she asked, crossing her arms over her apron, well aware that she was wearing a paper-thin cotton gown and no bra. It seemed strangely tempting to be so aware of what she wasn't wearing.

"I had to take a few boards out of my truck because I can't load the machinery I need at the Mitchells' tomorrow. Need my air compressor."

Rayne pretended to look at a nonexistent watch on her wrist. "And you waited till nearly ten-thirty to bring them over?" She raised her eyebrows like an impatient school marm.

He spread his hands. "Maybe I had ulterior motives."

"You saw the light?"

He grinned and nodded. "And smelled something cooking. Want to take a walk? As friends?"

She peered into the soft darkness that had settled around the shrubs and trees of the newly trimmed backyard. Luminescence fell onto the glossy leaves from the full moon hanging over the still landscape. "I'd like to, but I have a cake in the oven and compote on the stove."

He inhaled. "That's what I smelled."

She kept her hand on the knob as if she might not let him inside. But she knew she would, the way she knew she shouldn't have gone over to his house the last time she'd visited him. Temptation flirted with her, heated her blood, made her oblivious to all things rational. She thought about his parting words days before. *Until you want something more.*

She did indeed want something more.

Because sexy Brent Hamilton stood on her porch wearing a pair of well-washed jeans and a tight T-shirt that made his eyes looked even bluer than the delphiniums on the plates mounted on the wall. He was a Dolly Parton song waiting to happen.

"You want to come inside for a taste?"

His eyes actually dilated at her not so obviously stated invitation. But he knew. Yes, he knew. She wanted a taste of something herself.

He stepped inside and shut the door.

"Show me what compote is," he said, moving toward the stove.

A small radio sat on the baker's rack. Her aunt liked to can tomatoes and bake Christmas cookies with accompaniment. Rayne flicked the switch and tinny music filled the quiet. Nothing like country love songs to fill a void. Or give her something to sway to.

One of Brent's arms snaked around her waist and spun her toward him. He lowered his head and whispered in her ear, "Forget compote. I want to dance with you."

One of his arms curled around her back and pulled her into his embrace. The other pushed her curls from her face before grasping her hand.

Then he began to move to the music, to the man crooning about having never seen that look in his woman's eyes.

She felt mesmerized, caught in a magical place of memories and new paths. It was both frightening and exhilarating, but she knew she wanted to go there.

To a new place. With Brent.

She lifted her head and smiled. "Do friends dance like this?"

His gaze was hot. So were the hands he moved in circles on her back. "Depends."

"On what?" she said, laying her head against his chest with a small moan. He felt so good against her. Like he was made for her.

"On you."

BRENT LOOKED AT THE beautiful creature he held in his arms. Every part of her fit him. From the way her cute nose bumped against his chin to the way her bare feet planted themselves on his boots as he moved them around the room. She wore a thin white nightgown that fell past her knees, but held no secrets. He could feel the warmth of her skin through the thin material, had caught sight of the silhouette of her slim legs as they swayed in the glow of the undercounter lights. And, man, did he feel the sway of her unbound breasts against his chest.

He slid his hand along her spine, savoring the delicate flesh, so sweet and yielding. Yes, he felt her meld to him and her small surrender sent satisfaction rippling.

"I'll always be your friend, Rayne. But I want to be more."

She leaned deeper into the hardness of his body and absentmindedly stroked his back with her fingers. Her head rested almost on his shoulder and the warm moistness of her breath against his neck quickened his pulse.

Yes, he wanted more.

He turned his head toward where hers lay and caught her mouth in a sweet kiss.

Slowly she lifted her head, allowing the hands she'd twined about his shoulders to slide to his hair. The moment she ran her hands through his hair was the moment the kiss turned from sweetness to fire.

He caught her soft gasp with his lips, moving his hands up her side to capture her face. He drank from her. She was everything sweet and wonderful. It was like lapping up brown sugar and brandy. Passion inflamed him and he spun them both out of control.

He turned her toward the counter, pushing her against the edge, banging his elbow on the mixer, causing it to fall over. Vaguely he knew something had spilled. He felt the wetness.

But he couldn't stop kissing Rayne. It felt as if he'd waited forever for this moment. It was like coming home. It was like riding out liftoff in the space shuttle. Beyond description.

Rayne whimpered.

He broke the kiss.

"Lemon juice is running down my back," she whispered against his lips. "At least I think it's lemon juice."

Her breathing was ragged, matching his, mingling as they stood for a moment in each other's arms.

"Brent," she whispered.

"Huh?"

"Lemon juice is cold."

He laughed against her lips and pulled her from where she stood against the counter. She grabbed a towel and swiped at her back.

"Here," he said, taking the cloth from her. "Let me."

She turned and, oh, what a sight it was. The cotton had plastered itself to her, revealing the delicious curve of her waist and a sweet little thong on the nicest backside he's seen in a while. It seemed a shame to soak up something that gave him such an eyeful.

He pressed the towel to her and swiped. "I really didn't take you for a girl who'd wear a thong."

She tossed a few red curls over her shoulder and smiled. "What? You think I wear granny panties? Wanna come look in my drawer?"

He narrowed his eyes. "Is that an invitation to your lingerie or your bed?"

"Well, I know you like to peek in women's underwear drawers."

He rolled his eyes. "Real funny. Shoulda been a comedian. Especially since that stuff you're cooking smells like it's burning."

Rayne squeaked and hotfooted it toward the stove. She jerked the saucepan from the burner and clicked the flame off. "Shit."

"Such an ugly word coming from such a pretty mouth," he said, moving to peer over her shoulder at a purple-and-black lumpy...something.

"You sound like your mother," she said, shaking her head and using a scraper to rake the ruined fruit into the trash bin. "What a waste."

He took the pan from her and set it on a burner. "I wouldn't call it a waste at all."

He tugged her back close and nibbled her lower lip. "I wouldn't mind seeing if we could burn something else."

He dropped several little kisses on her lips.

"I never burn stuff." There was almost a purr to her voice. He could feel her warming up to him again as her nipples brushed the front of his T-shirt. He slid his hands to where her gown still clung to her backside. He pulled the fabric away so he could feel her skin. Her sweet bottom filled his hands and made her gasp. He caught that gasp with his mouth.

She opened her mouth and let him fan the fires. He moved his hips allowing his erection to slide against her belly. She moaned and his body started on that journey toward utter loss of control.

But he wasn't ready to go there. Not yet.

He broke the kiss.

Her eyes had been closed. They flew open. "Why'd you stop?"

He smiled and caught one of her curls. "Because you like labels. And so far we've established friendship. Friends don't kiss like we just kissed. Are you ready to move toward something else?"

Her mouth was still open, still glistening and beckoning. Her chest moved up and down, the nipples brushed the placket of the gown, so very visible, so very tempting. Not to mention, her ass had been made for his hands. For a moment, Brent wondered if he was the biggest idiot in Howard County.

"Oh, so you're not ready?" she asked.

He didn't know whether to be offended or flattered. "Well, it's pretty obvious I want you, Rayne."

Her gaze moved to his crotch, and it felt like a caress. His body tightened. His erection pulsed. So he tried to think about the hair in his third grade teacher's nose. Mrs. Gryder had displayed a veritable broom from each nostril. And Lenny Holden. He'd wiped boogers under his desk. And only yesterday Apple had rolled on a dead toad.

Better.

Rayne crossed her arms over her chest. It wasn't defensive, and, thank heavens, it covered her breasts from his hungry gaze. "I—I think you're right. Friends don't do what we just did, and I think we need to evaluate—"

"No." He shook his head. "I don't want it to be about thinking and planning, Rayne. Just knowing what is right for each of us. Timing. I've always thought more people should listen to their bodies, their hearts, their natural rhythm. Not necessarily what their minds tell them. Hell, the mind is a dangerous thing. I'd rather trust my gut."

"Hmm. Trusting instincts. I suppose. You'll have to understand I like knowing the score. I'm not good with mucking through."

"You used to be good at mucking through. At listening to what your gut said."

She frowned. "Listening to my gut or heart or whatever didn't get me very far last time. In fact, it got me hurt."

Brent didn't miss that she was referring to him. To his indifference to her the night she'd stepped to the mike to read the poem she'd written for him. It hurt. But he couldn't change the past. He wanted to move forward. "You're hurt anyway. Your husband died, your son is struggling. And what about you, darling? Where are you right now?"

She pressed her lips together. Nerve hit. But he could see her rally. She squared her shoulders. "I'm where I choose to be. I'm not hiding who I am. And I'm deciding where I'll go. There's a difference."

He gave her a peck on the cheek. "If you say so... friend."

Then, obeying his gut instinct, he turned and left.

His watch read ten thirty-seven and the moon still cast a glow on the quiet beauty of the night. Any other time he'd hurry to his office, plop into his chair and crank out a few more words on the scene he'd been fleshing out. But he didn't hurry down the steps. Instead he stood in the gloom and took a deep breath.

He could smell the sharp scent of earth unfurling. Spring had arrived and with it a great possibility for change.

He felt Rayne at the screen door.

"Night, Rayne Cloud," he said, using one of the childhood nicknames he'd given her.

"Night, Hambone."

It was not the name she'd given him. It was the name the cheerleaders had.

CHAPTER FOURTEEN

A WEEK LATER, RAYNE STILL hadn't resolved where she was heading with Brent. And she still hadn't heard from her agent. So no progress there. But things were progressing nicely with the inn. Brent had stopped work on the porches for a few days in order to finish another job. It had given her a temporary reprieve from his presence but not from the desire that sat hot and heavy in her belly. He was a Krispy Kreme doughnut and she was a dieter. The more she tried not to think about him, the more she did. So she kept busy trying to not think. Instead, focused on doing. The result was a completed menu for the inn, a first draft of the cookbook and a new website ready to go live when the inn reopened for business.

They had three weeks until the magazine writer's visit and they still had much to accomplish. Today Brent had returned to paint both porches. Which meant, of course, she kept looking out the window or going to check the mail…and the male. She was no better than the hootchie mamas down at Cooley's honky-tonk. Or the viperous Brandi, who'd hired Brent for personal eye candy.

She tore her gaze from the window and examined the parlor critically.

"Put the sofa under the window. I think it will

balance the room," Rayne said, motioning the two teenagers holding the large piece of furniture. They shot each other a look. It was a long-suffering look. She shrugged. They'd only moved it three times. She was helping them build muscles. Plus, they'd gotten out of school with the career shadowing program. Lifting a couch was better than doing calculus, wasn't it?

"Rayne, you know everything about running a restaurant, but I'm not sure you're great at decorating," Aunt Fran said, surveying the room with a critical eye.

Rayne felt herself bristle, but then realized her aunt was absolutely correct. "But this is our project. I don't want to call in a designer."

Aunt Fran shook her head, making her silver-streaked brown bob ripple. "We don't have to call in a designer. Let's ask Dawn if she'll come take a look. You should see what she's done to Tucker House. Not to mention, the bungalow she and her husband remodeled actually landed a page in *Southern Living.*"

Rayne smiled. "Perfect."

"Yes, all us backwoods folks don't have cotton for brains." Aunt Frances left the room and returned with a ragtag address book stuffed with note cards and scraps of paper. Rayne was certain her aunt had had the same one when Rayne lived with her years ago. Some things didn't change, which was oddly comforting.

"Whoever implied you were backwoods or cotton-brained? I happen to know Grandmother Rose was from Chicago, and you scored the highest in your class on your college admission test." Rayne motioned the two high school seniors to the kitchen where delicious zucchini bread rested on the baking rack. A glass of milk and three pieces later, she sent them outside to help Brent haul away the lumber scraps and rotten boards.

By the time she'd made it to the parlor, Aunt Frances had moved a side table to sit between two wingback chairs. "Dawn is going out of town tomorrow and said she'd pop by in about thirty minutes."

"If it's too much trouble..." Rayne narrowed her eyes at the newly arranged seating. Something wasn't right.

"Nope, she's taking her car to get the oil changed and said she'd swing by."

Rayne shrugged and went and made coffee.

An hour later, the coffee was gone and the room looked incredible.

"I like the way the chintz looks against the soft gold of the wall. Warm and inviting. I'll whip up a few throw pillows in a toile and paisley when I get back from Houston," Dawn said, nudging the sofa an inch more to the right so that it was perfectly centered across from the hearth. Her hair was gathered into a low ponytail and she wore a navy short-sleeved sweater set with a trim pair of plaid pants. A silver cuff on one slender arm along with a pair of Brighton wedges gave her a Town & Country appearance. But there was nothing remote or snooty in her warm smile.

"It's odd," Rayne said, wrapping several pieces of zucchini bread in waxed paper for Dawn's husband. "We shoved this furniture all over the room and couldn't figure it out. But you step inside and whamo you knew exactly where to place it."

"Sometimes it takes an outside person to see what ought to be," Dawn said, picking up her purse and surveying the room with a satisfied gleam in her eye. She

gave Aunt Frances a small squeeze before heading for
the door. "And I'll be glad to serve the outside person
role anytime. Tyson might start hiring me out if I come
home with treats like this. He'll mow through this bread
in seconds. Thanks."

"You're welcome—" Rayne's words were interrupted
by a crash on the front porch.

All three of them spun toward the door.

"What the—" Aunt Frances said, her hand clasped
to her chest.

A really dirty word and a tinny thump served as a
finale to the crash that had shaken the house.

Rayne was closest to the door, so she opened it and
stuck her head out. She couldn't believe her eyes. She
felt Dawn and Aunt Frances at her back, but didn't turn
around. She didn't think she could have ripped her gaze
from Brent if a pig had sprouted wings and flown into
the elm tree out front.

"Don't," he said, from beneath a thick coat of latex
paint that dripped down his face and streaked onto
his burgundy T-shirt. From the top of his wavy brown
hair to the tips of his well-worn work boots, Brent was
splattered with Cottage White paint. Nearby a bucket
oozed its contents across the porch boards. A small
ladder with a bent leg lay next to the railing.

"I—I—" She snapped her mouth closed. She tried
really, really hard not to laugh. Of course, the thought
of not laughing made her snort. Which made her issue
a most obnoxious guffaw. Really obnoxious.

"Son of a bitch," Brent said, wiping paint from his
eyes. "I should have replaced that damn ladder last week
when the leg— Oh, for Pete's sake, stop laughing."

But she couldn't. And it felt good to laugh so hard.

It was the pee-your-pants kind of laugh she hadn't used since she was a girl. And with Dawn and Aunt Fran joining in, they sounded like a chorus of hyenas.

Rayne finally managed to take a few steps toward the towel Brent had slung over the rail, then handed it to him. "Here, use this. It might—"

"So, think this is funny, huh?"

Rayne screeched as one of his paint-soaked hands clasped her arm. "Brent Jamison Hamilton! Let go!"

But he didn't. Instead he pulled her into his arms and gave her a squeeze. Then he gave a devilish laugh.

"I can't believe you," she said, struggling against his arms. "You're ruining my dress!"

"So? I'll buy you a new one. One that's tight and shows off those nice assets," he said, grinning at her. He looked like a crazy person, albeit a happy crazy person.

Her heart started thumping against her ribs. She caught his crazy happy bug and grinned. "I don't want one that shows my assets. This is highly... irresponsible."

Then he did something even more reckless. Something insane. He leaned down and kissed her. Not a peck. Nothing teasing. But a real kiss. Full of passion. Full of something she couldn't quite taste. And it wasn't the awful taste of latex paint. It was more like joy.

She couldn't stop her body from coming to life and it felt so good, so freeing, that she giggled against his lips. A rumble of laughter started in his chest. Pretty soon it emerged and their lips were no longer locked. So they stood there, wrapped in each other's arms, covered in paint, laughing as if they'd sniffed glue. Or latex fumes.

Eventually, Brent released her and she jerked her head around and took a look at her butt. Sure enough two white handprints marred the backside of her sundress. She looked like one of those cards Henry brought home with his handprints on them each Mother's Day. Except these were large male handprints...on her ass.

"Look at my dress," she said, spinning around to show him. She should have been disgusted. Instead she felt giddy. As though she was thirteen and crushing on a guy who made her heart flutter.

"Just putting my mark on you," he teased, grabbing the towel that had fallen and trying unsuccessfully to mop up his face.

"You do realize we're still here," Aunt Frances said.

Rayne spun toward her aunt. She could feel her face ignite. How had she forgotten her aunt and Dawn? Good gravy.

Dawn smiled. "Looks like a good way to forget the world. Little messy, but fun."

Brent delivered a trademark Hambone smile, his gaze sliding to Rayne. "Never say Hamilton Construction doesn't make sure the owner is satisfied with our work."

"How is this satisfactory?" Rayne quipped, rubbing at the droplets of paint on her arm.

"You didn't let me finish the job," he said silkily. He grinned the way Henry did when he'd done something naughty but worth it.

"Oh, brother." Rayne's groan caused the two others standing on the porch to snicker. She rolled her eyes but couldn't stop the silly smile. How did one get latex paint off oneself? Thank heavens, she'd worn a braid and hadn't had her hair curling around her shoulders. That would have been messy.

"Hey, Brent, I meant to tell you earlier that Tyson wants you to call him about the proposition," Dawn said, breaking the absurdity of the moment. She readjusted her oversize purse on her shoulder and dug inside, coming out with keys in hand. "I think he's definitely interested."

Brent nodded. "Good. Tell him I'll call in a couple of days. My parents are coming back from their trip tomorrow."

Dawn smiled. "Well, I'll let you two get back to your fun."

"Oh, no," Rayne said. "This is not my kind of fun."

Dawn laughed. "Oh, yeah? Well, in this designer's eyes, I'm seeing what you're not. I know when things go together."

She trotted down the front steps. "See y'all later. I'm off to Houston. Good luck getting off all that paint."

"Bye," Brent and Aunt Frances called.

Rayne didn't say anything. It wasn't as if she was stunned by Dawn's words. Brent had left everything up to her with regard to their relationship. She knew he wanted more. He'd said so. And she knew she wanted something more, too. But sharing that something out in the open felt too real. It made Rayne feel as vulnerable as a newly born fawn on shaky legs. She wasn't sure if the feelings Brent stirred were worth the problems that were sure to come. She wrapped her arms about herself, wincing at the stickiness of the drying paint.

"Well, I better rustle up some olive oil for getting the paint out of your hair. Best be glad it's not oil-based."

Aunt Frances gave them a knowing smile before slipping into the house. This time she didn't allow the door to slam. She closed it gently.

Brent stomped around a few moments more before pulling his shirt over his head and tossing it toward a cardboard box he used for debris. Brent still had a football player's body. One that had not gone soft. She thought about Brandi and the other women who used him for eye candy, and she turned away.

"I guess I shouldn't have gotten so carried away. I kinda outed us. Sorry."

She didn't respond. Wasn't sure what to say.

"Not to mention, I ruined your dress." He walked toward her and pulled the skirt that bore his mark away from where it hung at her side. "I don't think it will come out."

Rayne took the fabric from him. "It wasn't expensive. Don't worry."

"Rayne," he said, his voice probing her doubt. "Don't clam up on me."

"I'm not sure about this. I've gotten past the hurt I felt years ago. I'm big enough to overlook the fact you were embarrassed to let others know we were—"

"What are you talking about? I've never been embarrassed of you."

"I'm not trying to dredge up the past. I'm accustomed to being your secret friend. Not so out in the open."

He took a few steps away from her. "We really need to get this paint off, but I can't let that statement slide. First, we're not kids anymore. We've been to the Dairy Barn together twice. Henry's been with us, but that only enforces the idea that I'm serious about you, Rayne. I don't care if people know it or not."

She opened her mouth, but he held up a hand. "I'm not finished. Look, when we were kids, I didn't parade our friendship around the school because...well, because you were mine."

What the hell did that mean?

"I know it sounds crazy," he said, staring out at the empty street, "but when we sat in the swing or crashed on the grass and stared up at stars or clouds, it was the only time I felt like I was me. At school, hell, outside that fence, I played a part. I guess it's one I'm still playing."

He turned toward her. "But back then, I protected my piece of the world, the piece that had you in it. I wasn't embarrassed about you. I just didn't want to mix those worlds. I needed them to be separate because without you and those stolen moments I couldn't do it. I couldn't be that guy everyone thought I was"

Her heart crumbled at his words. He wasn't embarrassed about her? He wanted to keep their friendship, their first inklings of love a secret? "Well, thanks for asking me about it. I guess I didn't get a choice in the matter. Those three years of high school were freaking torture for me. I was teased about being a skinny, flat-chested freak whose parents were weirdos. I was called *bastard* and *retard* and everything else under the sun. I don't think you endured that, did you? Instead, you passed me by in the hallway with a cheerleader on one arm and an entourage at your back. Then after the world went to sleep, you met me out back to twist my hair and dream about a better tomorrow."

Brent opened his mouth. She held up her hand. "No, it's my turn."

He closed his mouth, but his eyes showed a dawning understanding. Had he really never thought about what her life had been like at Oak Stand High? Had he not realized what everyone else in town had thought about poor knock-kneed, skinny, redheaded Rayne?

She'd been like a broken toy that kept popping up. First, when she'd been in grade school, attending Oak Stand Elementary for three months before being jerked out because her parents found a place they needed to go in order to find peace, tranquility and people who'd buy their art. The town saw her parents as burned-out hippies, and she and Summer got lumped in by default. When she'd finally come to live with her aunt and uncle, she thought it could be different, but her mold had been cast.

Being different in a conservative, small Texas town was beyond difficult.

"You decided for me, Brent. You had your cake and ate it, too. You can say all you want about pretending to be another person to please your parents or whoever, but being Brent Hamilton was, and is, not a hard thing to be.

"I walked around this town with nothing but a bad case of hero worship. I didn't get to go to the Dairy Barn after games with you or drive to the lake and drink beer. I sat at home on that damn swing waiting on you like some pathetic loser. It must have been nice to make out with Katie Newman as Brent the Stud and then come to me for chaste little kisses as Brent the Philosopher."

"I didn't treat you that way, Rayne." His words were

tinged with irritation. No man liked to be called out. "Don't you realize you meant more to me? I loved you. You were my best friend. You gave me hope and peace and an anchor to my identity. When you left, I lost that. All those girls, football, drinking out at the lake—none of that was real."

"It felt real to me," she said, crossing her arms over her chest. "It hurt me."

"But I didn't intend to hurt you. You were my soul mate. I could be myself with you. It's hard to explain, but you were like this perfect rose, beautiful to contemplate, a symbol of everything that was pure and good in my life. You were like reading Emerson, seeing a thing of beauty, not to partake, but to observe. To treat you like other girls would be…sacrilege."

Rayne stilled her hands. "Are you cracked?"

He stiffened. "What do you mean?"

"Seriously? You're talking to me of Ralph Waldo Emerson? Of things erudite and fanciful? I wasn't a muse. Or a…a…freakish anomaly. I was a teenage girl who was in love with you."

"Emerson wasn't fanciful. Far from it." Brent moved to the rail. "And I know you were a girl. But you weren't like the other girls. It was a soul thing."

"But I'm not a symbol. I'm a woman. I have flesh. Flesh that needs more than contemplation."

"Rayne—"

"I'm not a paragon on a pedestal. Or a rose too perfect to clip. I'm tired of being this…this ideal flower for you. I can see it now. The way you saw me. I was your counterpart, too pleasing as the yin to your yang to be anything other than your testing ground for ideas, for dissertations on self-reliance and beauty and love.

You made me something you couldn't have. Some kind of—"

"No, that's not what I meant." He ran a hand through his hair, but it didn't go far. The paint had started drying, making his hair clump together. He sighed and pulled his hand from the mess. "I saw you differently than other girls. That's true. And, yes, you were a bit of an ideal. But I never wanted to hurt you."

She nodded. "I don't think you did. But intention is one thing. Reality another."

For a moment all was quiet on the porch.

"Now I can see why you were only content to kiss me. You always backed away. Still do. Just like in the kitchen last week."

"The only reason I stopped is because I respect your wishes. You know I want more than kissing, but I value you more than a cheap lay. You mean too much," he said. Damn if he didn't look as appealing as he ever had, bare-chested, streaked with paint and disillusioned. Rayne wanted to go to him, slide her hand up his chest, feel the springy hairs as she felt his heart beneath her hands.

But she didn't go to him. Instead she walked to the door and slid her feet into the flip-flops she habitually left outside.

"What are you doing?" he said, straightening. "We're not through talking."

She trotted down the steps. "I'm tired of talking. About the past. About the future. Instead, I'm doing what you said I should do. I'm following my gut instinct."

He watched her as she followed the path that led

to his parents' backyard. "And that's taking you where?"

"Through the French doors of your house," she said. A strong impulse had knocked over the rationales she'd used to protect herself. Not to mention longing, desire, passion and need—all balled up into one—had finished the job. If she and Brent were going to move in a direction, there was one path she wanted to walk down. And that path meant stepping through those doors literally and figuratively.

"Rayne," he called.

She turned around, flipped her braid over one shoulder, and unwrapped the elastic band that held it. She ran her fingers through the strands, releasing them so that they tumbled over her shoulders and back. "Quite honestly, Brent, I think it's time that you plucked me."

CHAPTER FIFTEEN

BRENT WATCHED AS RAYNE sashayed toward his house. At least he thought it was a sashay. Looked sassy and determined to him.

He paused for a moment. But only a moment.

He'd meant what he said. Rayne was different. So he hadn't wanted to rush the physical side of their relationship. Hadn't wanted it to be about sex. But neither was he dog-ass stupid. He'd wanted the sweetness of Rayne on his lips ever since he'd grown hair in unmentionable places on his body. Was he going to leave her hanging?

Hell to the *H* no.

He rounded the rail of the porch, stopping only to grab the bottle of olive oil that Frances handed him silently as he passed the front door.

"Keep an eye on Henry?" he said as he trotted down the front steps.

"No problem," Frances said before closing the front door.

He was certain he'd seen a smile on her lips.

He looked down at the bottle in his hand. Oil seemed a bit kinky, but they were covered in paint. So more of a necessity.

When he reached his house, the French door stood ajar. It was beckoning. An open invitation not into his house but into the mystery of a very complicated woman.

He stepped inside. No lights were on, but the afternoon sunlight streaming through the sheers showed him exactly what he wanted to see.

A very naked Rayne.

"Dear God, woman," he said, closing the door and turning the lock. "You're naked."

"You noticed." She stretched, raising her long white arms above her head, and arching her back. Her generous breasts rose and he nearly lost his breath. Nearly.

He exhaled and bent to unlace his boots.

"Do you want me to cover up with the throw you used last time?" she asked. Her voice was low, seductive. Very naughty. He loved it.

"Are you sure about this, Rayne Bow?" He purposely used one of her childhood nicknames. He wanted her to realize what she was doing. Once they made love, there was no going back.

She moved closer to him. He caught the scent of vanilla, the sweet goodness that was signature Rayne. His body tightened.

"I'm sure, Brent." She ran her fingers over his naked shoulder. It might as well have been a cattle prod, for it seared his flesh. He set the olive oil on the table and toed off his boots. Rayne stood boldly before him, red hair curling over her shoulders, framing the sweetness of her face. She held her lightly freckled shoulders back so that her rose-tipped breasts jutted forward. Her taut stomach tapered to round hips and long legs that seemed to go on forever. She propped her hands on her hips as he perused her body.

When he met her gaze, she smiled. This woman was

no shy, stammering girl. This woman was his match in every way. Made for him.

A rightness settled over him, along with a serious need to scoop her up, take her to his bed and do all the crazy wicked things he'd imagined in the wee hours of the morning.

He'd said they should listen to their gut instincts. His told him to do this and do it right.

"Okay," he said, allowing one finger to outline her collarbone. Her breath caught nicely and her cinnamon eyes dilated. She sucked in her lower lip and watched him. "Should we shower first? We're a little…messy."

"I like messy," she said, reaching out and running her hand lightly over the hair on his chest. His erection literally leaped at her touch. And for the first time in a long time, Brent felt nervous about being with a woman.

Not that he didn't know what to do. On the contrary, his moves were so practiced, his knowledge so vast, that he could likely write a book.

He knew how to have sex with a woman.

But he didn't know how to make love to Rayne.

It was unnerving.

He tumbled through time as he reached out a hand to test the weight of her breast. Once again, he was tangled with Rayne beneath the weeping willow, daring her to let him touch her, scared to get caught working on his moves. It felt new again. Yet incredibly familiar.

She rose on her toes and pressed her mouth to his. A hot weight settled in his chest before sinking deep into his loins. He wanted this woman in a way he'd never wanted a woman before. He'd spent forever waiting on Rayne, and now she would be his. It was almost surreal.

He threaded his hands through her curls, cupping her head, angling her so he could deepen the kiss. She tasted like innocence. She tasted like sin.

He groaned and allowed his hands to glide down the smoothness of her back, to cup her sweet bottom and haul her against his body.

She felt so good. So different. But his hands remembered the curves, the way she felt even if she had changed.

He broke the kiss and buried his head in the curve of her neck, inhaling her fragrance, nipping the sensitive flesh of her throat.

"Brent," she breathed against him, running her hands down his back. When she reached his waistband, she slid her hands beneath to his buttocks. Hot, glistening desire flooded him.

He ripped himself from her and reached for the fly of his jeans. "I'd like to do this right. So slow and sweet. Make you come, watch your eyes. I can't. I—"

Her hands stilled him. She caressed his shoulder, tracing a smudge of paint. "We don't have to go slow, but it's our first time. I've waited a long time for you, Brent Hamilton."

Her words slid over him. She was right. He was no randy teenager, no matter how she made him feel.

"Do you know how sexy you are, woman? Do you know how close I am to losing control?"

She reached down and clasped his erection through his boxers. "I've got an idea."

He nearly hissed at her touch. It was so warm and

womanly, so damn hot and good, he nearly exploded. "You're not helping matters doing things like that."

He wrenched her hand from his hardness. She laughed.

"Shower?"

"No," she said. "Bed."

He grinned. "I'll have to buy you a new dress and myself some new sheets."

She gave him a mysterious smile. One that was part Mona Lisa, part devil. "It'll be worth it. I promise."

"Damn," he breathed as she turned and headed for his room. "Where did you learn seduction?"

She turned, all her parts jiggling in all the right places. His mouth went dry. "From the best. I learned from you."

RAYNE COULDN'T BELIEVE how empowered she was. Couldn't believe how naughty she felt. But she had Brent under her power. It was heady and raw. She loved it.

For years she'd dreamed of his seduction, of his practiced lips trailing down her stomach, of his knowledgeable fingers strumming her like a lyre. But never had she imagined she'd do the seducing.

She turned and waited in his doorway, reveling in the way his gaze caressed her body. His normally icy eyes were the color of the blue in a flame. Hot, molten blue. She felt his gaze like a touch, burning her thighs, searing her breasts. His eyes were hungry and she was his feast.

So she offered herself to him, sliding her hands up to cup her breasts. She'd be his bounty, she'd feed the flames of his fire.

He stalked.

Their bodies crashed together in sweet collision as he swept her against him. She wound her arms around his shoulders and allowed him to lift her from her feet and carry her to the big bed that dominated the small room.

He'd made his bed that morning. Impressive. And he was responsible enough to tug the coverlet from the bed and toss it in a corner.

"New quilt," he murmured against her lips as he laid her across the burgundy sheets. He didn't join her immediately. Instead he lifted himself from her and stared at her lying naked before him.

She tugged her hair from beneath her and allowed it to fan out around her head. She kept her hands beneath her head and crossed her feet, trying for absolute casualness, though her heart raced in her chest. "Now you've got me. What are you going to do with me?"

His teeth flashed in the darkness of the room and a chuckle emerged from his lips. "Let's see. The toilet needs scrubbing, my khakis need ironing and the ice maker has been giving me—"

She made as though to get up.

He playfully pushed her back. "Oh, no. I think I'd rather sample your talents here. Let's see…what should I have you do first?"

"Kiss you?"

"Nah. That's too easy."

She reached out and ran a hand down his belly. "I didn't say where."

He laughed and covered her body with his.

And suddenly all playfulness fled. Passion took its place, and passion was all business.

Brent's body was deliciously heavy, meshing against

hers in all the right places. He wrapped his arms around her, pulling her so there was no space between them. She felt him everywhere. And it was so very right.

She twined her arms around his neck as his lips came down on hers. He plundered her mouth, giving her no time to think. She could only feel.

His hands moved everywhere. They stroked, they explored, they pushed the limit and then pulled back, knowing how to play her. And she allowed her hands to return the favor, to stroke the leanness of his hip, his muscled back, his sensitive thigh.

Finally, when she could hardly breathe, he rolled off her, stopping so he rested on his side. He loved her first with his gaze, then with his hand, stroking the parts he'd been unable to reach atop her. Seconds turned into minutes. Resolve turned to surrender. Like a magician he worked her, parting her thighs, teasing and playing until he took her over the edge. Not once, not twice but three times.

Her breathing was jagged. She wanted him inside her. Wanted all of him. But he didn't stop touching her, teasing her. In fact, he seemed most content to take his time making love to her.

She loved that his caresses weren't by rote. His motions weren't mechanical or practiced. Instead, they felt new and tender, almost tentative, as if he were touching a woman for the first time.

He lightly slid his hands over her, brushing the curve her waist, fanning her belly. "You're so beautiful. I feel like I've never done this before. Like I've never had sex, never touched a woman here—" he rolled her nipple between his thumb and forefinger "—or here."

He brushed the neatly trimmed hair at the juncture of her thighs.

She slid her hand to his bristly jaw and cupped his face. "It feels new to me, too. You didn't have whiskers the first time I kissed you."

He smiled and cupped one breast before dropping a kiss atop it. "And you didn't have boobs. Or at least not this much."

She reached down and clasped his erection, sliding her hand over the smoothness of him, causing him to suck in his breath. "I think turnabout deserves fair play, don't you?"

He smiled, but didn't stop stroking her. "Would I ever disagree with you?"

She arched one eyebrow, eliciting a grin.

"Okay, so I'm lying."

She punished him by taking her own sweet time torturing him, driving him so close to the edge, he literally grit his teeth. "Rayne, no more," he panted, pulling her from him.

"Condom?" she whispered into his ear, as she kissed the ridge of his ear.

"Drawer." He sighed, moving down to kiss her stomach.

Less than a minute later, he was sheathed and between her thighs. He gave her the smile of all smiles. She'd never seen one so pure from a man who had such an arsenal. "I feel like I've been waiting years for this."

She held up her arms, beckoning him to fill them. "You *have* been waiting years."

He bent one of her legs, pushed it so her knee nearly touched the tip of her breast and slid home. Rayne gasped as he filled her. It wasn't only a physical full-ness, but an emotional one. And it was strange and wonderful at the same time. Her heart felt as if it would burst and dampness gathered on her lashes. She felt overwhelmed by Brent and the fulfillment of having him inside her, joined with her. As hokey as it seemed, she knew it was more than sex, more than a connection. She couldn't even name it.

So she just rode it.

He moved inside her, a steady rhythm, building the tension, pulling it taut. He thrust slow and deep, pant-ing her name over and over in her ear like a mantra. And before she knew it, they arched over the backyard fence, up to the sun, exploding into a thousand lovely pieces.

She fell back, totally out of breath, totally enraptured by what had occurred between them. It wasn't as if she hadn't reached an orgasm before. She had. But this... this was so intense. She couldn't speak. No words.

So she didn't try for them.

She lay replete. Fulfilled.

The ceiling fan whirred above them, brushing their heated flesh with a gentle breeze. Brent shifted off her, fell to his back and breathed, "Wow."

"I know, right?" She smiled at the whirring fan be-cause she didn't have the energy to even turn her head. Her body felt like liquid.

They lay there for a good five minutes, neither saying a word to the other. Nothing but sweet silence. Until a buzzing interrupted.

"What's that? Your phone?" Brent said.

Rayne managed to lift her head. "Yeah."

"You going to get it?"

She sighed. It was probably Meg. She'd had some trouble with a supplier at Serendipity. For the fourth time that month. Rayne didn't want to get up. Wanted to pretend she and Brent were on a deserted island, a private oasis of delights. But she crept from the bed and padded the short distance to the living area and grabbed the phone from the pocket of her abandoned sundress.

The number on display was unfamiliar. It was an Oak Stand number, so not Meg.

She pressed the answer button.

"Mom?" His small voice was frantic and whispery.

"Henry, what's wrong?"

"The bus left me." A wealth of information in those words. Her son had been left behind. He was scared. And she was standing naked in Brent's living room.

"I'll be right there, honey."

CHAPTER SIXTEEN

RAYNE DIDN'T NOTICE THE scenery as she sped toward Oak Stand Elementary. All she could think about was how selfish she'd been not to give even a thought to her only child. She'd been so focused on taking her relationship with Brent to the next level she'd forgotten who she was.

Of course, forgetting everything had been easy when she'd been wrapped in Brent's arms. Always had been. But sooner or later, life intervened and reminded her.

First and foremost, she was a mother with a child who had severe anxiety issues.

She needed to remember why she'd come to Oak Stand and that reason was not to get tangled up in Brent Hamilton.

What had she been thinking?

The answer was she hadn't. She'd been feeling.

It wasn't as if she couldn't have a life of her own. She'd never play martyr, but she did need to prioritize. Being a mother meant putting her child before herself, something she wasn't sure she'd done enough of. After all, if she'd been less focused on her career and more focused on her family, she'd have been there for her son when Phillip died.

But she hadn't been.

She'd been in the studio at the local news channel

filming a segment on soufflés. She'd skipped out on
Henry's karate exhibition at the school, sending him
a smiley face cookie in his lunch to make up for it.
Phillip had gotten stuck in traffic and that's where the
aneurysm had struck. Henry had waited outside the
gym with an annoyed karate instructor until Rayne had
thought about him.

What kind of mother forgot her child?

Strike that. What kind of mother forgot her child
a second time while she was having hot sex with the
neighbor?

A bad one.

She pulled to the curb of the elementary school and
shut the car off.

Henry stood next to the duty teacher, drawing in the
dirt with the toe of his sneaker. His head popped up
when he heard the car door slam. The look on his face
spelled relief.

"I'm so sorry I'm late. How did this happen?"

The duty teacher gave her a smile. "It's no big deal.
Happens to a kid at least every month."

Henry's face didn't look as if it weren't a big deal.
But then again, Henry wasn't like most kids. Most
didn't worry obsessively about being left behind…and
then have it happen to them. His shirt was damp around
the buttons and Rayne knew he'd likely been chewing it.
She teased him about being a baby goat, but she knew
the compulsion was a result of perpetual worry.

She felt her heart break but plastered on a contrite
smile. "Not sure it's much comfort knowing children
get left often by the bus drivers."

The teacher, whose tag read Mrs. Frye, ruffled
Henry's hair. "There's no time to take roll on the bus.

Usually the drivers ask the other children to say if they don't see a particular student, but sometimes it's rowdy and the drivers get distracted. Things like this happen." She looked down at Henry and smiled. "Don't worry, Henry. We'd never leave you. You're safe here."

"Okay," Henry said, not bothering to look up at the teacher.

"You guys have a good evening. See you tomorrow, Henry." The teacher gave Henry a pat and headed toward the double doors of the school, passing Mr. Cleveland, the janitor who had been sprinkling vomit dust and unclogging toilets at Oak Stand Elementary for as long as Rayne could remember. She gave him a halfhearted wave and took Henry's sweaty hand and led him toward the car.

"Are you okay, buddy?" she asked.

"Sure," he muttered, tugging his backpack up to his shoulder. Rayne knew he lied, but didn't know how to make it better. She pretty much sucked at parenting. Obviously. She couldn't fix Henry with a cookie or a bowl of ice cream. She knew. She'd already tried food as a way to heal. It hadn't worked.

And coming home to Oak Stand hadn't helped. It might have made it worse. After today, it had definitely made it worse. How could she take him to New York City? Just thinking about the fast-paced city inspired anxiety in her. What would it do to Henry? How could she leave him in the care of a nanny or a day care while she worked long days in the studio? Then factor in the time she'd have to fly to Austin to take care of Serendipity.

She opened the car door and grimaced as Henry rounded the front of the car and opened the passenger door. He knew better than to try to ride shotgun. But one look at his face and she closed her mouth.

He dumped his backpack on the floor, fell into the passenger seat and buried his head in her lap. Sobs shook his body as he cried. Rayne could do nothing more than stroke his back and murmur, "It's okay, baby," over and over again. Even if she knew it wasn't.

"How did this happen?" she asked when his crying finally stopped.

"I don't know." He sniffed into her wrinkled skirt. "I had to go to the bathroom, and she left me."

She being Freda Ford, the bus driver. Rayne wished she had the bus driver's phone number. Maybe old lady Ford needed a good tongue-lashing. Then maybe next time she'd take a moment to check to ensure all the children were on the bus. Maybe a note to the ISD transportation office would work, as well.

"Will you pick me up from now on?" He lifted his tearstained face.

"Honey, you can't let this defeat you. It was an accident. The bus driver should have checked, and you should have told a duty teacher you needed to use the bathroom," she said.

"Please, Mommy. I don't want to be the last one here. What if they don't know I'm here and leave? What if there's a bad person who lives close? I saw this one guy on TV who took this little girl from the school and—"

"No one is going to take you. You have your list. The people on that list are your safety net," she said, smoothing his cowlick, patting his sweaty back.

Henry sat up and buckled his seat belt. "What good

is having Meg on the list? She's always in Austin. I want to put Coach Brent down."

Rayne started guiltily out the window. She'd just crawled from the man's bed and she didn't even know his cell phone number. That seemed wrong. She could get it, give it to Henry. But that seemed a bigger jump than kissing in front of Dawn and Aunt Fran. Even bigger than what they'd done less than an hour ago. Making Brent one of Henry's "safe" people felt binding. "We'll see about asking him to be on your list."

"I know he can take care of things. He's that type of guy."

Yeah, he was. She could definitely put him in that category. Odd, she'd spent so many years cementing him into a carefree, swaggering Lothario when she'd always known deep down inside that he was far more than that stereotype. Strange how being hurt colored a person's perception. It had been unfair of her, but she understood why it was so easy to hate him, to kick him over into the bad guy category and keep him there. But she'd been wrong to do so. He'd been a sixteen-year-old kid with baggage that weighed him down. "Okay, unbuckle and get into the back."

"Aw, Mom. I'm big enough to ride up here," Henry grumbled, apparently forgetting he'd lain in her lap minutes ago and cried like a toddler.

"Nope. In the back."

"I don't need a stupid booster, Mom. No one uses them in the second grade. People are gonna think I'm a baby." The disgust in his voice proved he was over being left behind. For the moment anyway. Begrudgingly, he climbed over the seat, nearly knocking her phone and bottle of water from the console.

Rayne smoothed her paint-spattered, wrinkled dress as if she could smooth out the wrinkles in her life. But it didn't work. On either count.

BRENT STARED AT THE WORDS he'd scratched on the page weeks ago. Coach of the Year was a big deal to the kids on his team. They'd taunted the last team they'd played with that tidbit, something he'd had to address. Bragging was something boys did as naturally as breathing, but they needed to learn humility and good sportsmanship. Something else a coach needed to teach, along with the lessons he'd written on the notebook in front of him—reaching far, trying hard and giving your best.

It was a decent acceptance speech. But now it rang hollow because he knew that for many years he'd not done any of those things. He'd been content to tread water. To give up.

Weeks ago the words had been platitudes. But today he wanted them to be true of himself. He was changed. He was no longer the Brent Hamilton Oak Stand expected. He'd metamorphosed. And Rayne had been the catalyst.

Rayne. With her soft hair and rigid spine. Glowing eyes and satin skin. Yesterday afternoon had been the culmination of a long-standing need to be with her. And it had been as good as any rousing daydream he'd had about the leggy, surprisingly fiery woman. Yes, he'd changed. Because of Rayne.

Although, he had to acknowledge, he'd decided to shed his good-time Charlie persona before Rayne had stepped back into his life. She'd simply given him more reason to toss away the fetters of his old life and try for what he really longed to be—strong and respectable. Proud and upstanding. A husband and a father.

Fear crowded his throat.

He swallowed hard as if it were easy to get rid of the nagging thought that the last two were unattainable. He wanted to be both...but only to Rayne and Henry.

The thump of the crêpe myrtle branch against his house jarred him from his heavy thoughts and signaled the arrival of his folks. The colossal RV always announced its entrance in the side drive with the same enormous thunk.

He pushed back his chair picked up the notebook and ripped the pages from the wire bindings.

"Two points," he said as the paper hit the rim of the wastebasket and fell in.

He stepped outside into the gloaming of Oak Stand twilight. His mother Donna smiled and waved from her perch beside his father in the RV. She looked happy and well-rested. His father looked grumpy and tired.

"Brent! Help your father before he knocks over the sweet olive hedge," she called from the door of the RV.

"Shut the damn door, Donna" his father shouted, turning the wheel too sharply, almost causing his wife to fall.

Brent dutifully guided his father in his parking efforts. Finally, the RV sat where it was meant to. His father and mother bailed out, squabbling about the tire marks in the side yard.

"Nice to see y'all, too," Brent said, following them toward the porch of their house.

"We're happy to see you, baby," his mother said, turning around giving him a brief squeeze. "It's just your father's prostate has been giving him fits and he needs to use the potty."

"Good Lord, Donna, tell everyone why don't you?" Ross grumbled, climbing the steps and fishing his keys from the pocket of his trousers.

"I'm telling your son. He's not *everyone*." His mother stopped and stuck a finger in the planter housing a hibiscus, presumably checking the moisture level. Brent must have watered sufficiently because she didn't say anything. She opened the screen door and gave Apple a belly rub. "Hello, Apple girl. We missed our baby."

Both he and Apple were her babies. Great. He was on a level with a dog that rolled on dead things and pulled stuffing from pillows. He'd never felt he ranked high on his parents' list unless he was winning awards or excelling on the field. It was an irrational feeling he'd carried with him for most of his life. He'd been a shadow for so long that he wondered if they saw him as one, too. He was the go-to guy for lifting furniture and feeding the animals when they were out of town. He was expected to step into the family business, live close enough to call upon and show up on all holidays to bring the ice. That was his role.

But no longer.

Because his parents would be the first to understand Brent was cutting ties with his past. He was more than they expected.

"I know y'all just got home, but before you settle in for the evening, I'd like to talk with you both," Brent said, watching his mother shift through the two stacks of mail on the granite countertop. She sorted the pile quickly.

"Sure it can't wait? Your father is a grumpy old bear.

His bursitis is acting up from all that driving," she said, not bothering to look up.

"It's important. I'd like to talk to you before tomorrow night."

"Tomorrow night?" she asked.

"The Little League banquet," Brent said, settling on a bar stool in the cozy kitchen and picking up the *Field and Stream* magazine she'd tossed aside. A deer with a target centered on his chest graced the front cover. *Been there before, buddy.* He tossed the magazine aside.

"Oh, of course," she said mindlessly.

"Did you call that fellow about the Chargers? What did he say?" His father's voice came from over Brent's shoulder. Ross Hamilton took a room by storm. The air seemed to be sucked right out of the kitchen. Large, domineering and the former offensive tackle for Texas Christian University, Brent's father bulldozed his way through life, bemoaning his traitorous knees and his propensity for putting on a few pounds by even glancing at a piece of cake or pie.

"That's what I wanted to talk to both of you about," Brent said, meeting his father's eyes as Ross squeezed by Donna and reached for the teakettle. His father always had a cup of chamomile tea before bed, the only even remotely feminine tendency the man had.

"Oh?" His father filled the kettle and lit the burner before rummaging around in the cabinet for the tea. Donna ignored them both, her lips moving as she read a letter. The paper looked to be one of her prison ministry letters. "Do you have some training camp dates? Do we need to talk to that agent again?"

"I never called," Brent said.

"Why the hell not?" his father yelled, causing Donna to jump.

"Please, Ross," she said, dropping the letter to the counter. "The whole neighborhood will hear you shouting."

"Why the hell should I care?" his father said, pulling a mug from the cabinet. He refocused his attention on Brent. "I went to a lot of trouble to get you that look-see."

"I know you did, Dad, but I don't think you realize I'm no longer interested in playing football. I'm not in shape for it and the possibility of actually earning a place on the team is slim to none."

His father held up a finger. "But it's still a possibility. You still have it, son. I can see it in the way you move, on the balls of your feet. You're fast and could easily be in peak shape by July. Don't pass up this opportunity. It's your last chance to live your dream."

"You mean your dream," Brent said quietly. He held his gaze on his father. No more looking away.

Brent's mother slid the mail away and zeroed in on the situation. She'd been in the same position many times. Between father and son. She loved Brent, but she had to live with her husband. "Now, Ross, if Brent's not interested, you can't force him. We've talked about how it's time for you to give the reins of the company over to him."

"Not if he can take one more shot at the NFL," his father said in a way that brooked no argument.

"I don't want another shot at the NFL. And I don't want the company," Brent said, rising from the stool. Sitting put him at a disadvantage. He always thought better on his feet.

"What?" his mother said.

"I don't want to buy into the company with Uncle Richard."

"Well, then what the hell are you going to do?" his father shouted as the teakettle whistled. "You can't make ends meet building damn bird feeders."

Anger bristled in Brent. He'd never been able to reason with his father. The man never listened to anyone but himself. "Who said I'm going to make a living building bird feeders? You don't think I'm capable of making a living any other way than what you decide for me? I have a degree, you know."

"In British literature," his father sneered. "What the hell kinda job can you get with that? All that time at UT and you get a degree in something that impractical." He spun toward Donna and jabbed a finger in her direction. "I told you not to encourage him to doodle around and make up poems and crap."

Brent's mother shrugged. "He liked to read and write. So?"

Brent slapped his hand on the granite, drawing the attention of both his parents. "I'm moving out of the carriage house. I'll pay you rent to cover the rest of this month and next. And I'll be giving my two weeks' notice to the company."

"Brent? What has gotten into you?" his mother asked. Her lined face reflected dismay, shock, perhaps a little aggravation.

"Fine." His father almost growled. "But I know you'll come groveling back when you don't have enough money for all those beers you drink down at Cooley's."

Brent closed his eyes and tried to push down the

anger rushing toward the surface. He knew this would not be easy. Nothing with his father ever was. "I won't change my mind. I've needed a change in my life for a long time. It's past time. I have a new direction and my financial status is secure at present."

"But surely you don't have to move? Where will you go?" Donna asked, spreading her hands in a pleading gesture she'd used most of her life. Mostly with his father, who was as immovable as a mountain.

"I'm not sure, but I'm tired of treading water, Mom."

A furrow appeared between her eyebrows, but she nodded. "Okay. I see. You feel trapped by us. By the company."

Brent's father poured water from the kettle into his mug, but didn't say a word. His face was florid, making the shock of white hair look even more pronounced. Brent had always seen his father as strong and invincible, but he noted that the man had aged considerably in the past few years. Time had stamped its mark on Ross.

"I've been talking to Tyson Hart about the possibility of merging the companies. It's something you might want to consider."

"The hell I will!" Ross shouted, sloshing the water over the lip of the mug. "Hamilton Construction belongs to me and Richard, and I'll be damned if I let some upstart come in here and try to buy us out."

Brent shook his head. "Dad, he's not trying to buy you out. Just merge. Two construction companies in a town the size of Oak Stand is one too many. He's been getting more contracts than we have. Business has been tough for us lately and joining with Hart will ensure there's a future. Tyson's a good man. I've drawn up preliminary paperwork. He's interested. Since I won't be continuing with Hamilton Construction, it's up to you. I'll send the proposal over and let you look at it. I didn't want to leave you hanging."

"Glad you thought about me," his father said. Anger blossomed between them. It was thick as a fur parka and just as suffocating.

"Yeah, I did think about you. And me. And how it's been tough between us for a long time. Ever since Denny died." Brent moved to the other side of the counter so he stood beside his mom. Donna stiffened at the mention of Denny's name. As she always did.

"I don't want to talk about it." Ross tossed down the spoon he'd used to stir sugar in his tea.

"That's fine. We don't have to talk about it. Just know I love you and Mom. But it's time I cut the apron strings. I've stayed here in Oak Stand because it was easy. And I've been slowly dying inside."

"Oh, Brent," his mom said, reaching out a hand to stroke his arm. "Don't say that."

He patted his mom's hand. "It's okay, Mom. I'm fine because I know what I want in life. It took me a while, but I can see where I need to go."

"That's a bunch of hogwash," Ross said, jerking the tea to his mouth. The liquid must have been scalding because he hurriedly set it upon the counter after one sip. "You've been fine. The company's fine. What the hell have you been doing? Listening to self-help crap? You been going to that singles' ministry over at the Presbyterian Church? I heard they're all into empowering young folks."

Brent almost laughed at the disgust in his father's

voice. He'd planned to tell his parents about his writing. A box of his newest book had arrived this afternoon. He'd planned on revealing his secret career and then taking them both to the carriage house to show them the books he'd penned. The awards he'd won. A copy of the five-book deal he'd just inked. But now wasn't the time. His father wasn't open to it and needed space to adjust to the abdication of his only remaining son.

"Not exactly, Dad. But I have been doing some soul-searching. And I guess that's been empowering." Brent leaned down and kissed his mother's head. Her graying hair smelled of some Estee Lauder perfume she'd worn since he was small. "I'm glad you're home. Get some rest. I know you're both tired."

His mother reached up and hugged him. "We love you, son. We'll try to understand what you're feeling. It's not easy and it may take some time." She looked pointedly at her husband.

Ross grunted. "Good night."

Then he left the kitchen, taking his tea with him.

Brent shrugged. "Guess that didn't go very well."

Donna returned his shrug. "Your father is a complex man. He'll come to accept it in time. He's always wanted so much for you. Maybe too much. But, Brent, he loves you. Never doubt that, sweetheart."

His mother whistled for Apple and gave him a light kiss on the cheek before disappearing into the den where her husband had likely gone to sulk. Or brood. Or perhaps watch the Rangers who were playing the Tampa Bay Rays.

Brent stared at the empty fruit bowl on the counter a moment before leaving. It could have gone better. Or it could have gone worse. Either way, he knew he'd taken the first step toward claiming himself.

He had more steps to take, including making Rayne see he was ready to be the man she needed.

But one move at a time.

He crossed the yard toward his small house. He needed to work up a new speech for the banquet. Something to reveal the man he now was. It was time. More than time.

A horrid smell filled his nose as he stepped onto his porch. He looked down at his tennis shoe. Dog poop caked the bottom.

Crap.

Literally.

Not the step he wanted to take. He jumped from the porch and headed to a thick patch of grass to scrape the mess from his shoes, hoping this wasn't an omen.

Lord, he prayed it wasn't an omen.

CHAPTER SEVENTEEN

BRENT WATCHED AS HENRY swung the bat. His swing was naturally graceful and the ball pinged against the metal bat before sailing over the second baseman's head and rolling into the outfield. Henry flew around first base, never breaking his stride as he took second and headed toward where Brent coached third base. His eyes had searched Brent's as soon as his foot hit the second base. The boy played heads-up ball.

It was the top of the fifth inning and the Warriors were up by nine runs. If he sent Henry home, the game would be over by the ten-run rule. So he held him up. It was too pretty a day to end the game so early.

Warmer weather had played hide-and-seek all spring long in the South, darting across a few days, baking them in warmth, then disappearing again, causing everyone to hunt for sweats to pull on. But this afternoon was warmer than the past few days, and Brent enjoyed the heat of the sun on his shoulders.

Henry shot him a smile and delivered some knucks.

"Good hit, bud," Brent said, glad to see Henry showed no ill effects from having been left at school the day before yesterday. In fact, he seemed back to himself. Thank God.

The bat cracked again, Brent waved Henry home, and the game ended.

Brent watched as Rayne's son celebrated with the rest of the team. The Warriors remained undefeated and there was general consensus among the boys that this could be the year they took the championship. Brent didn't want to encourage their cutthroat competition for first place, but he was proud of them all the same. They were a good team and having Henry aboard had rounded them out.

A tender something moved in his chest at the thought of Henry. He was certain it was pride, though he wasn't sure he was entitled to it.

The boy was an incredible athlete, but there was much more to him. A bone-tickling sense of humor, a sweet vulnerability and a thirst for someone to love him.

Brent walked to the pitching machine and unhooked it so he could store it in the equipment shed. Out of the corner of his eye he saw Rayne stand and gather her camp chair and a small cooler.

She looked as lovely as the rose he often compared her to. Deceptively soft as satin with protection designed to leave a person wondering how he'd come away with a prick of blood.

He dashed his once again too-poetic thoughts as he wheeled the machine down the first base line.

He and Rayne had not spoken since she'd grabbed her purse, twisted her tangled hair into a ponytail and hurried to the school to pick up Henry. Usually, he had no problem seeing women after he'd slept with them. Lord knew he'd had plenty of practice. But it felt dif-

ferent with Rayne. Maybe because of Henry. Or maybe
because he actually cared about Rayne.

Not that he had callously used other women in the
past. He'd always been careful to make sure the women
he'd had brief relationships with knew the score. Obviously, he'd failed with Tamara, who he'd not seen since
the night he'd stepped in it at Cooley's. It had almost
been as bad as what he'd stepped in last night. Damned
messy.

But making love with Rayne had been exactly that…
making love. And it had been the first time for him.
He'd never made love to a woman he wanted to keep.

And he wanted to keep Rayne.

And Henry.

Even if the thought of it scared the socks off him at
times.

He locked the shed and turned toward the dugout.
Rayne still stood among the other parents, no doubt
discussing what dishes they'd bring that night to the
banquet. He loved the way she moved her hands when
she talked. Henry ran around with Cameron Harp,
racing to the concession stand and back.

She and Henry looked as if they belonged here.

That thought buoyed him, so he headed her way.

"Hey," he said, touching her shoulder lightly, drawing her attention away from the other mothers. Was it
too intimate?

She turned and her cheeks bloomed with color. "Hey,
yourself."

Why was she blushing? Was it shame? Did she
regret what had happened between them? No. What
had occurred between them had been good, not tainted
with guilt. She'd been his equal in every way—not the

muselike specter she'd accused him of creating in his mind. Rayne had been woman to his man.

It had been absolutely good and right between them.

"You coming tonight?" he asked. His mind dipped right to naughty at his own words. Hers must have, too, for her eyes widened. Desire hummed in his veins as he noted the delicate pulse in her neck, the smooth slope of her shoulder, the smell of vanilla that was her essence.

"You mean the Oak Stand Athletic Club celebration banquet?"

"Did you think I meant something else?" he asked, trying to make it teasing, but failing. It sounded like an invitation.

Her cheeks deepened in color and she laughed nervously. "Of course not. I knew you meant the banquet."

For the past three years the Oak Stand Athletic Club had hosted a banquet at the beginning of May rather than at the end. Most families had little energy or enthusiasm for baseball parties in late May with the end of school and the launch of vacations. Trophies were awarded at the last game, but they held the banquet before things got suicidal.

"Well, our coach is being honored as Coach of the Year. I wouldn't miss it," she said with a smile as she glanced toward where Henry messed around with a few teammates. "Henry is excited you're receiving the award. He's talked about nothing else for the past week…just in case anyone around our house forgot about it."

She spoke so the other mothers could hear her.

Brandi and a few others laughed appropriately. Stacy even gave him a thumbs-up before grabbing Cameron's bat bag and trudging toward her minivan. Waves and "see ya tonights" were given as the crowd of parents thinned out.

Brent gave a wave or two and refocused his attention on the woman in front of him. "I'm supposed to sit at the head table tonight, but I can have a guest. Do you want to sit with me? Henry, too, of course."

"We can sit with you?" Henry squealed, skidding to a stop in front of them.

Rayne opened her mouth and then shut it. She stared at Henry and then looked back at Brent. He could read her eyes. She knew sitting with him would send a message. A very public message.

"Come on, Mom, we got to," Henry pleaded, nearly jumping up and down. "It'll be so cool."

Brent waited. Henry hopped about squeaking, "Please." And Rayne looked like a mouse in a trap.

Was showing everyone in Oak Stand that they were an item really that bad?

HOW HAD HENRY HEARD BRENT? He'd been airplaning around, whooping with the other boys. Jeez. Boys and their selective hearing. How could Rayne say no now? She couldn't. But it seemed another giant step in an unknown direction. If she sat with Brent, everyone would know they were dating. Was she ready for that? She supposed if she could sneak around and have hot sex with him she should at least be willing to sit with him at a baseball banquet.

Setting her plate next to him on a raised platform in front of Oak Stand's finest would have implications.

Was she afraid of them? Afraid that the town would see her as another notch on Brent's bedpost? Would they see her as easy or weak? Or merely like Brandi? A woman looking for a plaything.

Lord, she was tired of her self-doubts.

Brent watched her. She could see his thoughts, see his worry. He wanted her to say yes. He wanted to claim her out in the open. The idea both thrilled her and scared her.

She'd not told a soul that she'd slept with Brent, though naughty Aunt Fran had given her sly smiles and made juvenile innuendoes about sausage yesterday morning.

"I guess we could," she said, slinging her purse over her shoulder along with the cooler strap. Brent took the chair and carried it over to her car. "You don't want your parents to sit with you? It's a nice honor."

Brent shook his head. "I'd rather have you next to me."

Those words sank into her brain, rattled around and elicited a glow around her heart. It overruled the fear of becoming known as Brent's girl. "Okay. I'll be there."

"Let me pick you up. No sense taking two cars."

Henry had stopped to throw dirt clods at a Dumpster. No one else was around her car. Brent moved closer to her, caught her hand. She put the cooler on the back floor and shut the door. "You think that's a good idea?"

He smiled and the heat in his blue eyes told her he was thinking of more than baseball and banquet speeches. She felt her blood ignite. She could smell his subtle, clean scent. She remembered the way his skin felt against hers. She also remembered the way she'd called his name when she'd tumbled over into the most intense orgasm she'd had. Ever.

"I've been thinking a lot of things are a good idea," he said, his voice low, soft. Very, very sexy. "Like I missed taking that shower with you. I had plans for that oil."

His hand slid up her arm to the delicate spot in the curve of her elbow. He stroked there, causing liquid heat to unfurl inside her. He trailed one finger up her arm to where she'd rolled up the Warriors T-shirt before sliding it to the sensitive flesh beneath her arm. It should have tickled. It didn't. It inflamed.

"Rain check?" she said.

"Oh, yeah. Definitely." He smiled and she felt her toes curl in anticipation. Jeez, the man was sex on a stick. Hedonistic takeout. Drive-by orgasm. Not to mention, he'd been *Sixteen Candles'* Jake Ryan of her high school heart. The absolute in ideal guys. He was smart, good-natured and her kid was half in love with him. Was there any better prospect for a nearly thirty-two-year-old widow than Brent Hamilton?

Other than the fact he'd broken her heart once before?

And that's what stopped her.

That and the fact that she hadn't planned on Brent happening. Her life was beyond shaky. Well, not shaky. Uncertain. If the Food Network deal fell through, she'd go back to Austin and pop into Oak Stand only on occasion. It wouldn't make sense to stay in Oak Stand, unless... She scratched the thought from her mind. Brent implied he wanted more than friendship, more than hot afternoon sex, but what did that mean? Dating?

Commitment? Marriage? Those questions had clogged her mind over the past forty-eight hours. She'd visited them again and again. And received no answer.

"So when can I redeem that rain check?" He leaned close and she thought he might kiss her, but he merely wanted to tempt her. He knew she was revved up. The man was a tease.

"I don't know—"

"Let's go already, Mom. I'm starving." Henry edged past Brent and pulled the passenger door open. He tossed his baseball bag in then climbed inside before looking back expectantly. "Come on. Today."

Rayne stared at her son through the glass. She looked at Brent. He scowled.

"Watch your manners," Brent said, propping a hand on the top of the car and leaning toward Henry.

"Huh?" her son said.

Rayne could have been offended at having Brent fuss at her son. But something about it felt good. It felt like something a coach should address. Or a…father.

"It should be *sir,*" Rayne said.

"Oh." Henry said looking puzzled. "Huh, sir?

"You didn't say excuse me and you interrupted our conversation. You also shouldn't demand things of your mother. She deserves your respect." Brent's tone was matter-of-fact.

Henry's mouth fell open a little before shame crept into his cheeks. He turned as red as she had earlier. "Sorry, Mom. And, uh, Coach."

Rayne sighed. Another thing she'd gotten wrong in Parenting 101. She was raising a rude chicken. Great. But Brent was correct. She needed to pay better attention to how Henry addressed her and other adults.

Brent had pinched her toes a bit stepping on them. But he'd further cemented the idea that Henry needed some male guidance in his life. And she wasn't sure if Brent could be that form of guidance.

"Thank you for apologizing," Rayne said with a small smile. "Now get your fanny into the backseat."

Henry's shoulders sank and he blew out a disgusted breath. "Fine."

She cleared her throat.

"I mean, yes, ma'am."

Brent smiled at her when she gave a sigh to rival Henry's. "He's a good boy. Don't overanalyze."

She nodded and tossed Brent a weak smile. Things felt so heavy. She felt laden with too much and adding Brent to the mix had felt right in a sense, but her head refused to believe a love interest in the middle of up-heaval was a good idea. She'd always been good at following her head. This time she'd ignored the alarms and clanging bells of warning that begged her to slow down. Yes, she'd always listened to her head.

Her heart? Not so much. Hearts got girls in trouble.

"I'll pick you up at five-thirty. I should get there early," Brent said, closing the passenger door and giving Henry a wave.

She nodded and walked to the driver's side. "I'll be ready."

But her words felt hollow.

She needed to get away.

She couldn't think with Brent next door, on the porch, suggesting showers. And she felt like she needed to think. Get some space, some clarity. Especially before Monday hit. Before the deadline for the network to accept or decline her offer. Before she had to go to the mattress on her career.

She slid into her car and turned the key.

Coming to Oak Stand was supposed to clear the air, not muddy the waters. But she couldn't see her feet in the puddle she was trudging through.

She looked back at her son in the rearview mirror. He caught her eye.

"Mom, do you think you could marry Coach Brent?"

Her foot slipped and hit the accelerator. She nearly took out an overflowing trash can, but managed to brake and mutter a dirty word at the same time.

"Just asking," her son said.

"Why?"

"Because I like him. And I can tell he likes you. And you laugh a lot more around him. I think he'd be a good addition. We could maybe go live with him. I like that dog."

Rayne sighed. "You want me to marry a man because of a dog?"

Henry laughed. "No, not just 'cause of a dog. Because Coach is really good at playing ball. I could use a guy like him around. I'm tired of not having a dad."

She put the car in Drive. "Those sound like good reasons, but they're not good enough to change everything about our life."

"I thought they were," Henry said.

CHAPTER EIGHTEEN

THE OAK STAND RECREATION Center had been built five years before. It didn't smell of dirty socks or sweaty leather yet, so the baseball celebration banquet had been held there for the past few years. The tables were covered in white paper tablecloths and the food was potluck. Traditional Texas barbecue, coleslaw and fries weighed down the large tables to the side. Not to mention there were gallons of sweet tea, Tupperware containers of ambrosia and pans of decadent browns and gooey cake.

The chef in Rayne Rose recoiled. The country girl in Rayne Rose put extra butter on her corn on the cob.

"Mom, what's this?" Henry asked, pointing to a Jell-O salad.

"Not something anyone should eat, but you can try it if you want," she said, eyeing the head table where Brent sat wearing a sport coat and tie, digging into a plate of ribs. Rayne could have sworn she'd heard out-and-out gasps when she and Henry had taken the seats to the left of him. Presently, everyone was content to eyeball her and whisper.

Great.

She added a scoop of ambrosia to her plate and grabbed a tea. When in Oak Stand and all that.

She walked out of her way in order to avoid Brandi

and Stacy. She even hurried past Nellie, who was sitting across from Bubba Malone and trying unsuccessfully to wipe her daughter's mouth. Mae Darby, adorable in a hot pink T-ball shirt with matching bows in her pigtails, ducked under her mother's swipes and talked a blue streak. Bubba thoughtfully nodded his bald head to everything the little girl said. He caught Rayne's eye and grinned. She was glad Meg had seen what many in Oak Stand sometimes overlooked when it came to Bubba. He was a gentle giant with a spark of practicality.

Brent's parents, Ross and Donna, had made it back to town for the event and sat with several other members of Oak Stand old guard. They were lively and loud the way they'd always been. Good people, but they'd pushed Brent hard to succeed…in something he'd had absolutely no passion for. She waved to them, but didn't stop to chat. She knew they had questions about her and why she was sitting next to their son at the table of honor.

She set her plate next to Brent's and got Henry settled with a napkin in his lap. She cut up the pork loin he'd picked out and realized she needed to teach him how to cut it himself. There was so much she hadn't taught him. His shoes came untied all the time, washing hair was hit or miss and he still tore the bread when he tried to butter his toast. Her report card for being a parent wouldn't show A's across the board. Raising Henry would have been much easier with a tag team partner.

Her mind flashed back to Brent's admonishments toward Henry earlier that afternoon. And his words. *Don't overanalyze. He's a good boy.*

Maybe Brent was right. She hadn't done such a bad

job on her own these past two years. No mother was perfect and she was trying to put Henry first. If no one came along to tag up with her, she'd be fine. Henry wouldn't go to college unable to tie his shoes or cut his own meat. She needed to give herself a break.

She looked at her son and he smiled.

He was an awesome kid.

Brent leaned over. "You okay?"

She nodded, feeling a blip of comfort at his question. It felt nice to have someone who wasn't Meg or Aunt Fran looking out for her. "Everyone's watching us."

"Wanna give 'em something to talk about?" he asked with a wicked grin. Her serious thoughts melted away as she considered his words. He was as big as Texas, brazen, bold and so damn good-looking it made a woman want to hog-tie him and lock him in a back-room for twisted purposes.

"Not really. I'm accustomed to people looking at me because I cooked the food, not because I'm with the hometown hero."

He looked at her strangely but didn't say anything more. Merely tucked into some macaroni and cheese she'd obviously missed out on. She hadn't had something with that much butter since she left Oak Stand years ago, so she snagged a spoonful off his plate.

He didn't mind.

Twenty minutes later, the president of the Oak Stand Athletic Club, Griffin Doyle, strolled to the lectern and cleared his throat. The hardware store owner began rattling off mind-boggling statistics about the man sitting beside her. She didn't know what half the things meant, but Brent's parents seemed to sit taller. He, however, did not. At the conclusion of the accomplishments, Griffin mentioned the number of years Brent had coached base-ball and football. Ten years. Almost the entire time since he'd left college.

"So join me in giving a big round of applause to Oak Stand's own all-American…the Coach of the Year, Brent Hamilton."

Henry nearly killed himself joining in on the thun-derous applause, and as Brent rose, he caught her gaze. The expression on his face was a mixture of embar-rassment and resolve. An odd combination for someone who should be proud of his accomplishments.

Brent walked to the lectern and shook Griffin's hand, accepting the gold plaque that came with the annual honor.

"Thank you for such a nice tribute," he said, motion-ing everyone to quiet down.

"I want you to know that I've received many awards over the years I've been involved with athletics, but this award means much more to me because it represents my contributions to the future of organized sports."

Several people clapped and one man whistled.

"Yes, it's appropriate to applaud the future of sports because these little guys sitting with you here today—they are our future Hall of Famers, future Heisman winners, future running backs, forwards, shortstops and gold medalists."

He paused and took a deep breath. "But me, I'm the past and my contributions can only be given as someone who molds an athlete. It's a weighty job, and one that is important, more important than any role I've ever played, which is why tonight I want to come clean about some things."

There was a small murmur in the audience, and

Rayne felt something inside her snap. She was pretty sure it was trepidation. What was the man doing?

"When I was growing up, I loved playing sports, but there was something I loved even more."

Oh. No. Rayne's heart sputtered then sped. Surely he wasn't going to declare his love for her? Not here. Not now.

"I loved to read and write. Growing up, I spent hours out in my backyard with my best friend making up stories, creating, building, reading and dreaming. I carried that love with me all my life."

Rayne gave an inward sigh of relief, but then watched as he pulled a crumpled piece of paper from his inside jacket pocket. Something niggled in the back of her mind. When she caught sight of the faded red heart sticker, she knew. And it caused a prickly awareness to wash over her, a sense of planets aligning. Or something.

"A while back a friend gave me a poem about having the courage to be who you really are. It's a poem about daring to leave what others think of you behind, about reaching for dreams and holding fast to them. She spoke to my heart with those words and I've kept it in a special place, pulling it out to read when I sometimes lost faith in myself."

A keen warmth stole into Rayne at his words. It burrowed deep in her heart and caused a clog of tears to form in the back of her throat. She looked around the recreation center. Most people looked confused, but intrigued. Even toddlers stopped wiggling as if they knew this was a profound moment.

"I tell you this for a reason. Being who you truly are is important. I was afraid to do that for many years because I didn't want to disappoint the people who loved me. I didn't want to let people down."

Brent's parents squirmed. They were the only ones. Everyone else looked mesmerized by the admission of the former all-American.

"But in doing that, I let myself down. And I let down a person I cared very much about, the person who wrote this for me."

Rayne centered her gaze on Brent. He swallowed and cut a glance her way. She smiled and he returned it. It was a poignant moment and she really didn't give two flying figs if everyone else shared in it.

"So I want to encourage all of you boys and girls out there to embrace who you are. If you dream of being an NFL quarterback, then go for it. If you want to dance on Broadway, polish up your shoes and tap your way there. If you want to be a writer, park your bottom in a chair and write a story. No one can tell you who you can be, and if you're lucky, you'll have someone along the way who will challenge you to be all that you can. It could be your mom or dad, or a teacher, or a coach or maybe a special friend who sees beyond the outer wrappings to the real gift inside you." He paused and seemed to fidget, as if bracing to take the next step.

"Tonight I'm going to come clean on something. A secret."

Another murmur started and a couple of kids starting talking. Their parents quieted them. Brent waited.

"My dream when I was young was not to play in the NFL as many would expect. My dream was to be a writer. And for the past six years, I've been living my dream. I have twelve middle-grade sports books on the shelf. In fact, most of them are in your school libraries.

I write the Buttontown Boys series under the name B.J. Hamm."

Rayne felt as though someone had hit her with a golf club. Brent was a writer? He was a *published* writer? He was the writer whose books Henry had been devouring? Good Lord.

She knew her mouth was open. She looked out at the audience. Most of them had their mouths open, too. A few people had bulging eyes.

But Brent's parents, well, they appeared shocked. Like heart-attack onset shocked. His dad turned to his mom and the look they shared was almost comical.

Brent, with a natural instinct for timing, allowed a moment to pass. He pulled a book from his jacket pocket. It was a copy of one he'd not yet loaned to Henry. He held it up so the audience could see it.

"This was my first book. It's about a boy who tries so hard to be a good basketball player he nearly misses the opportunity to learn to play the guitar and find his true talent. I had seventy-three letters sent to me by boys and parents who told me how much my story had meant to them. I find that much more satisfying than someone telling me how great the catch I made in the Texas A&M game was or how cool it was when the Longhorns won a National Championship.

"So my message to you tonight is to not let anyone hold you back in following your dreams, least of all yourself. If you want something, have the courage to go and get it."

With those last words, he looked at her, and she felt the weight of them. Felt that he wasn't talking about writing or football. He was talking about her.

Brent's parents still looked astounded. Donna had

her head cocked and a bewildered expression on her face. But then as Brent stepped back from the podium, his mother smiled. It was the biggest, proudest smile Rayne had ever seen a woman wear. In fact, it was catching. Like the flu, that smile spread throughout the recreation center. Rayne couldn't stop her own lips from turning up in sheer wonder.

Then Donna stood. And she started clapping. Rayne didn't fail to notice the tears streaming down her face. She was joined milliseconds later by Ross, who seemed a bit choked up himself.

Then the rest of the attendees rose with a clamorous scraping of metal chairs and clapped not for Brent Hamilton, the guy who broke records and put their town on the map, but for Brent Hamilton, the writer.

Rayne felt frozen in place. Brent looked flabbergasted. He glanced at her with a what-do-I-do look. She shrugged, stood and clapped.

Henry whooped. "That's so cool! I love his books!"

What a secret to keep all those years. Pride flooded her as the impact of Brent's achievement crept in. Brent had spent many years among people who expected very little of him, and yet, he'd been successful. Secretly following his dream. But why had he kept being a published writer a secret? One would think Brent would want the people around him to know he'd done something so…what had Henry said? Cool?

She didn't understand. Maybe because everything she'd done had been out in the open, heavily promoted by first Phillip and now her agent along with everyone else in her company.

She pursued opportunities like a tenacious bulldog which was why the New York deal was so important to her. Two times before she'd been turned down. The network's refusal had only made her more determined. She could be content with what she had now—a successful restaurant, cookbook and apron line, not to mention the soon-to-be-opened inn. No one would look askance at such a measure of success. But getting a show into production would be the feather in her otherwise brimming cap.

Brent shook Griffin Doyle's hand again and made his way to the chair beside her. The audience sat and Griffin made a few parting comments about how the season had progressed so far and a plea for parents to stop parking on the new sod they'd planted.

But Rayne couldn't focus on Griffin's words. Her mind spun, trying to wrap itself around the revelation the man beside her had made. An author. Rayne tried to beat down the twinge of hurt that appeared when she realized he hadn't shared his secret career with her. What right did she have to know? His own parents hadn't even known.

"Why did you hold out on me?" she whispered. "This is a big deal."

"I don't know. Why are you still holding out on me?" he asked out of the side of his mouth.

"What?" she whispered, a bit too loudly if Erma Doyle's frown was any indication.

"You hold back. You won't let yourself jump over the fences you've built."

Rayne sank back in her chair. *Fences?* What the hell did that mean? "I don't have secrets."

He smiled as Doyle once again congratulated him on his Coach of the Year honors. He even held up his hand and mouthed "Thank you," before leaning close to her. "You may not have secrets, but you're hiding from yourself. Hiding from what you really want."

Rayne straightened and whispered. "No, I'm not. I'm deciding. That's different."

He nodded to several of the others sitting at the table. People around the room rose from their chairs and made their way toward Brent, including his parents. No time to talk when others demanded his attention.

"Later," he said, wiping his mouth with a napkin and rising with a smile. "Meet me out back tonight?"

She barely had time to nod before Brent was consumed by well-wishers, leaving her feeling discontented and discombobulated by his words.

She hadn't come to Oak Stand to hide. She'd come for a break. Or something.

She looked at Henry. He was fully engaged in some kind of dessert with crumbled chocolate cookies and gummy worms. It looked disgusting, but he crammed it in his mouth like a contestant in a pie-eating contest.

She had Henry to think about. Her career. Her employees. Her house in Austin. Her line of hand sanitizers and polka-dot rubber dish gloves. She couldn't toss her life to take a chance with Brent. People only did that in chick flicks and half of those ended with moviegoers crying in their popcorn. Real people had real repercussions. They couldn't chase waterfalls and rainbows. Or handsome old flames.

She glanced at Brent, who now had an arm curved around his beaming mother and shook hands with a guy in a crisp police uniform. The guy was attractive in a buttoned-up, military way. She assumed he was the new police chief some of the mothers at the ballgame had been talking about. Bubba held Mae Darby under one arm, and she accidently kicked Brent's father as he chatted with Mayor Tom Sutton. Smiles, laughter and kids galloping about the room.

It wasn't a bad place to raise a family. Quite good actually.

Her phone buzzed in her purse signaling she had a text message. She slid it from its case and pressed the button that opened her texts.

It was from her agent.

Talked to Tate. Good news. See you Monday.

She stared at the screen then at Brent. At the way his wavy hair dipped over his brow, at his sparkling blue eyes, at the curve of his mouth.

She should be ecstatic. Her agent Holly Munsen never made a peep unless it was noteworthy. So for her to declare good news meant an offer was on the table and it was an excellent one.

They wanted her.

It meant New York. It meant her face on TV. It meant more money not only for her but for her team of chefs, restaurant managers, assistants and agents.

It was big.

So how come she felt like crying?

CHAPTER NINETEEN

BRENT STARED UP AT THE star-strewn sky and inhaled. Cut grass. Mr. Hines had likely mown at twilight as was his custom, and the air carried the clean, earthy scent. The crescent moon hung high in the sky, a fingernail throwing the gentlest of light. It should have soothed him, but he felt too keyed up to allow the quiet night to calm him.

After his speech revealing his alter ego, B.J. Hamm, he'd been inundated with people who wanted to talk to him, to congratulate him on his success. A few kids had declared his books to be "supercool" and Hunter Todd wanted to know if he could be in one. When Brent had told him he'd been the model for Skyler in the basketball book, the boy had gotten so excited he'd knocked a cup of iced tea into his grandmother's lap.

Overall, Brent couldn't have wished for a better coming out.

The soft look in Rayne's eyes had made it all the better. She'd looked so happy, so surprised…yet not surprised. Rayne had always expected the best of him. Somehow, even though she hadn't been around when he'd begun writing, her belief in him had kept him going. He hadn't lied when he'd drawn out her crumpled poem from long ago and told everyone how she'd encouraged him with her challenge to be who he was.

And now he felt extremely comfortable in his skin. For the first time in a very long time.

"Hey." Her voice was low behind him.

"Hey," he said, not turning around. He had his hands in his pockets and kept them there. He wanted to reach out for her and draw her into his arms, but waited.

The expanse of lawn between his carriage house and his parents' huge screened-in porch was draped in shadows. His parents never left the porch lights on because they bothered him. He was glad for the darkness, glad for the mystique that shrouded them.

"Want to sit on the swing?" he asked, cocking his head in her direction.

"Sure," she said, moving toward the sturdy cedar swing sitting beside the willow tree.

"Let me grab a blanket. It's a little cool," he said, jogging the short distance to his door. He'd left it unlocked so quickly snatched the same throw he'd used to cover his nakedness weeks before and returned to where she sat. "Here."

She took the woven throw and twined it about her shoulders. The sleeveless dress she'd worn was vintage Rayne—soft, flowing and feminine. It draped across the swing and made her look like dessert. He sat next to her and draped his arm over her shoulders, pulling her into his embrace. It was a position long familiar to both of them. She snuggled into the curve of his arm and sighed.

They spoke no words for a while. He inhaled the clean scent of her hair and idly twisted one of her curls about his finger. The way he'd done a hundred times before.

Peace stole across his soul.

"Henry is beside himself at the thought you wrote those books he read," she said, finally breaking the tranquility.

"Mmm," Brent said, brushing a kiss on her forehead.

"You surprised a lot of people," she said.

"Mmm," he said again, not wanting to relinquish the moment. It was too perfect. Too good to hold her and just be.

She turned so she could see his face in the glow of the moon. "Are you going to talk to me?"

He smiled. "Talking is overrated."

She smiled. "So you showed me."

He couldn't stop the chuckle. "Well, you weren't too bad yourself."

She nodded. "I *was* bad, and that's what made it so good."

"Yes, you were," he said, dropping another kiss atop her head.

"I'm really proud of you. Not because you've made it as a writer, but because you let everyone see a glimpse of who you are, the man you always should have been. I think old Rita Ratcliff's teeth may have fallen into her plate when you pulled that book out."

He laughed. "I guess it was shocking for many. Most people can accept that I shoot a mean game of pool or know the difference between single and double malt scotch, but stringing sentences together? Yeah. Brent Hamilton as an author. Hard to comprehend."

He kicked the swing into motion. She slid her sandals off and tucked her toes into the hem of her dress. "I love that you surprised people. It must have felt good."

"I didn't do it to surprise them. I did it for you."

He felt her stiffen against him. "For me?"

"Yeah, for you. I wanted you to know I'm ready to be the man you always wanted me to be. I want to be your future."

He watched her press her lips together. "I've always known what kind of person you are. What you announced didn't surprise me as much as it surprised others. But I can't promise a future right now. I know you don't want to hear that, but I can't—"

"Why not?" he asked. Fear gathered in his chest. He'd thought they were moving to something bigger than a moment in time. He hadn't made love to her with the thought it was only a roll in the hay. It had meant more. At least to him. And he'd thought it had meant more to her, too.

She sighed. "I can't allow myself to get carried away, Brent. There is much more at stake than my heart. There's Henry, my staff, my career. I can't promise this thing we're doing isn't just a slice of my life."

"A slice of your life?" He pulled his arm from beneath her head. "What do you mean?"

"You said yourself we weren't going to plan or label this thing between us. I'm trying hard not to do that. My heart leads me one way, but my head pulls me another. I wasn't supposed to fall for you. Not again. I can't."

He put a foot down, stopping the movement of the swing. "So what we've shared is a moment in time? A sort of makeup for what you missed when you were fifteen? Please tell me you weren't using me for sex or for some misplaced revenge for not escorting you to prom. Please tell me I'm more than a detour on your journey to wherever the hell you're going."

"I'm not using you. I've tried everything in my power

to stay away from you, to stop my heart from wandering down that road again. Last time that road led to heartbreak."

"Well, that's up to you. I'm not breaking your heart. Roles are reversed, sweetheart." He scooted away from her as if he could move away from the pain she'd caused him. Never in a million years would he have thought putting himself out there would hurt so bad. The J. Geils Band was right. Love did stink.

"I'm not breaking your heart, Brent. I'm trying to do what's right. I don't want to put on dancing shoes just to walk down a rocky, pitted road."

"What road? What are you talking about?"

"You. Your track record with women. I know you think you want something more now, but—"

"I'm not thinking. I'm doing. I'm offering you commitment," he said, wondering if he rushed things a bit. He'd wanted to give her time. Take things slowly, but they'd reached a new level. "I want a life with you. And Henry."

She closed her eyes and shook her head. She actually looked anguished at his words. He couldn't believe she didn't want him. Or rather wouldn't have him. The irony was bitter.

"I can't make a commitment now. I can't. As I've said before, this is not about only me. It would be irresponsible for me to throw all caution aside and dive into something without looking."

He stood and walked away from her. Moments before he'd been perfectly content. How had it gone south?

Rayne followed him. Lord, the woman pushed even as she pulled away from him. "Brent, don't."

"Don't what? Don't be disappointed? Don't feel like

I've put myself out there only to be trampled on? I've finally shed everything. Every bit of the cloak I've wrapped myself in for so long. Babe, I'm more naked here than on that day you caught me unaware in my house."

Her hand brushed his forearm and moved to clasp his hand. "Please. I'm not saying no. I'm just not saying yes."

He pulled his hand from hers. He'd never known hurt like this. Not really. He'd felt an emptiness when Rayne had left him years ago. He'd been angry, confused, but had known why she'd left. He'd been on a different path, one that he couldn't get off. He'd not had the will to toss away his blue-chip, five-star status for puppy love. He hadn't had the strength to go against his parents, his coaches or the town to follow a dream.

But that was then.

And this was now.

He'd laid it all out for her. Because he loved her. Not because he'd always loved her. But because he'd fallen in love. Real love. With Rayne Rose.

"I love you," he said.

She actually gasped.

"I fell in love with you. Go figure. My heart has been sitting on a shelf, way up high, dusty and faded. But a baseball flew over my fence and everything changed. The moment that gate flew open and you stood there, pretty as a bluebonnet and mad as a hornet, I knew. You were here for a reason."

"But maybe that reason wasn't what you thought," she whispered. She sounded so sad. So resigned to over-thinking everything about their relationship.

"No," he said, spinning toward her. "I don't think

it was for any other reason but that we were meant for each other. From the beginning."

"Maybe," she said, staring into his eyes. Dampness hovered on her lashes. "And maybe I came to encourage you to a new place in your life."

He shook his head. "And what about you?"

"Maybe you are my one loose string. The one thing I'd never had completion on. Maybe my coming to Oak Stand was about pulling that string so I could move on and not think about you at the strangest times. Maybe this hasn't been about a new beginning but about closing the book on what once was."

He thought about shaking her until her teeth rattled. "Are you shitting me?"

She stiffened. "I'm trying to look at all sides of this. I can't throw everything away because you think you're in love with me. I have a child. I have a—"

"A career. Yes, I know," he said. He kept his arms around her. Wanted to kiss her senseless, shake her, then kiss her until she melted, until the doubts were gone.

"I don't take that lightly," she said, looking plum miserable, her heart evident in her big brown eyes. He knew she felt pulled in too many directions.

He looked hard at this woman.

She was not the same girl. She didn't think with her heart. She didn't leap without looking. She checked and double-checked. It had become her nature. But even as he knew this about her, accepted it, he knew she was wrong about seeing their relationship as something fleeting.

But he didn't know what to do about it.

Because every little move she made told him she

loved him. Told him that this could be forever. Told him that he was right. But to push her was to lose her.

"Hell," he murmured, lowering his head. He pressed his lips against hers, tugging her lips apart, loving the way she tasted, mixing the honey of her taste with the saltiness of her regret. Of her doubt. Of her pain.

He pulled her to him, loving the way she fit him.

He'd have to let her go.

Had to.

He couldn't manipulate her. She had to choose him because she wanted him, wanted a life with him.

He wanted a heart given. Not taken.

He broke the kiss.

"I don't *think* I love you. I do," he said, stepping away from her and colliding with the weeping willow's graceful branches. How appropriate they stood next to a crying tree. Symbolic. "And I know you love me."

She pressed her hands to her face. "Brent, I never said I didn't love you. I want to be sure. I have to be sure."

"Okay. So be sure."

Her head jerked up. "What do you mean?"

"You need time. Okay. I think what we've got is worth waiting on. I'm going with my gut here, but if you need to double-check your heart with your head, then I'll be patient."

She stared at him for a moment, her eyes glazed with emotion. "How did this happen?"

He shrugged. Rayne blowing into his life was a godsend for him, but not for her. She'd come to Oak Stand to clear her head and he'd clouded her vision more. He understood.

"It's not bad. I'm not asking you to choose me and

Oak Stand over your career. I'm asking you to open yourself to the possibility of a whole new direction. A path we can blaze together. I don't want you to stop being you. I like the adult Rayne. You're responsible, levelheaded and fiery. But there's nothing wrong with merging her with the girl who made origami birds and daisy chains. With the girl who took chances and chased dreams. This isn't a do this *or* do that sort of thing. It's a be this *and* that sort of thing."

She pulled the blanket tighter around her shoulders and stared at the moon. She looked lonely and lost. "Have you been watching *Dr. Phil* or *The View?* Because you're making a lot of sense. Not that those shows always make sense."

He let go of a smile. Maybe things would turn out okay. He had to believe that they were meant to be. "Dr. Phil has me on speed dial."

She laughed softly. "I'm leaving for New York tomorrow. My agent texted me earlier tonight. The executive producer of *Emeril Live* is interested in developing my show. I have a meeting Monday because the network has an offer."

Suddenly, his heart didn't feel so secure. It felt like it had jumped with no parachute. Not good. Not good at all.

"This is it. It's what I've been waiting for. Once in a lifetime opportunity for me and everyone associated with Rayne Rose Enterprises," she said, shaking her head in a resigned manner. "You'd be here in Texas, and I'd be in Manhattan working umpteen hours a week. It wouldn't work."

He stood like a statue, trying to pretend disappointment hadn't lodged in his gut. Trying to pretend her words were untrue. That they didn't prick him like thorns. Irony had raised its head and laughed. "You'll have to decide what you want, Rayne Rose. Go to New York and see what they say. I'll be here when you come back."

She raised her gaze to his. Her dark eyes filled with regret. "I may not come back."

He couldn't stop the flinch that came with her words. He felt as if he should try and get his feet beneath him, for the rug had been yanked out from under him. He pulled his gaze from hers and searched the night sky as if he could find some help from the celestial bodies glowing above him. No shooting star fell. Just a void.

"Even so, you'll have to decide," he said to the moon.

CHAPTER TWENTY

THE STREETS OF MANHATTAN had been brutal with hundreds of bodies pressed together moving like salmon up a stream. It was as if after an endless stretch of ice and snow, every New Yorker decided to leave their winter-weary burrows and venture out along all the numbered streets they could find. And there were a lot of numbered streets in New York City. For three days, she pressed against strangers while balancing a cup of chai tea, trying to keep her game face on.

Playing the corporate game had exhausted her.

When the plane hit the tarmac at Dallas-Fort Worth airport, she literally felt the stress melt from her shoulders. Back in Texas. Back to slow talking, open land and sweet iced tea.

And now, as she climbed into her Volvo in the long-term parking lot of DFW, she took a moment to relish the warm leather seats, the faint scent of fresh cotton from the fragrance clip and the possibility of miles and miles of open road.

She took a deep breath.

She'd come back to Oak Stand. Sort of.

After paying the exorbitant fee for parking, she headed southeast toward the small town where her son waited. Where Brent waited. Nerves settled like lumps in her stomach, but she ignored them. What she'd done had been for the best. Everything would be okay. It had to be. The decision had been made.

As she looped around I-635, she noticed dark clouds hanging over East Texas. Dark and ominous, they swelled larger and larger over the silent prairie, causing unease to grow inside her each mile her car traveled. About an hour into her drive, the sky grew darkly pregnant and the wind picked up.

She drove thirty minutes more into the darkening sky before reaching for her phone and giving the voice command that would dial her aunt's cell phone. Screw the warning against using a cell phone while driving. Something told her she needed to check on things in Oak Stand.

The phone rang endlessly before finally she heard her aunt's voice. The connection wasn't good, but she managed to ask about the weather conditions.

"Honey, I'm leaving Longview with Mrs. Upchurch. Her endodontic appointment ran late and the weather's bad here." Her aunt's voice faded in and out.

"I'm worried about Henry. The bus will pick him up at the school soon, and it looks like a storm is coming."

"I should be home when he gets off the bus. I think. Isn't Meg there? She said—" Rayne couldn't hear the rest of her aunt's statement after the first drop of rain hit the windshield. Several more large ones plopped against the glass before a deluge opened above her.

"Aunt Fran," Rayne yelled into the phone even though she knew her aunt couldn't hear her. "Aunt Frances!"

The connection had failed. No sense phoning her back. Not when the rain had gotten so heavy Rayne could barely see out of the glass. To try and dial in those conditions would be stupid.

Meg wasn't in Oak Stand. She'd left hours ago for Austin to head up the staff meeting Rayne had postponed four days ago. Rayne had approved the menu, but some staffing changes had to be made before the weekend and a distributor contract had to be renegotiated. She and Meg had talked extensively about what needed to be done during Rayne's time in New York. She agreed Meg needed to fill in for her and sent her to the restaurant never imagining Aunt Frances would get held up in Longview. Nor had she foreseen an unsettled weather forecast.

She set her iPhone on the console and sent up a quick prayer. *Please let Henry be okay. Help him not to be afraid.*

Maybe Brent would think about Henry and check on him.

But why should he? After the way they'd left things, what reason did he have to do her any favors? She'd basically taken his offer of a future together and shelved it. The man who'd haunted her dreams since she'd reached puberty had offered her his heart and she'd shoved it back at him.

Well, not exactly shoved, but she certainly hadn't snapped up the offer. To a degree, it baffled her she hadn't tossed everything aside for a chance with Brent. Hadn't she secretly dreamed about having Brent to love, even when she wasn't supposed to be dreaming of him? Even when it seemed impossible? On the other hand, it made perfect sense to think hard about what taking a chance with him would mean.

It would mean tossing her career ambitions to the

side, refusing the network deal, changing her whole life—where she lived, how she worked, who she was. And there was no guarantee that Brent would or could commit to her and Henry.

The most shocking thing was he'd seemed to understand her reasoning. He got that she came to the table with more than a mere hope for the best. She came with baggage. Baggage she loved and cared about. Her decision wasn't capricious, and his willingness to see things from her point of view had only endeared him more to her.

The force of the rain made it hard to hear the words John Mayer was crooning on the radio. Fear leaped in her belly.

God, please let Brent think about Henry. Please let someone remember I'm not in town. Let my baby be okay.

She glanced at the clock on the dash—2:35 p.m. Only twenty-five minutes until the elementary school bell rang and the buses fired up. She'd never make it in time to pick up Henry before the buses departed. And the storm would scare him. But maybe the storm wasn't even near Oak Stand. Maybe it had passed the small town. Just because the weather was horrible along I-20 didn't mean it had even rained a drop in her former hometown.

But her gut told her differently. Something felt wrong.

She punched the button that would give her the FM band and scanned until she found a local station. Eighties rock filled the car—ironically it was "Rock You Like a Hurricane" playing. She sighed and fought to keep the car in her lane. The wind had increased and the gusts swooping over the open pastures on either side of the highway had her gripping the steering wheel for dear life.

A long harsh alarm sounded on the radio, interrupting the iconic song. A flat voice informed her that the National Weather Service had issued a tornado warning for Howard County. Several funnels had been spotted over North Havens Road moving southeast toward the town of Oak Stand. All persons in the area were to seek cover and stay tuned to the radio station for further details.

The storm was ahead of her. And it was deadly.

"No," Rayne said to the emptiness of the car. "No. Please. No."

Her heart thumped against her chest. Her baby was in the path of a tornado. Dear God.

She looked at the phone sitting in the console. She needed to call somebody, but she hadn't programmed in Brent's number. And she couldn't very well search the internet while she drove in hazardous conditions. No time to pull over. She had to get to Oak Stand.

Just as her hand hovered over the phone, the marimba ringtone jangled, vibrating the phone against the leather holder.

She snatched the phone, pressing the answer button. The number was unfamiliar.

"Hello," she said.

"Rayne?" Brent called over the thready connection.

"Brent! There's a tornado. Henry's at school. Can you get to him?" she yelled over the pounding rain. A gust caught her off guard and blew her car toward the shoulder. The sound of the rumble strips on the shoulder had her jerking the wheel, nearly overcorrecting. She steadied the car, clutching the phone, unwilling to toss it down even if it meant her own safety was at stake. Keeping Henry safe was more important.

She heard Brent saying something, but couldn't make out anything he said.

"What?" she called into the receiver. "Please say it again."

His voice faded in and out. She thought she heard the name "Henry" but couldn't be sure.

"Please get to him, Brent!" she cried into the receiver.

The connection died and she threw the phone onto the passenger seat next to her purse. Fear pierced her, but she vowed she wouldn't dissolve into tears. She had to keep it together. Keep her cool. Get to Oak Stand.

God, how could this be happening? It was like a bad movie.

She couldn't drive any faster than she was because visibility was down to almost nothing. A few cars had pulled to the side of the road while others crept like tortoises on the normally speedy interstate. Five miles after she'd lost her connection with Brent, the rain eased slightly. Rayne gunned the car, increasing her speed to eighty miles per hour. She knew it was dangerous, but no longer cared. She had to get to Henry. He wasn't like most kids. With her out of town, he'd be petrified. The Tyler exit appeared in front of her swishing windshield wipers. She breathed a sigh of relief.

Almost there.

Rain still fell and the wind gave periodic gusts, but overall the fury of the storm had fled east toward Louisiana. The music on the radio rattled her nerves but she didn't switch it off in case there were reports from the radio station about the weather. Finally, after Blondie crooned an angsty love song, the local news came on.

"There have been reports of two tornadoes touching down in Oak Stand. We've been in touch with the police chief Adam Bent, who told us one ripped through the center of town doing damage to several businesses in the area. The other touched down outside of the town and the amount of damage there is undetermined."

"No," Rayne said, hitting the steering wheel so hard her horn sounded, making her jump. "Please let him be okay. God. Please."

She swiped at the dampness in her eyes. She wouldn't cry. Henry was okay. He had to be. And Brent, too. There wasn't an alternative.

And suddenly as the gray landscape rushed past her, all the things she thought so important weren't. Her career, her fears, her hesitation in life. Did she need a hit cooking show on television? For that matter, did she need a successful restaurant? None of those things were more important than her family. None were more important than Henry. Or Brent. How had she ever thought fame and fortune the only path for her? Somehow she'd lost sight of the true meaning of life and let the passion she felt for cooking become the determinant for who she was.

Did she love her work?

Of course.

Did she love it more than a sleepy hug from her seven-year-old? More than a sexy kiss from Brent?

No.

"I'm a dumbass," she said to the interior of the car. Yeah, she was talking to her car. But somehow it didn't matter. All that mattered was getting to Oak Stand so she could make everything right again.

About five miles from the city limits of Oak Stand, she saw the first signs of the twister. A swath of trees lay broken in half as if an angry child had snapped them out of spite. A piece of tin roof lay in the middle of the lane and she swerved around it, uttering yet another prayer to a God she'd spent so little time conversing with she wondered if He could remember her name.

She hoped He hadn't forgotten her because the damage scared her silly.

A mile from town she saw more debris—limbs strewn like broken toys, a patio umbrella and outdoor furniture cushions. A tree had fallen across one portion of the road and it was passable only if she took her small SUV on the side of oncoming traffic. She plowed ahead, chanting a mantra of "Please, please," under her breath.

She drove past the city limits sign without seeing much damage, causing her to give a momentary sigh of relief. But when she passed the Westside Baptist Church and hooked a left, the direction the storm had taken was plainly evident. Broken boards, clothing and shattered glass filled the first glimpse she had of the town square. She rounded the square, proceeding cautiously around the brick streets, swerving around fallen branches and people standing in the road staring slack-jawed at the smashed window fronts of the businesses. Several signs hung drunkenly, many more lay tossed aside, broken.

The rain and wind had stopped and the small town was absolutely still.

And very much devastated.

Rayne felt her heart contract with apprehension. She

didn't know when she'd ever been so scared. Not even when Phillip had died and she'd awakened the next morning to a sobbing five-year-old and the reality of life without her husband. The emotion that swamped her now was sheer terror. What if something had happened at the school? She remembered a school in Alabama that had its roof blown off, killing several students. Surely, something of that nature hadn't happened in this small Texas town.

"Oh, no," she moaned as she spotted a car crushed by the auto body shop's sign. The steeple was missing from the Oak Stand United Methodist Church. It lay upside down on the newly planted Hope Garden funded by the Ladies' Auxiliary.

She wanted to close her eyes. Pretend the devastation in front of her was a bad dream. How could she have gone from sitting in first class drinking tomato juice three hours ago, to now staring at the raw potency of an angry Mother Nature? Rayne clutched the steering wheel tighter as she turned on Crabtree Street and saw an electrical line lying over the sidewalk. She was only one street from her aunt's. She hesitated for a moment before passing the entrance and veering toward Oak Stand Elementary. As she traveled through the neighborhood that harbored the recently constructed school, she noted thankfully that the damage sustained in this area looked moderate. She drove the puddle-strewn streets dotted with leaves and the occasional limb.

She pulled in front of the school and put the car into Park. The outside of the school was hopping. Parents, clutching the hands of children, hurried away toward idling cars. A few children sat in rows against the brick walls of the school, minded by vigilant teachers milling

around looking purposeful. The principal stood outside with a handheld radio. She simultaneously waved
through cars blocking the bus loop and gave directions
to the security officer who also had a handheld radio.

"Mrs. Trimble," Rayne called, knowing she interrupted the principal's conversation with a harried-
looking bus driver. At this point, she didn't care. She
needed to see Henry. Needed to be assured he was
completely whole and unharmed. "Henry? Is he okay?
Did he get on the bus? Or did Aunt Fran—"

The principal held up one hand, halting Rayne's
rambling questions. She pointed the driver toward her
bus and spun around. "Deep breath, Mrs. Albright. All
of the children are fine. A little shook up, but fine."

Rayne nearly hugged the tall, spare woman.
"Henry?"

"Your aunt picked him up about twenty-five minutes
ago. He's fine."

Rayne didn't wait. She turned and sprinted toward
her car. She did manage to call a "thanks" over her
shoulder. She'd apologize for her rudeness by baking
the woman a cake or two. Better yet, she'd make brown-
ies for the whole staff. But right now, she needed to feel
her son in her arms.

She fumbled with the keys, nearly dropping them
into a puddle, before unlocking the car and turning the
ignition. She made a U-turn in the middle of the street,
bypassing a news van from Shreveport. Word traveled
fast.

She backtracked her route and swung onto the street
where her aunt's home had sat for thirty-three years.
She pulled into the drive and released the pent-up
breath she'd held all the way down the street. The house

had not sustained damage. Small limbs were scattered across the yard and dogwood petals dotted the grass like confetti tossed haphazardly, but the structure was sound. She shut off the car and opened the car door. The world that met her was damp and raw.

Aunt Frances bolted out the door. "Rayne! Oh, thanks be!"

Rayne slammed the car door and headed toward the house but didn't even make it up the steps before her aunt enveloped her in a hug. She rocked her back and forth as if she'd been in mortal danger. Come to think of it, she had been in mortal danger. She'd never thought about how perilous it had been for her to drive in such a storm. Her thoughts had been only for her loved ones.

"Oh, sweet girl, I was worried sick. I knew you were on the way home, but with this wild weather, I had this horrible notion you were in a ditch somewhere. Or in a tree."

Rayne managed a laugh. "I'm fine."

With one last squeeze her aunt let go. "Thank God."

Rayne moved past her aunt. "Henry? Where is he?"

Her aunt smiled. "He's fine. Better than I would have expected."

Rayne didn't look back. Just moved toward the open door.

"He's not inside. He's over at Brent's helping him clean up a tree that fell."

Rayne spun around. "With Brent?"

Her aunt nodded. "That man. You know I got to the school just as the bell rang and he was already there."

"Who was already there?" Rayne asked, retracing her steps.

"Brent. I walked up to mass confusion. Parents running hither, thither and yon. Kids crying. Teachers about to pull their hair out, and right in the middle of that bedlam were Brent and Henry sitting on the ground up against the wall in the hallway reading a *Sports Illustrated* magazine."

Rayne literally grabbed her heart. Brent had gone to her son. When he needed someone the most. When she'd not been there. "Reading a magazine?"

Her aunt nodded, staring out at the front lawn with a frown. A fat branch sat on the newly planted butterfly bush next to the mailbox. "Yeah. He said he couldn't check Henry out because he wasn't on the list of people who could, but he didn't want to leave him. So he got a magazine out of his truck and waited until I got there."

Rayne pressed her lips together and fought the emotion unfurling inside her. That man, indeed. "That was more than—"

"Yeah," her aunt interrupted, crossing her arms and contemplating the canopy of the oak above them. "It was almost parental. And that from a man whore."

Rayne stiffened. "He's not that."

"Only repeating what I heard," her aunt said, moving her contemplation from the leaves overhead to her niece. Her gray eyes were like bullets, piercing and deadly. "I don't know too many men who'd do that, unless they were daddies or family relation. He's neither of those. Just someone who cares a great deal about you and that boy."

Rayne looked away. As if she didn't know. As if

his declaration of love hadn't been on her mind night and day for the past three days. As if she could get the images of Brent beneath that willow laying his heart bare out of her mind. Even New York City couldn't distract her with its bright lights and strong drinks. When she lay in that hotel in Manhattan visions of Brent had danced in her head. A dream come true. But one she'd been unsure about.

She looked back at the woman who watched her. "I know."

Her aunt nodded. "Good. Very good."

Then her aunt turned on a worn sneaker and walked quickly up the steps of the house. Before entering the front door, she spun and stabbed a finger toward the property next door. "What you're looking for is over there."

Rayne almost smiled.

She needed to see her son. Thread her fingers through his hair and drop butterfly kisses on his sweet face. She also needed to see the man who'd come to her son's rescue.

She had never needed a white knight.

Henry had.

And Brent had not disappointed. He could have done nothing any better than taking care of the treasure of her heart.

Pretty good heroics from the man whore of Oak Stand.

CHAPTER TWENTY-ONE

Brent watched as Henry prodded the baby squirrel's mouth with the eyedropper. He'd located an unopened can of formula his mother had used last fall with an abandoned kitten she'd found. He wasn't sure a baby squirrel ate the same thing a baby kitten did, but it had to be close.

"He won't eat," Henry said, a furrow between his eyes. "Shouldn't he be hungry? I think I would be if I fell out of a tree."

Brent took the eyedropper from the boy and tucked the old dishrag around the baby squirrel that had been tossed from his nest during the storm. The poor thing looked more like a small mouse. He and Henry had discovered him beneath one of the limbs they'd been stacking in the corner of the yard. It had scared the hell out of him when it had moved. It was a wonder one of the cats or Apple hadn't gotten to it. "It's probably stunned and wanting its momma."

The words were out of his mouth before he thought better of them. He didn't want Henry thinking about his mother not being there. Hell, he didn't want to think about Rayne at all. Too damn bad his heart, head and body hadn't got that memo.

Henry looked wistful for a moment before shrugging the feelings off and picking up the small cardboard box they'd placed the little squirrel in. He looked down at the big-eyed animal. "I know how you feel little guy. I miss my momma, too."

Brent patted Henry's shoulder. "She'll be back soon. The Yankees are looking for a new pitcher. You up for the task?"

Henry smiled. "I can't pitch for the pros. Yet."

Brent laughed. "That's the spirit. Always expect you'll get where you want to go, Hank."

The boy looked down at the animal Brent had forbidden him to touch. Who knew if baby squirrels had rabies...or other diseases? "I'll tell you where I don't want to go. New York. Only thing good about that place is they get snow. I never got to build a snowman before."

The heart in Brent's chest constricted at the thought of Henry and Rayne living in New York. Without him. When had he gotten so damned attached? Oh, yeah. The day both of them walked into his backyard.

He sent Henry to his parents' porch with the box and instructions to set it on the table and pull the screen over the top to prevent hungry cats from finding a snack. Then he turned toward the large limb that had fallen onto the rope hammock, breaking the frame.

As he broke off the branches that snagged in the ropes, he heard Henry singing to the squirrel. It was the "Good night" song Rayne had always sung to him when they were young. The sound made his heart lighter.

He'd make it work. Somehow.

New York was the capital of the publishing business. Moving there wouldn't be a bad move. He could lunch with his agent, meet with his editor rather than have long telephone conversations about revisions and visions for more books. He could write anywhere. He didn't really want to. He'd never loved city life the way many did. Didn't give a rat's ass about Starbucks on every corner, good martinis or designer clothes. Hated the constant noise and congestion. And, hell, Central Park was always crowded with those stroller-pushing jogging nannies and homeless nutjobs looking to score some blow. At least that's how they portrayed it on TV.

He couldn't see himself there. Were there old men in feed stores to drink coffee with? Bass fishing with Talton and Bubba? Sunsets and sunrises that took the breath away? Crickets? Cows? Eight-dollar haircuts? Betty Monk's chess pie?

He didn't think so.

But surprisingly, after his parents and uncle met with Tyson Hart, they'd agreed to sell half the company to him. Their construction company was now Hamilton-Hart Builders. With that move, Brent had been pretty much freed to go wherever life took him.

If that meant New York, then so be it.

"Brent?" Her voice sounded like the velvet night sky. Or the calm after the storm. Or merely the woman he loved.

He turned and saw Rayne framed in the gate, the way she had been that day over a month ago.

"Where's Henry?" she asked. Tenseness knotted her shoulders; worry creased her brow.

"Mom!" Henry shrieked, flying off the porch and into her arms. She dropped to her knees, closed her eyes and held her son tight against her. Then she kissed his face all over while simultaneously checking him with her hands. She pulled back, looked at him, and then pulled him back into her arms for another hug.

"I was so worried about you, pumpkin. So afraid that you were scared to death," she said, giving her son a shaky smile. "You okay?"

Henry nodded. "'Course. Brent came and got me. Well, not got me 'cause he can't check me out. But he stayed with me and we read an article on the NFL draft. See, I told you he would be a good person to put on my list."

She nodded, briefly meeting Brent's eyes. "So you did."

Henry disengaged himself from Rayne, grabbed her hand and tugged her toward the porch. "Come see what me and Brent found."

"What Brent and I found," she corrected, flashing him a hesitant smile before following her son to the box sitting atop the wicker table.

"Yeah, that's what I said," Henry said.

Brent couldn't stop a smile from twitching at his lips. He wanted to go to her, take her in his arms, especially when he realized she'd likely been on the road in the middle of the storm when he called her. Fool woman. Should have found shelter and waited.

But what could stop a mother's love?

Not anything as measly as an F-2 tornado.

He tried to pretend he wasn't watching her ooh and ah over the baby squirrel they'd rescued. He broke more branches, finally untangling the large limb before dragging half the hammock with him across the yard.

Rayne appeared at his elbow as he tossed the remnants of the old Carolina hammock on the discard pile.

"Hey," she said, brushing his back. It was like hot flames licking his skin, a mixture of pleasure and pain.

"You came back," he said, not yet meeting her eyes. He didn't want her to see how much he wanted her. How much he needed to grab hold of her much as she'd done to Henry minutes before.

"Yeah," she said, snaking her arms around his waist, squeezing him. "Thank you. Thank you so much. For taking care of Henry. For being there for him when he needed it."

Wrapped in Rayne's arms was exactly where he wanted to be, but he couldn't allow himself the pleasure. Not when he stood in limbo.

He unwrapped himself from her and stepped away. "You're welcome."

He could feel her question in the silence. He didn't look at her and instead thought about the many times he'd left a girl feeling much the way he felt that instant with Rayne.

Hurt and determined not to feel used.

Even if the temptation to toss his defenses away ate at him. It would be so easy to take whatever she offered. Even if it were merely an hour of her time. But he wanted more from her. This time he needed her to choose him.

RAYNE WATCHED AS BRENT moved away from her. He'd pulled away. Physically. Mentally. And it hurt. The vibes were deep and after the afternoon of near-exhausting emotions, she didn't want to churn through more with Brent. Not yet.

But obviously she wasn't getting what she wanted.

"Why did you pull away?" she asked, latching her

hands behind her back and keeping an eye on Henry as he tossed a ball for the Boston terrier that belonged to the Hamiltons.

He didn't answer. Just stared at the sagging gutter on the side of the Hamilton's house. He seemed so not himself.

"Brent?"

He turned toward her. "Did you come back for Henry? Or for me?"

Rayne opened her mouth, but Henry chose that moment to run toward them. He galloped full speed tugging on the dog's rope toy. "Hey, Mom. Can we get a dog? I think I need one."

Brent glanced at Henry and then back at her. Did he expect her to answer in front of her son?

"Apple's not yours, is she? She's your mom and dad's, huh?" Henry went right on talking as he tugged the now-growling dog in circles around them. "Maybe I can get one just like her. I mean she's cute with her mashed-up nose, huh? Can I, Mom?"

"Henry. Please stop pulling that dog. Brent and I need to talk. Take her to the porch," Rayne said, trying to tamp down the irritation she felt at being interrupted. Ten minutes ago she'd kissed Henry all over his sweet little face. Now she felt exasperation creeping in. The timing was off. She couldn't talk to Brent about their complicated relationship after a tornado had swept through town. Not with Henry whirling around them much as the storm had done. Not in the side yard of his parents' house with rain dripping from the trees.

"I can't, Mom. She might eat that baby squirrel. She likes to eat frogs, too. Brent says they make her throw up. So—"

"Now, Henry," she said trying not to yell.

Henry gave her a hurt look but slunk toward the porch, dragging the dog with him. Apple had her teeth clamped on the rope and shook her head ferociously.

Guilt flooded Rayne. "Um, after I finish talking to Brent, I'll get you one of the Pop-Tarts."

Henry visibly brightened. Great. She now used processed food to bribe her child. She'd sunk to a new low. She opened her mouth to say "nevermind" as Brent's mother stepped onto the porch. She called for Henry to come have some gingersnaps and milk. He threw Rayne a questioning look before looking back at Mrs. Hamilton.

The older woman didn't give Henry time to refuse. She turned and disappeared into the large house. Apple, who obviously knew what gingersnaps were, took off, abandoning her rope toy in the wet grass. Henry followed.

Rayne glanced at Brent. He brooded. She hadn't seen him do that in quite a while. "Brent?"

He looked at her, his light blue eyes so indecipherable. "What happened in New York?"

"Before we talk about me and New York, let's talk about what happened here. What have you heard about damage? Is everyone okay?" She looked around but there was no place to sit. Everything was wet including her feet. Strappy sandals weren't the best choice for slogging through storm-strewn yards.

Ever in tune to her, Brent jerked his head toward the carriage house. "Let's sit on my porch and talk."

They walked silently toward Brent's place and sat on the edge of the porch, side by side, but not touching. No comfortable sliding into favorite blue jeans feeling between them. Rather the air was heavy. Tense. As if the storm wasn't really over.

Brent broke the awkward moment. "The town is messed up, but we'll survive. I'll need to go help with the cleanup later, but I felt it was more important for Hank to feel safe. Even after your aunt picked him up, he looked freaked out. I figured putting him to work helping me clean up around here would keep his mind occupied."

"Thank you for thinking about him."

"Why wouldn't I? You don't give me much credit, do you?"

Rayne stiffened; her chest tightened at his words. "You know that's not true."

He met her response with silence, his gaze much more telling than any words he could speak. She'd hurt him and he'd carried it with him. He tore his gaze away from her. "I didn't know you were coming home today."

"Coming home," she said, smoothing the tight skirt against her thighs. "Sounds weird. For the past few years my vision of home has changed quite a bit."

He didn't say anything. Didn't even look at her. On one level it made her angry. He didn't know anything about what she felt, and yet, he pulled away. On another level, she understood. He was trying to protect himself. She'd done the same once. She'd written that poem challenging him to be who he longed to be and challenging him to love her. When he did neither, she'd packed up and run. She supposed he thought she was doing the same now, except the shoe was on the other foot.

He'd declared his love and wanted her at his side.

"You know," Brent said, interrupting the plop of rain dripping from the eaves. "So many times I gave girls the boot. I wasn't an asshole about it or anything. But I never knew how they felt. How they wanted more from me than what I could give. Now I get it. I see how bad it sucks to put your eggs in a basket only to have them dropped and cracked. Joke's on me."

Rayne slid her hand over to his. "Who said I'm cracking your eggs? Now who's the one not giving the other a fair shake?"

He straightened but tightened his grip on her hand. "I can't make you stay here. You've been working hard for a long time to get to this moment. You need to take it. You have to take it."

She nodded. "Yes, I do. I mean, I am."

"So, New York it is," he said, turning his hand over and grasping hers. "I guess I'll get used to the noise."

"What?" She nearly broke her neck she turned her head toward him so fast. He looked almost smug sitting there in tight blue jeans, a damp T-shirt and a knowing smile.

"If you're going to New York City, then I'm going, too. I told my dad I won't be buying into Hamilton Construction. I'm rolling the dice and trying writing as my full-time job. I may end up sleeping on benches in Central Park, but I believe in us. So, where you go, I will go."

She couldn't believe his words. He'd move to New York for her? She couldn't imagine him living anywhere else but where he now sat. He loved Oak Stand. He loved Texas. But he loved her more.

Whatever the heck cockles were, well, hers were warmed.

"You mean you'll move to New York City with all those cabs and crowded streets. With the lights blinking on and off all the time and horns honking and—"

"Way to make me embrace the idea," he said, heavy on the sarcasm. But he didn't let go of her hand.

"You're serious about making this work, aren't you?"

He shrugged. "I've spent years here merely existing. I love this little town. I have lots of good memories here, but when you walked back into my world, everything changed. What I wanted changed. What I needed changed."

She blinked at the emotion lacing his words. It made her humble...and happy.

"But what I really need to know, Rayne bow, is if you want me there with you."

Rayne felt a clog form in her throat. Tears perched raw and unshed in the back of her throat. A huge sweeping warmth flooded her and she couldn't have talked if it would have saved her life. She shook her head and waved her hands, trying to rein in her emotions. But they wouldn't be held. Today had been too much. His words had been too much.

"Hey, babe. Don't cry," Brent said, his voice gentle. He moved closer, sweeping an arm around her shoulders and gathering her into him. She fell against him, making noisy half sobs into his shirt. She wanted to stop crying. To make him understand how much his words meant to her, but her body didn't obey. So she went with it. She let out all her fear from the past few hours, all her regrets with Brent, all her pent-up frustrations.

After a minute or two, she pulled away and wiped

her cheeks. Oddly enough, she felt much better. Cleansed.

"Sorry," she croaked. "I guess everything got to me."

Brent withdrew his arm and gave a heavy sigh.

She lifted her legs from where they hung off the porch and tucked them beneath her. She grabbed Brent's hand and tugged until he focused those gorgeous baby blues on her. "I have always loved you. Maybe from the very beginning. From the moment I saw you. We clicked. Like we were supposed to go together. Even when I married Phillip, I didn't feel that same connection."

Something moved in his eyes. Something possessive. Something that said he knew what she felt.

"I loved Phillip. He was a good man. Had a good sense of humor and he loved me. I would never have left him for you. He wouldn't have deserved that."

She pressed her lips together and looked away from his probing gaze. Looked at the tiny spiderweb in the corner of the porch. Laying her heart out, even with Brent, made her feel naked. So vulnerable.

"But Phillip isn't here anymore. And I think God gave me a second chance with you."

She riveted her eyes on his and tried like hell not to cry anymore. "I don't want to let that chance go, but you can't come to New York with me."

"But I will. I don't mind leaving Oak Stand if it means having you and Henry in my life." He rifled a hand through his dark hair, making it stick up. The pain in his eyes nearly undid her.

She smiled. "No, that's not what I meant. I don't

want you to move to New York because I won't be there. I'll be here."

"You'll be here?'

She nodded. "Yeah, here. In Oak Stand."

"How? I thought you said you took the job?"

"I did."

"So…?" He spread his large calloused hands apart. She took them in her own, marveling at the strength. The tenderness of this man who'd given his heart away. Finally.

"So the show is going to be produced here in Oak Stand. At the inn. The main reason why the offer didn't progress several months ago was because the network had too many instructional shows and viewers were flipping channels and not sticking around to watch how-to shows. The network has been brainstorming new ways to bring in viewers."

Brent's eyes narrowed. "So you had no idea they would do something regional?"

"Not really. What my agent pitched was more of an 'on the streets of New York' sort of thing, but when we sat down to talk in the production meeting, the producer already had Austin in mind. He likes the eclectic culture of the city. When I mentioned the launch of the inn, he really got excited. He liked the duality of the rural and urban settings.

"So, instead of a cooking show, mine is going to be a regional travel slash food show with one cooking segment. Since Texas is a huge state with many cultures and we sit close to some of the best cooking in the South, the producer wants my show based out of Serendipity Inn but with segments filmed all over Texas,

Louisiana and Arkansas. With studios that film reality shows in Shreveport, it's an almost-ideal scenario."

Brent looked shell-shocked. "You're kidding."

Rayne grinned. "Nope. I'm staying here. Of course, I'll have to travel some. But we'll film most segments from the inn with a few in the restaurant in Austin. The show will be called *A Taste of Texas* and we'll start filming in the fall. So Henry can go to school here. Play for your baseball team. I will—"

She didn't get to finish. Mostly because Brent's mouth had covered hers. His mouth was hungry, driving her back. She stuck out one elbow to catch herself and wrapped her other arm around Brent's neck. He tasted so good. He tasted like coming home. For real.

Brent ripped his mouth from hers and looked deep in her eyes. "Why the hell did you wait so long to tell me?"

She contemplated his lips. They were wet and tempting. She wanted to kiss him again. So she did.

He tasted as good as he had the first time.

"Rayne," he mumbled against her kiss.

She broke the kiss, but stayed in his arms. "Maybe because there was a tornado. And Henry. And a dog. And your mother. And—"

"Okay, but you drew this out. Like torture," he murmured, kissing her jawline, not bothering to pull away from her, and she knew he had to be uncomfortable. An acorn poked her in the back.

She shook her head. "What did you expect? For me to blurt out everything?"

"Yeah," he said, falling so he lay flat on his back, tugging her atop him. He cupped her face and pulled her lips to his. Tenderly, he kissed her. Again. And again.

A flare of desire burst inside her as he loved her. She slid her hand to the raspiness of his jaw, enjoying the difference in their skin.

"Whadda you guys doing? Kissing?" Henry's voice crashed into them, cooling her ardor.

Brent lazily tore his mouth from hers and looked at her son. She turned her head, too. Henry stood beneath them with a disgusted look on his face.

"Don't you know you're not supposed to interrupt a guy kissing a pretty woman?" Brent said, sitting up and pulling Rayne with him. "It's guy code."

Henry frowned. "It is?"

Rayne shook her head and lifted her gaze to the heavens. Or what would be the heavens if they weren't blocked by the many trees between the carriage house and the back of the Hamiltons' house.

"Are you guys getting married or something?" Henry asked.

Brent shrugged. "Maybe. How would you feel about that?"

Rayne felt her heart contract again. For the umpteenth time in the past few months. "Henry, would you mind if Brent were my…boyfriend?"

Henry smiled. "I told you, Mom. Remember? I told you to marry Brent. He'd be a good addition. Remember?"

"How could I forget?" Rayne said.

Brent stood and tugged her to her feet, not missing the opportunity to brush her forehead with a kiss. "So you've been talking it over already."

Henry nodded his whole body. "Yeah. I already

decided you'd be a good guy for my mom. And you're pretty good at throwing ball. And you write good books. And—"

Rayne didn't hear all the other good attributes her son rattled off about Brent. She knew all she needed to know. Brent Hamilton loved her. And she loved him. They may not have a happily ever after, but they'd get as damned close as they could.

"I love you," she said, looking up at the man she loved.

"And I love you. I always have."

They linked hands and walked down the steps to the prattling seven-year-old who was on attribute number twelve which included something about knowing how to tie shoelaces so they didn't come undone.

Rayne felt a sense of absolute rightness flood her as she took Henry's hand. They stepped together toward the Hamiltons' house. Toward, hopefully, Mrs. Donna's homemade gingersnaps. Toward a new future together.

"So, since you're going to be my new dad, can I have a dog?"

Rayne looked at Brent.

Who looked at her.

They both looked at Henry and said, "No!"

"Aw, man," Henry said, scooping up the dog rope toy and waving it in the air. "Guess I'll take those Pop-Tarts then."

Apple ran circles around them, barking at Henry. Brent curled his arms around Rayne's shoulders, and Rayne looked up at him. "You don't know what you've gotten yourself into."

He smiled. "Oh, I know. And it's exactly where I want to be."

"Better late than never," she said.

"Amen," Brent said.

* * * * *

COMING NEXT MONTH

Available June 14, 2011

#1710 FINDING HER DAD
Suddenly a Parent
Janice Kay Johnson

#1711 MARRIED BY JUNE
Make Me a Match
Ellen Hartman

#1712 HER BEST FRIEND'S WEDDING
More than Friends
Abby Gaines

#1713 HONOR BOUND
Count on a Cop
Julianna Morris

#1714 TWICE THE CHANCE
Twins
Darlene Gardner

#1715 A RISK WORTH TAKING
Zana Bell

You can find more information on upcoming
Harlequin® titles, free excerpts and more at
www.HarlequinInsideRomance.com.

HSRCNM0511

REQUEST YOUR FREE BOOKS!
2 FREE NOVELS PLUS 2 FREE GIFTS!

Harlequin

Super Romance

Exciting, emotional, unexpected!

YES! Please send me 2 FREE Harlequin® Superromance® novels and my 2 FREE gifts (gifts are worth about $10). After receiving them, if I don't wish to receive any more books, I can return the shipping statement marked "cancel." If I don't cancel, I will receive 6 brand-new novels every month and be billed just $4.69 per book in the U.S. or $5.24 per book in Canada. That's a saving of at least 15% off the cover price! It's quite a bargain! Shipping and handling is just 50¢ per book in the U.S. and 75¢ per book in Canada.* I understand that accepting the 2 free books and gifts places me under no obligation to buy anything. I can always return a shipment and cancel at any time. Even if I never buy another book, the two free books and gifts are mine to keep forever.

135/336 HDN FC6T

Name	(PLEASE PRINT)

Address	Apt. #

City	State/Prov.	Zip/Postal Code

Signature (if under 18, a parent or guardian must sign)

Mail to the **Reader Service:**
IN U.S.A.: P.O. Box 1867, Buffalo, NY 14240-1867
IN CANADA: P.O. Box 609, Fort Erie, Ontario L2A 5X3

Not valid for current subscribers to Harlequin Superromance books.
**Are you a current subscriber to Harlequin Superromance books
and want to receive the larger-print edition?
Call 1-800-873-8635 or visit www.ReaderService.com.**

* Terms and prices subject to change without notice. Prices do not include applicable taxes. Sales tax applicable in N.Y. Canadian residents will be charged applicable taxes. Offer not valid in Quebec. This offer is limited to one order per household. All orders subject to credit approval. Credit or debit balances in a customer's account(s) may be offset by any other outstanding balance owed by or to the customer. Please allow 4 to 6 weeks for delivery. Offer available while quantities last.

Your Privacy—The Reader Service is committed to protecting your privacy. Our Privacy Policy is available online at www.ReaderService.com or upon request from the Reader Service.

We make a portion of our mailing list available to reputable third parties that offer products we believe may interest you. If you prefer that we not exchange your name with third parties, or if you wish to clarify or modify your communication preferences, please visit us at www.ReaderService.com/consumerchoice or write to us at Reader Service Preference Service, P.O. Box 9062, Buffalo, NY 14269. Include your complete name and address.

HSR11

"THANKS FOR NOT TURNING ON THE LIGHTS," Tyler said. "I'm a mess."

"Not in my book." Even in low light, Alex had a good view of her yellow shirt plastered to her body. It was all he could do not to reach for her, mud and all. But the next move needed to be hers, not his.

She slicked her wet hair back and squeezed some water out of the ends as she glanced upward. "I like the sound of the rain on a tin roof."

"Me, too."

She met his gaze briefly and looked away. "Where's the sink?"

"At the far end, beyond the last stall."

Tyler's running shoes squished as she walked down the aisle between the rows of stalls. She glanced sideways at Alex. "So how much of a cowboy are you these days? Do you ride the range and stuff?"

"I ride." He liked being able to say that. "Why?"

"Just wondered. Last summer, you were still a city boy. You even told me you weren't the cowboy type, but you're...different now."

He wasn't sure if that was a good thing or a bad thing. Maybe she preferred city boys to cowboys. "How am I different?"

"Well, you dress differently, and your hair's a little longer. Your face seems a little more chiseled, but maybe that's because of your hair. Also, there's something else, something harder to define, an attitude…"

"Are you saying I have an attitude?"

"Not in a bad way. It's more like a quiet confidence."

He was flattered, but still he had to laugh. "I just admitted a while ago that I have all kinds of doubts about this event tomorrow. That doesn't seem like quiet confidence to me."

"This isn't about your job, it's about…your…" She took a deep breath. "It's about your sex appeal, okay? I have no business talking about it, because it will only make me want to do things I shouldn't do." She started toward the end of the barn. "Now, where's that sink? We need to get cleaned up and go back to the house. Dinner is probably ready, and I—"

He spun her around and pulled her into his arms, mud and all. "Let's do those things." Then he kissed her, knowing that she would kiss him back, knowing that this time he would take that kiss where he wanted it to go. And she would let him.

Follow Tyler and Alex's wild adventures in
SHOULD'VE BEEN A COWBOY
Available June 2011 only from Harlequin® Blaze™
wherever books are sold.

HBEXP0611

Finding Her Dad

Janice Kay Johnson

Jonathan Brenner was busy running for office as county sheriff. The last thing on his mind was parenthood...that is, until a resourceful, awkward teenage girl shows up claiming to be his daughter!

*Available June
wherever books are sold.*